DAMAGED FRUIT

Hazel Reed

For a dear friend Lyn

10.12.2019

Michael Terence
Publishing

First published in paperback by
Michael Terence Publishing in 2019
www.mtp.agency

ISBN 9781913289409

I would like to dedicate this, my first novel to The Thursday evening Meat Ball Club, for giving me the encouragement to carry on.

A series of murders, in which the victims are mutilated, presents a challenging case for Detective Chief Inspector Jenny Trent. As the body count rises, and with the clock ticking, can Trent stop a determined killer before he turns his attentions to her?

Prologue

I must have stared for a full five minutes at the two ripe peaches in the bowl on the small kitchen table.

'Which one of you is perfect?' I asked, without expecting an answer.

I went to the one on the right and picked it up carefully, stroking the silky-smooth skin. 'Not you, I'm afraid.'

I threw it into the waste bin, hearing the satisfying squelch as it hit the side. 'I love that sound,' I said to myself, shivering with excitement and turning my attention back to the remaining peach. 'You, now, are perfect. You'll do very nicely.'

I picked the fruit from the bowl, bringing the soft, fleshy orb slowly to my mouth. The first bite was always the best. The sharp, sweet juice sliding down my throat. I worked with a systematic focus on the peach until only the sticky stone was left in my fingers. I carefully placed it on my tongue and closed my mouth to suck hard on the rough surface until every fibre of fruit was gone.

Satisfied that the peach stone was clean, I removed it from my mouth, hurrying to the sink to wash it, scrubbing carefully with a small soft nail brush, not wanting to harm the outside. It had to be clean, very clean. It had to be beautiful and big. More critical still, I had to be able to feel its rough edges.

'Now ... you are perfect ... in every way.' I placed the perfect peach stone next to two others. All three identical in height, size and colour.

I felt exhilarated as I stared at each one. 'Yes, you will all do nicely. Just one more to find.' I thought for just a moment. 'Or maybe two.' Happy, I giggled quietly to myself. 'You will be famous, my little peach stones ... you will be famous ... soon.'

CHAPTER ONE

Broomleigh House School

The gates opened and the car moved quietly towards the imposing entrance. There was a space next to a silver Rolls-Royce. My father carefully manoeuvred his car next to it.

As we walked towards the entrance, the large double-fronted glass doors opened silently onto a grand hall. There was a red face girl crying and a lot of other kids wandering around the hall, most looking frightened and some trying hard not to cry, their parents talking with each other paying little attention to what was going on.

A door at the side of the hall opened and a man shouted loudly. 'Good morning, everyone.' He waited for silence. 'My name is Dr Brian Cook.' He glanced quickly around, waiting for all eyes to look at him. 'Will all parents please say their goodbyes now?' He stood waiting through the murmured goodbyes. Some of the children clinging nervously to their parents.

My father took my hand, shaking it firmly. 'Good luck, son,' he said. 'Your mother will be here to meet you at four o'clock, enjoy your first day.'

'Dad, can I—?'

My father raised his hand. 'No! We have discussed this before, and your mother has made it very clear that you must use your name properly.' He let go of my hand and turned to join other parents making their way out.

I wanted to scream at my father to tell him how much I hated my mother for giving me the worst name in hell! But I just stood and watched as he walked towards the exit door of the grand hall. He turned once, raising his hand in a short wave before passing through the open door. I couldn't raise my hand in response, even though I could see the sadness in my father's face and felt another, stronger pang of hatred for my mother. I often did.

'Children!' Dr McAllister waited until all we turned to look at him. 'Please follow me to the large room at the end of the hall. Those of you who are boarders leave your luggage at the front of the hall before you come. It will be delivered to the dormitories allocated to you shortly.' He turned and headed towards the room at the end of the hall, his shoes clicking noisily on the polished wooden floor.

The room had a high ceiling with sparkling chandeliers. There was a stage with deep red curtains drawn back to reveal the wooden boards of the stage. The children moved towards the stage and stood quietly in nervous apprehension waiting for the next instruction.

Dr McAllister walked solemnly up the stairs and to the centre of the stage holding a clipboard tight to his chest.

Another man was already on the stage. He stood with his back straight and his arms folded. Dr McAllister held up his hand and the room went silent. All eyes were on him. He pointed to the tall man next to him.

'I would like to introduce your housemaster, Mr Charles Weldon.' The tall man moved two steps forward. 'You will have a lot more to do with Mr Weldon than you will with me.' He stopped and looked around the room. 'Especially if you misbehave,' he said loudly, with a hint of a smile.

'Now, listen very carefully, please. Mr Weldon will call out everyone's full name and, after the name, he will give a number, which will be one, two, or three. When he calls your name please do not forget the number that goes with it.' He looked over his glasses, scanning our faces to ensure everyone had understood him. The housemaster stepped forward to the front of the stage. Dr McAllister handed him the clipboard and marched off the stage, disappearing behind the curtains.

'Good morning, boys and girls.' said the housemaster. 'Here we go.' He raised his voice and spoke slowly and clearly. 'Please pay attention, or your very first meeting with me may well be a little unpleasant. As Dr McAllister said, my name is Mr Weldon, and as he also said, you will have a lot more to do with me than with him. Now, listen carefully for your full name and remember the number that goes with it.' He looked around the room to ensure we were all paying listening. I was listening very hard, but I was frightened as well. What was I doing here? I wanted to go home.

'Amy Sarah Brown three, Jonathan Peter Chillers two, Peter James Hudson three, James Samuel Chambers one.' While others waited for their names to be called, I shut my eyes and wished I was somewhere else –

anywhere… 'William James Booker two, Einstein Luther Smith two.' He gave a short muffled sniff.

A quiet snigger came from the row in front of me, and a few other boys shifted their feet, hiding soft giggles with their hands. The housemaster didn't notice or pretended not to. The list of names and numbers took several minutes to finish.

'Now, listen again, very carefully. I want you to fall into three lines.' He pointed to the right of the stage. 'All the number ones go this side of the stage. The twos go to this side.' He pointed to the opposite side of the stage. 'The threes line up in the middle.'

We took a few minutes to get into our lines, new shoes shuffling noisily. I pretended not to notice the stares and smirks.

'Miss Jones will take the ones to their classroom. Mrs Gale will take the twos and Mr Banister will take the threes.' We were led away by Mrs Gale. She was very tall and walked fast. I had to take a few running steps to catch up. This didn't help me feel any better.

William Booker was sitting at the desk next to me. 'Is your name really Einstein?'

'Yes,' I said. *So what?* I thought to myself.

'Well, it's a weird name, I must say,' said William. 'I'd like to be called Wills.' He thought for a few seconds. 'I shall call you Ernie if it's okay with you?'

'Fine with me.'

A boy behind us sniggered.

Lunchtime took an hour. Students that boarded had their lunch in the dining hall. Others, like me, had packed lunches brought from home. We went to a smaller room with a long table and wooden chairs. My mother made a good lunch, sandwiches, crisps, a drink and every day a peach, which was my favourite, the fruit so sweet and soft. If I'm completely honest the peach was the only thing I liked about my mother. There was nothing else, just the peaches. If the weather was good, packed lunches could be taken out to the large playground at the back of the school.

That's when it started.

One boy, a little older and taller than me, came up to me while I was sitting with Wills on a wooden bench, both of us about to eat our lunch.

'Is your name really Einstein Luther Smith?' He stood right in front of me, so close he was almost touching my knees.

I looked up at the tall boy, who was grinning widely, waiting for an answer.

'Yes.'

The boy turned to look at another boy and a girl behind him. He sniggered loudly. 'Did you hear that? His name really *is* Einstein Luther Smith.'

All three started to laugh. The girl held a hand in front of her mouth.

'After a few moments, Wills touched my arm. 'Come on, Ernie, let's go, they're just being stupid.'

The tall boy stopped laughing and turned his eyes towards William. He bent his head low so that they were nose-to-nose. His teeth were clenched. 'What's it got to do wiv you, then?'

William moved his head away from the screwed-up red face.

'If you ever say that me and my friends are stupid again, I'll bash you up.' He leant in closer to William again. 'Stupid.'

Without answering, William stood up, turned, and ran, leaving his lunch to fall onto the wet ground.

The tall boy stood up straight again and turned towards me. He took my sandwich box from the bench, threw it high into the air and, as it came down, he gave it an almighty kick. The box broke and the contents scattered, landing some way away in a large, dirty puddle.

'And what's this soft, juicy thing?' He picked up the peach I had placed beside me on the bench and threw it to his friends. The girl caught it.

'Ooh! I'll enjoy this a lot,' she said as she raised the peach to her mouth.

The bell rang, signalling ten minutes to the end of the lunch period. As they ran away, they sang very loud,

'Einstein … Einstein … Einstein Luther Smith,

Silly name … silly name,

We'll be back again,

Silly name ... silly name.'

I didn't care about the sandwiches – and I am used to my name being laughed at, but I did care a lot about the peach being taken.

Lunchtimes got worse. The tall boy and the girl always helping themselves to my lunch, and every day they took the peach. The girl would suck loudly on the fruit before spitting the stone out in front of me. She always screamed after she had finished. Her screaming was almost as bad as losing my peach. It made my head ache. Once I asked her to stop.

'I can scream much louder than that,' she said, putting her face closer to my ear. 'Silly name... Silly name' ... Another scream, even louder. It hurt, it really hurt. I couldn't stop tears filling my eyes. The other boy hung back, just staring at me. I told Wills to stay away and even thought about telling my parents what was happening but decided not to. My mother probably wouldn't believe me, and my father would only do what my mother told him to do anyway. He always did! He was pathetic.

One day, the girl came up to me without the others. I decided to try to make friends with her. *Perhaps she will be nice because her nasty friends weren't with her.* I thought.

'Would you like to share my sandwich?' I smiled as I offered her the sandwich box.

'Share your sandwich?' she shouted. 'Share your sandwich?' she repeated, even louder. 'Of course, I don't want your rotten sandwich.' Her face came close to me, eyes staring. 'But, I will have your peach.' She pulled the peach from the box and started eating it, pouting, her mouth wet with juice as it slid down her ugly face. Her laughter was like a witches cackle. My head was aching as I put my hands to my head, covering my ears, as the girl continued screaming. 'Ooh! It's so lovely,' she said, licking her lips and sucking the peach stone. She was screeching at me, her voice cutting through the air.

'Silly name ... Silly name.'

Then, another loud screech.

'Lovely peach ... lovely peach ...'

My head was aching, and I fought back furious tears.

'Einstein Luther Smith ... you really are a pain.

'Einstein Luther Smith … funny name … funny name.

'Einstein … silly name, we'll be back again … silly name.'

She was now singing as loudly as she'd screamed.

As the bell rang and the lunch period came to an end, she spat the peach stone at me. It hit my face. Wet juice and spittle splashed down my clothes. She turned, laughing as she ran into the school building.

I brushed the stone away, feeling hurt, angry and ashamed.

I hated her. Almost as much as I hated my mother.

Just as I was about to get up a girl ran towards me. I had seen her before, speaking to one of the bigger boys after they had left me and ran into the school. She stopped me by the sports hall door.

'Are you alright? She asked as she reached me.

'Yes, I am thank you.' I said quietly.

'I saw that girl bothering you again I really should report it.'

'No, please don't.' The thought of what they would do to me if it was reported, really made me scared.

'My name is Jenny, I am three years ahead of your year. I think I saw three children before. They looked as they were being horrible to you then.' She stood in front of me waiting. 'I really should report it. What's your name?' I didn't answer her. 'Please' she said. 'They really shouldn't behave like this and Mr Weldon really wants to know about these things.'

I didn't want to tell her my name, but I blurted it out. 'My name is Einstein Luther Smith.'

'Hello, Einstein. My name is Jenny Collins and if you really don't want me to report what is happening I won't, but they shouldn't behave so badly. I will report if I see anything like it again. No matter what you say, Einstein.' She turned to walk away and looked back. 'Do you understand?'

'Yes, 'I said.

The lunchtime ordeal continued day after day, even though Wills and I tried sitting in different places. They always found us. The peach would be stolen and passed around for my tormentors to eat. Once, it was thrown heavily at a wall. I was made to walk to the wall and lick the juice from the bricks. The girl stood behind me, pushing my face closer.

'Go on stupid, lick it … lick it.' She pushed my head even closer to the wall, screaming in my ear. 'Is your tongue bleeding? Oh dear, yes, it is … look … his tongue is bleeding!' Her laughing became screeching, louder and louder. Her face was redder and darker. My head felt as though it would burst, causing a pain, which was excruciating. I hated them, so much. *One day … One day … I thought.* My anger was getting worse and staying with me longer.

Wills tried to stop the bullying but ended up with a bloodied nose. 'Guess what, Ernie? I hit the biggest boy really hard this time and made his mouth bleed.'

They laughed together.

'Trouble is, Ernie, one of the boys warned me that they'll make it worse for me and you if I don't stop. We really should tell someone about what they're doing. I know Mr Weldon would like to know. I heard him telling a girl off for being nasty to someone, and I can tell you he was very angry with her.'

I looked at my bloodied friend. 'Wills, I'm so pleased we're friends, but I would like to fight this battle and I really, really don't want you to get hurt.'

'Don't bring in a peach every day.' Wills suggested as they walked home together one afternoon.

'I'm not giving in to them!' I was angry, my voice louder. 'I'm sorry, Wills, but I just can't. I'll sort it out one day, I promise you. One day.' I couldn't stop my voice from shaking, and fiercely rejected any suggestion that Wills should tell anyone about my tormentors.

There was a time when I was pushed into a dark cupboard, I heard the laughter from the girl as she locked the door.

'Try and get out of that, silly name!' she had shouted, and then banged forcefully on the door before walking away, laughing.

Someone must have heard her, I tried to believe, but no one came to open the door. The cupboard was small and damp and every attempt I made to open the door failed. I hated the dark and began shaking with fear. Twice the girl came back, but it was just to tap on the door and offer a whispered *'Einstein, Einstein … You really are a pain … Einstein … Einstein, silly … silly silly name.'* She continued singing as she ran away.

I shouted louder and louder, but no one was there to hear. I yelled as I lost my temper, which was happening a lot lately. I tried hitting the door until my fists were bruised and sore, so I kicked the door instead, my feet now my only weapon.

The door moved, but not because of my efforts. Someone had opened it and the sudden light hurt my eyes. I gasped loudly as fresh air rushed down my already sore throat.

'Who's there? What on earth are you doing in here?' It was the girl who had helped him once before. I remembered her name, Jenny. 'Who's in here? Come on out and tell me what happened. Oh, my goodness, what on earth has happened to you again Einstein? How did you get yourself locked in here?'

As the door opened fully, I rose and pushed clumsily past her, without speaking. I ran to the cloakroom, dragged my coat off the hook and turned to face her. 'Don't tell anyone.' I shouted angrily. Please, it will just make it even worse for me if you do. I'm dealing with it myself.' I made my way to the outside of the school as fast as I could.

'Einstein! Einstein!' shouted the girl called Jenny, 'Come back … please. I want to know what happened.'

I couldn't look back, I was terrified, my heart beating fast, my legs now weak and trembling, but I kept running, clumsily, until I found a wooden bench on the side of the road leading to home. I sat there until I could breathe easier, but I couldn't stop trembling. I clenched my hands so tightly they hurt. 'I will get them one day, I promised myself. One day!' Now I had to go and face my mother again. I staggered to my feet, kicked the bench hard and stomped home, wishing I was dead.

✳✳✳

I didn't like sport. Wills was a very good cricketer and did his best to get me interested in the game, but he soon realised that I was clumsy and uninterested so he didn't try very hard.

I often walked alone across the school playing field. When no one else was on the field I found the quiet and the freshness of newly cut grass relaxing and could forget my misery. One day, I was walking towards the middle of the field when I saw the tallest of my tormentors running towards me. I tried to run away but was quickly caught.

The boy held a large thick stick in his hand. 'Go on, silly name, run.' He began hitting my ankles. 'Go on, Einstein Luther Smith, run fast, run faster.' The stick pounded at my feet as the boy ran beside me. 'You really are stupid, as stupid as your name.'

I ran as fast as I could, my legs aching, my feet covered in the blood seeping through my socks. But he kept up with me. Hitting me over and over, my ankles were getting so painful from the beating I just wanted to stop and fall, but I didn't, I just couldn't. I wanted to scream, the pain from my ankles now beating at the sides of my head.

'Hey, stop that!' a girl yelled. 'What do you think you're doing?'

The beating suddenly stopped as the weapon was dropped. I fell to the ground, putting my hands to my bleeding legs and feet. I pulled at my socks, which were soaking wet with blood.

The girl ran to him. As she got closer I realised it was Jenny. I felt embarrassed and angry that she had seen me like this again.

'You need help, Einstein' she said, anxiously. 'Wait, I'll get a first-aider. Just sit here, I won't be long.'

'No, no! I'm fine,' I said as I shook myself from her grasp. 'We were just playing and I got hurt, I'm okay, really. I'm not in any trouble, honestly.'

She frowned her forehead wrinkling, but not spoiling her pretty face. 'Are you sure? Your legs and feet are bleeding, I really should get someone to help you. In fact, I need to get a first aider and then I will go and see Mr Weldon. He must be told now Einstein, he must.'

'I said I don't need anyone. Just leave me alone,' I shouted. 'Leave me alone, I can deal with it.'

'Alright, but I shall make a note of it in the first aid book. I think Mr Weldon should know about this. This is the second time I've seen you being attacked. How many other attacks have you had that I haven't seen Einstein? How many? She repeated. 'And it won't be the last if it is not stopped.'

'Please don't tell him. I told you – I'm alright and I'll sort this out myself. I will have more to worry about if he is told,' I was shaking with anger. 'My mother can deal with my feet as soon as I get home.'

'Okay, but if something like this happens again I won't even mention Mr Weldon to you. I'll just tell him. I shall be watching you very closely from now on Einstein. Someone's got to make sure you're alright.'

'Thank you,' I said, quietly, as she walked away. I looked down at my feet, blood was still coming through my thin socks. I'll have to throw them away and worry later about what my stupid mother would say about missing socks.

***

The regular school trips to the local swimming pool were sometimes more than I could bear. I hated the water, I couldn't swim, and I didn't want to. The cold water was always a shock. My constant shivering was ridiculed, not only by the bullies but also by the swimming instructor. But today was a swimming lesson day, no one escaped the swimming lesson day.

As I was walking and shivering along the edge of the pool, someone punched me hard in my back and I fell into the water. I swallowed gallons of water, the metallic tang of chlorine and bleach stinging my throat. I struggled harder and harder to reach the surface, feeling sick and terrified. I tried to put my feet on the bottom of the pool, but they slipped and my body sank further into the water. I began thrashing my arms and managed to burst through the surface, 'Help! Help! I can't swim!'

No one seemed to hear him. They just carried on walking past, talking and laughing. *They want me dead*, I thought as I went under the water again.

I emerged, through the water spluttering and coughing, and heard voices calling me.

'Come on, Einstein Luther Smith …

Come on …Einstein Luther Smith …

Use your arms, stupid …

Use your arms …

Come on, Einstein Luther Smith …

Use your arms stupid …

You really are stupid …

As stupid as your name.'

Everybody was singing. No-one stopped them. They were all laughing as they ran around the pool. The swimming instructor made no effort to stop the noise. I made a desperate grab for the side of the swimming pool, gasping for air. 'Come on Einstein keep your arms moving,' shouted the Swimming Instructor. I reached the edge, hung on to the tiles and pulled myself up. He clapped slowly as I stood up. I wanted to die quickly.

My mother's face was in front of me.

CHAPTER TWO

She rubbed her wedding ring with soft, circular motions. Jonathon's slow and painful illness had taken over her life. Her sadness was unsuccessfully hidden from the husband she adored. His last days were spent at home, her hands clutching the frail but firm hands of his. He knew she was there, he knew she would be with him, forever.

Her grief was overwhelming and re-adjustment for her life without Jonathan was hard. There were times when she thought she could take no more. Her role of Chief Inspector was challenging under usual conditions. Sometimes the loss of her mentor, her confidant, her lover and adored husband, had been too much. She was overwhelmed with grief. But, the tap on the shoulder of an understanding colleague, a tear wiped away quickly and the thought of Jonathan's response to her sadness urged her to continue the career they had both wanted and enjoyed. She had a team that worked hard and supported her throughout every step of the difficult days. Even though there were some that found it difficult reporting to a woman DCI, they soon warmed to her professional and thorough attitude to them and the job in hand. Time was slowly becoming a good healer.

Chief Inspector Jenny thoughts turned to the tasks of the day, a robbery, an accusation of domestic abuse, shoplifting. *A normal day's work* thought Jenny, as she stood to straighten her short jacket and new trousers, bought just the day before.

Jenny picked up her phone on the first ring.

'Get down to Marden Close immediately.' James Morgan-Jones said bluntly. 'Someone's been murdered, and from the sketchy details so far it sounds unpleasant. The victim's wife found the body and is in a bit of a state. You're the Senior Investigating Officer on this one, Jenny. As usual, I want your fullest attention and a quick result.' The line went dead. Superintendent Morgan-Jones bluntness was well recognised throughout the force, as was his determination for successfully resolving difficult cases.

'Did anyone hear anything earlier this morning?'

'No one seems to have heard a thing.' Peter turned back the pages of his small pad. 'I get the feeling he was not very well-liked around here, sort of kept himself to himself. Spoke to no one much, and no one spoke to him. Seems they had quite a few visitors on and off, but nobody seems to know or care who they were, and not many people appear interested enough to have asked.

'There were a lot of people gathered around and I heard a man in the crowd say 'Everyone gets what they deserve in the end.' By the time I turned around, everyone was quiet and no one moved. I asked who'd spoken, but got no response. I have the feeling that no one's interested in helping us find the killer. 'Peter closed his notebook and looked at Jenny. 'Are you okay?'

'Well, I've seen a few murder scenes in my time, but this one's the worst.'

'Thanks for the warning Jenny. I'll take a look myself as soon as I've finished here.'

He gestured towards a half-open door. 'That's where his wife is now. I'd like to go back outside and see if I can find anyone who may have heard the comment and who it came from.'

'Great,' said Jenny. 'I'll be talking with Mrs Williamson. Keep me informed. I need to know that everything is in place for a thorough investigation of what's happened here. Officer Yates is the CSO. If anyone is unsure of what they must do, let him know immediately.'

Emma Williamson was sitting on a large dining chair, with Dr Joe Barton, the police doctor on the scene, seated next to her. A young PC was standing close to them, notebook in hand. Mrs Williamson was sitting upright, wiping her eyes with a crumpled handkerchief.

'Mrs Williamson, I'm Detective Chief Inspector Trent, the Senior Investigating Officer. I'm afraid I have to ask you some questions,' Jenny said softly, sitting on the other side of the woman.

Emma Williamson raised her head towards Jenny, but didn't reply.

'I'm not sure she'll be much help at the moment,' said Joe. 'She just keeps saying she found him in the bedroom when she went to take him a cup of tea. I've given her something to calm her down. It may be better if

Damaged Fruit

you try to talk with her once she's had time to settle. Whatever she says may not make much sense at the moment.'

'I understand Joe, but, I need to be able to rely on what she says and need to get some answers as quickly as possible. This is obviously a murder investigation. Let me know as soon as she's able to talk.' She turned to the young PC. 'What's your name?'

'PC Spencer, Ma'am.'

'Okay, Spencer. Stay with her, and call me immediately when Dr Barton says she is able to talk, or if she says anything to you. It's not surprising she is finding it hard to speak about it after seeing her husband like that. It must have been a terrible shock. Just call me immediately if she does manage to say anything at all.'

'Yes, Ma'am.'

As Jenny reached the front door to leave there was a commotion outside. A large crowd had gathered behind the police cordons.

'What's going on in there?' someone at the back shouted. 'No one's telling us anything.' A murmur of agreement passed through the crowd.

Jenny approached them, and held up her hand. 'I'm afraid I'm unable to say too much until our investigations have continued for quite some time yet.' The crowd moved to allow her space. Above the diminishing sounds from the crowd, she heard Ben's angry, demanding voice. He had just left the house and was walking towards the police officers waiting on the path near the entrance.

'I knew you lot would stamp over everything. How many times have my team arrived to find everything trampled to death? Get out of my way and let me see if I can get even the smallest amount of evidence that may give us a clue as to what happened up there.'

Peter caught up with Jenny. 'It seems as though the killer may have been here for some time after the murder,' said Peter. 'There are bloody footprints on the grass.'

Ben overheard. 'Show me exactly where,' he said, as he pushed past Jenny. 'I'll need to take swabs.' He turned to the crowd. 'Can you please move out of the way? I'm sure you have better things to do than to stand here gawping.' He glared at the two men.

One of them straightened his back and took a step towards Ben. 'Now look 'ere, mate'

'I'm not your mate, and if you don't mind, I'm doing the looking.' He turned away, and strode off behind Peter, with Jenny following as she held up her hands to placate the two men.

They walked with care towards two forensic officers already occupied with taking swabs of blood from the footprints deeply imprinted in the grass.

Ben pulled a swab of his own from his pocket and reached for a plastic bag from one of his team. Jenny watched the careful scrutiny of Ben and his team, picking and scratching at the ground, she felt an urgent need to speak with Mrs Williamson again.

'You carry on out here, Peter, I'm going to see if I can get some answers from Williamson's wife. I know she's traumatised, but even a little bit of information from her will help. Also, see if anyone is looking for signs that might indicate how our killer got into the house.' She walked back through the front door and straight to the room where Emma Williamson was still sitting rigid in her chair. Dr Barton and PC Spencer remained close by.

'Still, too early, I'm afraid, Jenny,' said Joe. 'Still can't get two words out properly at the moment. Why don't I call you when she's able to answer your questions?'

Jenny looked at the stricken woman and walked a few steps towards her. 'Can you hear me, Mrs Williamson? I'm so sorry, but we urgently need to know more about this awful situation, and anything you can tell us will be very valuable in helping us find out who did this to your husband.'

Mrs Williamson looked straight at Jenny and tried to open her mouth. 'I'm… I'm …' her eyes closed and she slumped as she sank into the cushions.

Jenny looked at Joe. 'Just let me know when she can talk to me. I don't have to tell you how important it is to speak to her and get some answers. I'll get a Family Liaison Officer to release PC Spencer as soon as possible.' She turned to address the officer, 'Please stay here until someone else comes.'

'Yes, Ma'am.'

Through the large window in the dining room looking out to the front of the house, Jenny saw the coroner's van arrive, ready to take James Williamson's body away.

Outside, Peter joined her again. 'Still, a few people hanging about, despite the cordons. Probably waiting for the body to be brought out. Some are still being questioned, though. I've let them know that they may be asked to come to the station for more questioning later. Didn't go down well.'

'Peter, I want all the names of the people who live in this close. I need to know what they do for a living, how long they've lived here and what they know about the Williamsons. Everyone in this street is a suspect. We already know he wasn't liked, find out why. Use as many officers as you need. Make sure the crime scene log is kept up to date, and that everyone who has made an entry has timed it and signed it.'

'All in order. He smiled at Jenny. 'Are you okay Jenny you look a bit … well as though something is bugging you.'

'Not really bugging me Peter. It's just that his name. It seems as though I know it somehow.' She shrugged her shoulders. 'I need to give it a bit more thought'. She said quietly to herself. 'I'd better call the Superintendent. He'll want to know what's happening,' said Jenny, taking her a large handheld phone from her jacket pocket. Her call was quickly answered.

'Morgan-Jones here. Update please.'

'The scene has been secured and cordoned off, Sir'. My team are talking to the neighbours. They're trying to find out more about Williamson and his wife. The body is shortly to be moved to the pathology department. Ben Seldon and his team are still here gathering vital evidence.'

'Has anyone thought to speak to the wife yet?' he said.

'The doctor is with her now and has advised me to try and speak to her later, she's very shocked and unable to respond to any questions yet.'

'Any prime suspects?'

'Not yet, Sir. I'll talk to his wife as soon as I can. From what we've gathered so far the victim was not very much liked around here. Someone was heard to say that he's got what he deserved. Could have several possible suspects.'

'Keep me informed.' As usual, the contact was swiftly closed.

'It's going to be a long day,' said Peter.

''Fraid so Peter. Not much I can do about it. We have to have a conversation with Williamson's wife very soon.

Jenny's phone buzzed. 'Hi, Jen, Joe here. Mrs Williamson is able to talk to you now, but not for long. She's still in a bad way, so if you can keep it short.'

'Where is she now?' asked Jenny.

'She's still in the dining room. I'll take her to the lounge. I think she'll be more comfortable there and she may respond better if she's more comfortable.'

'Okay, I'll be there in just a minute. Do you know if the body has been taken away yet?'

'I've just seen it leave, but there are still a lot of forensic people here,' said Joe. 'How long will you be?'

'About ten seconds.'

Jenny and Peter arrived in the entrance hall just as Dr Barton and PC Spencer were assisting Mrs Williamson across the hallway to another room.

'That was quick said, Joe although she's better, it's still difficult for her to respond to too many questions, so take it easy.'

With help, Mrs Williamson entered the lounge and moved towards a large upholstered chair. As she sat down, Jenny followed through the door. The room was well-furnished and, in spite of its size, it was warm and welcoming. Jenny still felt no liking for the house. Emma Williamson was sitting upright again. She held her handkerchief to her mouth but had stopped crying. PC Spencer was standing close to her.

Jenny walked towards Mrs Williamson and held out her hand. 'DCI Trent, Mrs Williamson. As I said earlier, I'm in charge of the investigation relating to your husband's death.' Her outstretched hand was taken shakily by Mrs Williamson. 'I'd like to talk to you about your husband, if that's possible. It shouldn't take too long.

Mrs Williamson looked frightened and tired. Tears had stained her face and her hair was tangled where her hands had pushed through in desperation. She nodded.

Jenny turned to PC Spencer. 'See if you can find a drink of water for her, please.'

Emma Williamson began to speak, softly. 'James was due to come home late last night, he had a dinner meeting with an important client, so I told him not to worry about me, and that I would sleep in one of the guest rooms.' Her voice broke and sobs covered her words.

'Do you normally sleep in the guest room when your husband is not at home, Mrs Williamson?'

'Yes, I do, when he says he's going to be late,' she said slowly raising her head. 'He drinks quite a lot when he has his business meetings. It makes him very fidgety when he gets into bed. Together with the smell of drink, it keeps me awake.' She stopped and took a small sip of her water. 'Not that he would've noticed if I was there or not.' Jenny heard the anger in Emma Williamson's voice and observed her shoulders straighten as she added the last point. 'I went to bed at about eleven and got up at about early this morning. I made a cup of tea for both of us and called James to ask if he wanted anything else, but there was no reply.'

'During the night, or the early hours of this morning, did you hear anything, anything at all?' Jenny said.

'I don't sleep very well, so I took something to help me. I didn't hear a thing.' Her head dropped. 'If I hadn't taken the sleeping pill I might have heard something, but I didn't.'

'Mrs Williamson, when your husband comes home drunk from these meetings, he couldn't drive himself, so who would bring him home?'

'I really don't know. I did ask him once because he hadn't even closed the front door properly, so it was open all night. It wasn't the first time he'd done that. He just said it wasn't my business and he was home anyway, so what?' She gave a small gasp. 'To be honest I didn't care. I would rather he hadn't come home at all, smelling so horrible.'

'What was your relationship with your husband like, Mrs Williamson?'

'I don't know what you mean, my husband's dead, Chief Inspector.'

'I know Mrs Williamson, but your husband has been murdered. I am afraid I must learn everything I can about him. There is a lot of information I need to make sense of this and to find his killer. Only you, as his wife will know some of the answers. The sooner we have the information, the quicker we will find the person who carried out this vicious murder.'

'My husband had a very important job, Chief Inspector, which is why he was out a lot. We got on alright.' She sniffed and drew the handkerchief up to the side of her mouth. 'Some found him difficult to get on with, but that was because he worked so hard and demanded a lot.' She wiped the creased square of embroidered white fabric across her mouth, this time pressing hard. 'He didn't suffer fools easily.'

'What do you mean by that, Mrs Williamson?'

'Just what I said. He was arrogant, and a lot of people didn't like him.' Her voice was shaking. Jenny thought she saw another flash of anger in her eyes.

'Why didn't they like him?' she said. 'Can you give me an example of how you know he wasn't liked? Did you ever meet any of the people *he* didn't like?'

'You can ask people around here, Chief Inspector. There're plenty of people around here that would have nothing to do with him. Made me feel rather lonely, to be honest.' She put a hand to her mouth as she coughed quietly.

'How long had you been married, Mrs Williamson?'

'Almost twelve years.'

'Any children?'

'No. James didn't want children.' She sighed, and her shoulders sagged as she closed her eyes. 'I did, but I really had no choice.'

'What do you mean by you "had no choice"?'

'Just what I say. I wanted children, he didn't, so we didn't. That's the way it was, Chief Inspector. Whatever my husband wanted … he got. What he didn't want, he didn't get. It was as simple as that.'

'You say your husband had a very important job, Mrs Williamson. What was his job and where did he work?'

'He was an investment banker. He worked in London. Other than that, I knew very little about his work. He just told me it was important.'

'You said that his colleagues found him hard to get on with, can you be a bit more explicit?'

Mrs Williamson took a deep breath. 'Everyone found him difficult,' she said. 'Everyone.' A little louder. 'He demanded a lot from the people who worked for him. But he was very good at what he did, so they put up with it.' Turning away from Jenny, her body straightened. 'I don't know any more.'

Joe touched Jenny's arm. 'I really must ask you to stop, Jenny. I need to get her to the hospital.'

'Just one more thing, Joe.' She looked at the woman in front of her. 'Mrs Williamson, you've been really helpful – thank you so much. Just one final question - do you know of anyone that had a key to your property?'

'No, I don't. That doesn't mean there wasn't someone who had the means to get in, though. He had visitors that I knew nothing about. And when he came home late, drunk, which was quite often as I have already said, he nearly always just left the door open. Sometimes, if I woke up, I'd go and check, but last night, as I said, I took something to help me sleep.' She sagged as her eyes closed once more.

Jenny regarded the woman for a moment.

'Let's go outside for a moment, Joe there's a lot Mrs Williamson isn't telling us, Joe, which is not surprising. She must be feeling really terrible.' She walked towards the door and turned to PC Spencer. Please come with us Officer. The door closed quietly behind them.

Does she have anyone who can be with her Joe? It is very important that I get more information as quickly as possible.'

'She has a sister, and she is on her way now.'

Jenny looked at PC Spencer. 'I would like you to stay with Mrs Williamson here, and when she gets to the hospital. Don't leave her side until an officer gets there to guard the door to her room. Immediately her sister arrives, I need to know.'

'Yes, Ma'am.' PC Spencer nodded.

Thank you. You may go back to Mrs Williamson now.

Jenny returned her attention to Joe. 'As soon as her sister gets here, I want to speak to them both.'

Joe nodded his agreement and walked with Jenny to the front door. As they were about to leave, a scream vibrated throughout the house.

'I hated him! I truly hated him. I don't care … I don't care … he deserved to die. I'm glad he's dead. Glad, I tell you!'

'It's her,' said Joe, as they rushed towards to open the door of the lounge. They saw the terrified look Emma Williamson's face and watched as she broke into another deep-throated scream and fell to the floor, her body shaking with uncontrollable sobs.

'He w–was a monster …… I'm g–glad he's dead … he deserved to die! I h–hated him,' she spluttered. Joe moved quickly to her side, pulling his mobile from his pocket, already calling for an ambulance.

Jenny blinked. 'Did she say what I thought she said?'

'Yes, she said she wanted her husband dead. But you'll have to deal with that later. I need to get her out of here as soon as possible.'

'I need to know more about why she hated her husband, Joe,' Jenny said, and she took a few steps towards him.

Joe held up his hand. 'Sorry, Jenny, it will have to wait, I need to get her to hospital.' This time his voice was sharp and demanding.

Jenny moved back.

She turned to look at the police officer standing just behind her, who had evidently come to investigate the commotion. 'I want you to go with her as well, officer, don't leave her, and ensure that I know the minute her sister arrives. PC Spencer is already accompanying her, I want you both there at all times.'

'Yes, Ma'am.'

CHAPTER THREE

Jenny had responded to Ben Seldon's call, agreeing to his request that she come to the pathology unit as soon as possible. She arrived at the senior scientific support laboratory, part of the pathology unit twenty minutes later.

The laboratory was a severe-looking place with a large sink and iodine bottles stacked on an overloaded draining board. The white floor tiles spotless and gleaming. Microscopes, voice recorders, computers, medical and surgical equipment, all neatly arranged on a long white table, for fast access and efficient use. Although bodies were usually kept in closed freezer drawers, there were always a few lying on wide tables, loosely covered with black plastic sheets, chilled and unattended. Jenny shivered, even though she wasn't cold.

Ben was bending over a naked body on a metal autopsy table, the post-mortem in an advanced stage. His assistant, Dr Andrew Baines, was at his usual desk checking samples and making notes. He had worked with Ben for the past two years. During this time he had generally kept himself to himself. No one knew very much about him and he wasn't known for socialising with colleagues, which was probably the reason Ben liked him and wasn't rude to him. He acknowledged Jenny with a wave and a warm smile.

'Morning, Jenny,' said Ben. 'Thanks for coming so quickly. Few things to bring you up to date with.' He stood straight and walked a few paces away from the table. 'Well, as you can see, the coroner agreed that an autopsy could be carried out without any further action or questions, so we just got on with it.'

Jenny moved towards the table, where the body of James Williamson lay.

'Nice to see you again, how are you?' said Andrew, with a smile.

'I'm fine thanks. What about you?'

'Great. This one seems a bit more interesting than others.'

Ben scowled. 'Let's just look at the physical evidence, shall we? Because of the apparent lack of disruption anywhere else in the room where he was found, I would say that there was only one other person in the room with the victim. We haven't found any evidence of fingerprints on the body, which suggests the murderer probably wore gloves. There's no report of anything being taken from the room, which, if this remains the case, eliminates interrupted burglary as a motive for the murder. There is no evidence that the body was brought into the room because, as you know Jenny, there was blood splattered all over the place where he was found, and a lot of it too, with not a spot anywhere else in the house. It doesn't look as if he struggled much apart from his fingers tearing at his throat. From my first observations, at the moment, it looks like his feet were removed in just one fast, heavy motion by an incredibly sharp blade. However, I need to know a lot more about how the amputations were done, so more to do yet.' He thought for a few moments and then pointed to a small enamel bowl. 'We removed that from his throat,' he said. 'A peach stone. It's there in the dish. Andrew's had a look at it and logged his report. Though I haven't gone through it with him yet though.'

Jenny moved towards the bowl to see the stone and glanced back at Ben.

'It appears from the bruising that the stone was pushed down into his throat, blocking it and his attempts to breathe made him swallow it so far in, that it caused his death. The blood coming from his nose and mouth were caused by the edges on the stone cutting into the soft flesh of the throat.' Ben pointed to the neck. 'You can see the deep scratches where his fingers tore at his throat. When the brain lacks oxygen it will begin to die, generally taking four to six minutes. The heart takes a little longer. I think the stone was lodged first, and the feet severed as he grappled to release it, which is why there was so much blood. Other than that he was in good shape.' He gave a short laugh. 'Mind you, with his feet being severed at the ankles he would eventually have bled to death and died. So the puzzle is … why the peach stone?'

'How long has he been dead' said Jenny? Her mind in turmoil as she again looked at the mutilated body in front of her, now with even more wounds from Ben's investigations.

'Eighteen to twenty-four hours, which makes it early morning yesterday.'

'Have you any clues as to what the killer was like?'

'Not really, at this stage, except to say that whoever removed the feet used an extremely sharp, heavy object, although there's something a bit unusual about it.' He looked up at Jenny. 'As I said, I need to make a thorough judgement on how the feet were removed and what with. It's up to your lot to find out why and by whom.'

'I have a briefing to give later this morning,' said Jenny. 'Do you have any specifics that the team and I can work on?'

Andrew looked closely at Ben. 'What about the peach stone?' he said.

'What about it?'

'Well, he obviously wasn't eating the peach before he was attacked,' said Andrew.

'How do you come to that conclusion so quickly?' Ben said. 'I agree there's no surface juice apparent anywhere near the cut I've already made across his throat, but I haven't yet examined the face or deeper into his throat or stomach to see if there's any indication of fruit juices elsewhere.'

'There won't be,' said Andrew as he picked up the peach stone with gloved hands. 'Not a speck of peach juice on the stone. Lots of blood sticking to it, but underneath the blood, the stone has been scrubbed clean. Our victim was not eating a peach, he didn't swallow the stone accidentally. It might have been placed in his mouth, but it wasn't pushed down his throat. It was his gasping and efforts to breathe that dragged it further down.'

'Thanks,' said Ben tersely, as he turned back to the body, scalpel already placed on the chest, waiting to make the long incision which would expose a large part of the dead man's torso. 'A lot to find out yet, Jenny, but as I've already said, and it's been confirmed by Andrew, it was the peach stone that killed him before anything else, not the hacking off of his feet or even the loss of blood. Why? As I've said before, that's something your lot will have to find out. It does seem as though the peach stone was very important in this murder though.'

Jenny decided to leave Ben and Andrew to their grim task. 'Thank you.'

The two men were engrossed in their work, so Andrew didn't respond while Ben managed a grunt in reply.

CHAPTER FOUR

Jenny arrived early at her office to find Peter waiting for her.

'Jenny, the meeting has been brought forward to ten o'clock.'

'Yes, I know,' said Jenny. 'Morgan-Jones, I'm afraid. Although he won't be at the meeting, he wants to hear from me earlier so he can report progress at the meeting he has soon after ours. Have the crime scene pictures arrived?'

'Yes, they're all here, I've put them in the incident room.'

'Before we put them on the board, Peter, I need to bring you up to date with the details of the autopsy being carried out by Ben and Andrew. They found a peach stone lodged in the victim's throat and believe that's what killed him, and why his hands and fingers were so tightly fixed to his neck. Of course, they haven't completed the autopsy, but that information is particularly interesting and can be passed onto the team at the meeting later.'

'Great,' said Peter. 'Never heard of that before. Should get everyone's attention. See you there. Just got one or two things to catch up on.'

Jenny walked the short distance to the empty incident room. She moved to the table by the side of the large empty whiteboards which were waiting to be filled with pictures of the victim and possible suspects.

The photographers had done a good job and she started pinning them to the boards. The first was a portrait of the victim. He was smart and good-looking with the smile of success, but a strong look of arrogance in his eyes. *You only have to look at him and you can see why so many people didn't like him,* she thought.

There was also a portrait photo of Emma Williamson, when not ravaged with shock and grief. She was an attractive woman in her late thirties with light blonde hair and clear blue eyes. She obviously cared a lot about her appearance. Jenny stared at her for a moment, seeing sadness and fear in her eyes, despite the bright smile. It reminded her of the anger she'd witnessed when interviewing her. She pinned the photo of Emma

Williamson next to that of her husband, and drew a thick red line between them, adding an arrow at each end. Hearing movement behind her, she turned to see that Peter had arrived with two steaming cups of coffee.

He smiled. 'I knew you'd be in here before anyone else. Here, have some breakfast with me.'

'I wondered where you'd gone,' said Jenny, taking a coffee from him. She smiled 'Just what I needed Peter, Thank you.'

He produced two giant-sized chocolate muffins from his jacket, placing them next to his coffee on one of the chairs.

'Can't say I'm looking forward to the meeting with the Super. Not a lot to go on at the moment have we?' She waited for Peter's answer and was about to repeat herself when she noticed his eyes were downcast and sadness was evident on his face.

'There's something wrong, Peter,' she said. 'What is it? You know I will gladly help if I can.'

Peter hesitated for a few seconds. 'Maggie's finding it difficult to cope with the hours I spend away. I think she has someone else.' He stopped. 'Sorry, I shouldn't have said that. We have more important things to worry about at the moment.' He looked hard at Jenny. 'I'm going to see this one through and I'll be with you every step of the way. After we've solved it, I can sort things out for myself.'

'Your happiness and well-being is always important to me Peter. Just let's get through this and my priority will be you, and sooner you will have time to focus on your own concerns, the better. If there's anything I can do to help, you know I will, just ask.'

She had always appreciated Peter's loyalty, attention to detail and the ability to get the team working together. His concerns about his wife were understandable, but she was afraid that Peter would be persuaded to leave the force. She didn't want to lose him, but her instincts were telling her that once this case was over, he would prioritise his marriage. How could she blame him, when the loss of her own husband still haunted her every day?

She pushed any more thoughts out of her mind and turned to look at the photos in front of her, knowing this case would need all her focus. The ones taken in the bedroom were hard to look at. In full colour, they showed various shots of the feet placed beside the victim's head, the wounds vivid and colourful, the blood dark and plentiful.

There were several pictures of Williamson's head, his eyes were wide open and bulging. The bleeding vessels were pronounced, and the pupils enlarged like big black holes trying to pull the pain deep into the centre of his body. Some of the images showed his hands on his throat and the deep bloody lines where his fingers had gouged the skin in trying to move the stone. There were pictures of the room where Williamson was found, and pictures of the inside and outside of the house.

'As you can see, there's a lot going on here, said Jenny. Thanks, Peter, the photography boys have done a great job.'

∗∗∗

The room was buzzing. There were now seven officers and detectives assigned to the case. Jenny nodded to them as she rose. 'Right, let's get started, shall we? Thank you for coming in early. You will all know by now that we're investigating the brutal murder of James Williamson. At the scene of the crime, you had your instructions, and your findings have been given to DI Branden and me. Please make sure you've logged the information too, and that it's available for anyone on the team to read. You will all receive further instructions and tasks when the meeting is finished.' She pointed to the photograph of Emma Williamson on the whiteboard.

'It appears that Emma Williamson hated her husband, and she has already said that she's glad he's dead. Unfortunately, as yet we were unable to find out more and she's in hospital at the moment and hasn't yet been available for further questioning. As soon as I have reported progress to the superintendent, I will go to the hospital with the intention of speaking to her. But, it has become quite clear from a lot of people in the local area that the victim, James Williamson, was disliked by almost everyone in the vicinity of his home. That makes everyone in the close a suspect. I want all residents interviewed and I want to know why he was not liked. Go back to the ones you have spoken to already. They would have been shocked by what had happened when you first spoke to them and may well have other things to say now.' She turned to face Peter. 'DI Branden will go through all the information we have. Please ask any questions you think would assist the investigation.'

She stood to the side just as Ben came in and stood at the back of the room. There was rarely any need for him to be there at the start of the investigations but he always insisted on being present. This time she was pleased to see him. There could be questions he may be able to answer.

Peter walked towards the whiteboard. 'As DCI Trent has already said, we have very little more to tell you at the moment, except to say that this murder was extremely violent.' He moved to the side of the board so that he could point out the information they had so far. 'Let's go through the few things we do have, no apologies if some of it is already known to you.'

'James Williamson,' he prodded the photo, 'was an investment banker working for the Standard Elite Bank in London. He was successful and very wealthy. Lived at number 6 Marden Close with his wife for the last ten or so years. They had no children and no pets.'

A hand went up. 'I was told it was twelve years, not ten years they'd been married, probably not important though.' Jenny recognised him from the murder scene. He had been speaking with the neighbours.

'Everything is important,' said Peter. 'Even the slightest detail means we get closer to solving what's happened here. To be absolutely clear Williamson had been married twelve years and had been living in the close for two years. I do hope it's not only Sergeant Hughes who remembers that.' A soft murmur filled the room.

He pointed to the face of Mrs Williamson.

'Emma Williamson. She found her husband dead in the morning and up to now hasn't been able to say much to us. She is traumatised and at the moment is in hospital,' he paused for a few seconds. 'As you've already heard from DCI Trent, she didn't like her husband either. She used the word "hated". The team from the scientific support unit has been working hard at the scene, and are still there, so we may have more from them soon.' Peter glanced at Ben Seldon. There was no acknowledgement.

'What was the cause of death?' The question came from the middle of the gathering in the room.

'I was just about to come to that,' said Peter acknowledging the question. 'A peach stone was dropped into his mouth so far down that he swallowed it,' he said, pointing to the photograph of the stone. 'Unable to dislodge it, he choked to death, but not before his feet were cut off and placed by his head. 'How do we know the peach stone was dropped into his mouth?' He shrugged. 'He could just as easily been eating the peach and the stone just slipped down his throat.' He looked at the detective who had spoken earlier. 'Perhaps you can enlighten us, sergeant?'

'Detail,' said Hughes.

'Carry on,' said Peter, as he motioned for him to come to the front.

Hughes walked forward and stood by the photographs. He pointed to the photo of Williamson lying on the floor. 'There are no signs of the peach juices around the body or on the floor, no signs of peach flesh. Nothing to indicate that he was eating a peach. Try eating a ripe peach without juice or flesh going anywhere other than in your mouth.'

There was a sound from the back of the room. Ben held up his hand.

'Another important detail,' he said. 'His feet were not just cut off. You're making it sound as though a pair of scissors did the job. They were sliced off, with a very sharp, heavy object that has not yet been found.'

'Thank you,' said Peter. 'And thank you, Sergeant Hughes.'

'Sir,' said Hughes as he went back to the group.

'As Dr Seldon says, it was a very heavy sharp instrument that took the feet off the victim's legs. So we need to find out where it came from, see if any of the local ironware stores have sold anything sharp and heavy that could do the job.

A hand went up from the back of the room. Peter recognised DC Roberts. He stood up. 'Do we know why Mrs Williamson hated her husband so much?'

'That's why DCI Trent will be visiting the hospital today. Mrs Williamson's sister is also arriving today, so we are hopeful of getting the answer to your question. But we also need to know why he was not liked around where he lived, and that's for some of you to find out. Any more questions?'

A hand went up. 'He obviously didn't drive himself home, so what about the person who did?'

'Again, a good question, and one we're working on. We'll inform you once we know more.' The room was quiet. 'Right, I'll hand you back to DCI Trent.' He returned to his chair as Jenny moved towards the whiteboard once more.

'What we've just run through, and what we have on the board, is what we know. I can't tell you enough times how important it is that we talk to the neighbours again, every one of them. Find out more about James Williamson's life. We already know that he was disliked … why? What did he do when he wasn't working? Who were his friends? What are the neighbours are like? I'm hoping I shall find out later why his wife hated him so much. There will be neighbours who know more than they've already said. We also need to find out if there are other members of the family who can shed any light on what kind of people they were and are.' Jenny looked around the room at the intense faces of her team. She'd worked with some of them for a long time and they worked as a relentlessly together. Questions and answers exchanged enthusiastically. 'Someone wanted to kill him and be noticed. Someone has made a statement about the victim and we need to know why. Thank you, everyone.'

She turned to face Peter. 'If there are no more questions, ensure that everyone knows what they have to do.' She motioned to him to join her for a moment before he began allocating tasks, murmuring, 'Get someone to start looking at the bank and the victim's associates there. But as a priority, I would like more information from the neighbours. Take as many officers with you as you need. Someone's got to know why this happened. Someone said he got what was coming to him. Find out who it was. I'm sorry, Peter, but this is urgent, at the moment it looks like our only way into this case. Get back to me as soon as possible. Your phone can wake me at any time.'

CHAPTER FIVE

A Nightmare

My mother was holding my hand just a little too tightly as we arrived at my first school. We went through the wide glass doors, which opened without being touched. I managed to pull my hand away from her grip. We sat down on the tall chairs placed neatly in the corridor of the large hall in front of us. Other boys and girls were sitting with their parents, all looking, well … a bit strange and silent.

A girl with bright red hair, glasses and a big brown spot on her nose came up to me, stared and went away. After a few moments, she came back. 'My name's Mary, what's yours?'

Before I could say, my mother spoke, in the stupid voice she used when she thought she was the most important person in the room. 'My son's name is Einstein Luther Smith.'

First, there was silence, and then the girl with the big brown spot giggled. 'Is that your real name?' she said, staring at me, holding her hand over her mouth, smothering an ugly, wide grin.

I looked at my mother, who was smiling at big brown spot. 'Einstein Luther Smith is his name. It's a very important name.' She sniffed loudly.

Big Brown Spot's silly giggle turned to a laugh.

Other children and their parents were looking at my mother and me. They started to giggle too. One small boy tried to say my name, but the words came out very peculiar and he rolled onto the floor holding his stomach and laughing. His parents also started to laugh, and very quickly everyone – parents and children – were laughing so much that tears were running from their eyes.

I looked at my mother again, who appeared not to have noticed the scene in front of her. I tugged her hand. 'Can we go, please? I don't like it here, everyone laughing at me.'

She looked surprised. 'No one is laughing at you. Don't be silly, we haven't seen the teachers yet.' She tried to grab my hand again, but I pulled away from her and sat watching the children rolling around on the floor. The laughter was so loud my ears were hurting.

I raised my hands to my head, covering my ears, trying as much as I could to drown out the noise, they were starting to sound like snorting pigs, so my head was beginning to ache. 'Stop it … stop it … please, please stop!'

No one heard me. If they did, they took no notice.

'Einstein Luther Smith, Einstein Luther Smith, Einstein Luther Smith.' Not laughing now, just chanting. 'Such a strange, funny name … funny name … funny name … funny name.' I pressed my hands harder against my ears, the pain and the sound refusing to go. My anger growing with every passing minute.

The door to a small room opened and a tall man with untidy thick black hair and a large moustache appeared. 'Next, please.' Ignoring the commotion in front of him, he stared at my mother. 'Come in with your son.'

My mother took my arm and pulled me roughly through the door.

The screeching laughter continued but, like my mother, the tall man with the moustache didn't take any notice of it. He closed the door, and as we walked further into the room it became quiet again.

'Please, take a seat.' He pointed at two chairs in front of the desk he was now sitting behind. My mother smiled her silly smile and sat heavily down on one of the chairs.

'Right, let's have some details,' said Moustache as he pulled a piece of paper from the top drawer of his desk. 'Your son's full name, please.'

'Einstein Luther Smith,' said my mother, smugly with the usual sniff.

The man laid his pen on the paper, stared at me and then at my mother. 'What did you say?'

'Einstein Luther Smith.' Sniffing even louder, she repeated, 'Einstein Luther Smith.'

'That's what I thought you said.' He raised his hand to cover his mouth, then a sympathetic smile as he turned from staring at my mother to me.

'What's wrong with his name?' Her face, at last, showing concern.

'Nothing. It's just that, well … ah … nothing, really.' He stopped staring at me and turned back to my mother. He hesitated, 'It's just that … well … I'm sorry it's just that … Smith,' he emphasised loudly. 'Smith … it's such … such a ghastly common name.'

My mother's face turned a deep shade of red. She fainted and rolled off the chair, landing with a thud on the floor in front of me.

I woke, sweat dripping down my face. The nightmares were still coming. I wanted to cry and scream. More than anything, I was angry that I couldn't stop them. Mother … 'Mother!' I cried. 'Let me go, please, let me go …' I curled myself into a ball and pulled the thick duvet over my head. *I'll kill my mother one day … one day.*

CHAPTER SIX

Lynn Moore pulled over on the narrow road, which seemed much longer than she had anticipated. She decided to check the details Mr Brown had given her. Taking the red folder from the passenger seat, she turned to her handwritten description of the house she was to view. She was definitely at the right house.

She had tried to contact Sarah to let her know she was visiting a property, but so far had not been able to reach her. *Probably still got the hump over the argument we had at Mum's,* she thought. *That's why she hasn't tried to contact me. Don't see why I should be the one to keep trying to get in touch with her, though.*

The agent had advised her that it was worth her viewing the property as quickly as possible. 'An opportunity not to be missed,' he'd said with great enthusiasm.

The house was derelict, which was reflected in the selling price and, being well under their upper limit, would leave them plenty of money to complete the renovations, with some to spare. 'I think it's just what you're looking for,' Mr Brown had said.

Just a little too fervently, Lynn had thought, still feeling a little puzzled by his statement, as both she and Sarah had said that they were looking for something that was in good order and that they would also consider newly built houses. But he had been so excited she'd felt obliged to see it.

Placing the red folder on the seat next to her, she started the car and crawled further along the road, looking for anything that would give her a clue as to where the property was situated. She came to a rusty iron gate and stopped. On the post next to the gate a crooked sign read 'Tregarth House'. 'Found it,' she said softly.

Parking on the verge just a little past the gate, she gathered the file and walked hesitantly forward, looking around for someone to greet her. Stopping at the gate she could see the big house in front of her. It was, as Mr Brown had said, in a bad state of repair and looked as though no one had lived in it for a very long time. Windows were broken, ivy was creeping wildly into cracks. It felt abandoned. *Why on earth would Sarah and I want to see this? There must be a reason!* She shivered. Curiosity overtook her, and she pushed open the gate. The path leading to the house was wide, with weeds pushing through the cracks and holes in the tiles. She picked her way along it with care, the sharp click of her steps resounding noisily from the uneven and dirty tiles beneath her, until she reached the front door. The door knocker was cast in the form of a large owl's head. It had a newly-polished look, the brass glinting in the weak sunlight pushing through the trees and overgrown bushes. Lynn glanced upwards at the dark heavy clouds forming in the distance and shuddered. *There must be something fantastic inside that I must see.* Her thoughts trying to justify Mr Brown's insistence on her seeing this ungodly house.

She lifted the owl's head and brought it down twice on the door. The door moved slightly, opening just a fraction. Lynn stepped back and looked at her watch, she was a few minutes early and didn't feel like pushing it open and going in alone.

She turned and took several steps down the path to look at the house and wondered again why she was here. It definitely wasn't what she and Sarah were looking for. Perhaps Mr Brown had mistaken them for someone else. But … she was here, so she might as well look it over. She imagined it had once been a magnificent family home. With money and careful planning, it could be beautiful again. *Perhaps we could have the house we've always dreamt of, after all,* she thought, and her mood started to lift.

Lynn looked at her watch again, he was now five minutes late. She wanted to know more about the house so that she could maybe encourage Sarah to view it as it *could* be, rather than the depressing ruin it was at the moment. Her curiosity overcame her as her interest grew. She nudged the heavy door open a little, as a rush of adrenaline spurred her on. She took a tentative step across the threshold, and into the dead silence of the hallway ahead of her.

Although it was almost dark, she could see what once would have been a splendid hall. There was a wide, carpeted staircase, broken in the middle, polished bannister rails on each side inviting her to make the climb to the first floor. Instead, she moved carefully along the hallway, split floorboards creaking with every step she took. There were doors on each side, all in a poor state of repair. Cold fingers of damp worked their way through her coat, and she shivered again. *It doesn't welcome me,* she thought.

Lynn stopped. She wished that Mr Brown was there to take her around the house. This could be a really lovely home. If Sarah likes it we'll be able to do such a lot with it, and have the type of house that we would never imagine could be ours in a thousand years. Her excitement over the potential in the grand building suppressed her unease. She moved further into the soft shadows. A sound came from behind the last door at the end of the hall, she hesitated and listened. The noise of someone moving in the room encouraged her to move towards it.

'Is that you, Mr Brown? It's Lynn Moore here. I've come to view the house, I didn't realise you were inside. I was waiting outside for you. I'm sorry if I'm late.'

She took a few more steps towards the source of the sound and, hearing it again, was emboldened to move further along the corridor until she reached the large double door at the end of the hallway. The door was old and warped. The black paint had mostly vanished, leaving dark-grained, swollen wood. At a slight push, it moved, moaning like an injured animal. Halfway open, it shuddered to a halt and she moved hesitantly through the aperture and into the room.

'Are you there, Mr Brown? I was waiting outside for you, I didn't realise that you were inside already. I really would like to see the rest of the house. If it's at the right price ...' she paused. 'You obviously know that it needs to have a lot of work done on it, so that's why the price would have to be right for us.' There was no answer, and she moved a little further into the room. It smelt of decay and damp timber. It was dark and gloomy except for a sharp beam of sunlight pushing its way through the dark clouds onto a filthy broken window. The room should have been cold, instead, it was warm, as if still occupied.

Light from the broken window shone on the opposite wall and lit up empty picture frames with dirty broken glass, some hanging perilously, appearing to be held up only by the grime on the wall. Patches of the floor were picked out by the sunlight, which revealed chipped and worn boards covered with a silky black slime. The room stank of dirt and sweat.

The sunlight receded to a light grey shade, just enough to briefly to illuminate another door in the back corner. Like the huge main door, it was swollen and twisted, with a large rusty iron lock, no key, and no handle. The swelling looked as though it had been created by something pushing in from behind, but the door had held tight, the black paint cracking and peeling under the strain.

Lynn was gripped by an overwhelming urge to run from the room. As she turned and took a few careful steps forward, the half-open door back to the hallway swung swiftly shut. Trapped and afraid, she cried out. *Her cry would be heard by the person in the house,* she thought, but it just echoed around the filthy room, bouncing off the walls and ceiling. She ran to the double doors and pulled with all her strength. They didn't move. She scratched at the doors until her nails were worn and her fingers bled from the roughly broken paint and exposed wood. Exhausted and terrified, she finally collapsed onto the slimy floor. Bile rose in her throat and pulsed in grim time with her accelerated heartbeat.

The door with the iron lock, but no handle or key, slowly began to open, brushing the muddy slime beneath it. It creaked to a halt. Lynn heard the movement and turned her head to face the door, where she saw the shadow of a man. She was going to get out of this filthy room, relief flooded through her body.

Through the failing light, she could see him edging closer. As he got nearer to her she raised her arm towards him. 'Please, help me, I can hardly move.'

He stood for a few moments. Then, as she was about to plead with him again, he bent down, his face almost touching her.

'Please … plea …' Lynn stopped as she saw his face through the dim light, a glimmer of recognition flickered in her mind. She fought hard to recognise him, so close was he to her. As a crooked smile spread across his face, old memories swarmed through her head. Her scream filled the room, followed by abrupt silence as something dropped into her mouth, it was hard and smooth. She drew breath to try to move it, but it slipped further to the back of her throat. Every breath she tried to take was excruciating. The object in her throat becoming painfully sharp, as it cut deep into her flesh. She raised her fingers and dug them deep into her neck trying to push the pain upwards and out. Dark shadows flew past her. As she moved her hands to touch them her mother appeared and then drifted away into a soft grey swirling mist. As she tried to call out, Sarah appeared in front of her, arm outstretched trying to pull her closer. Lynn raised her arms to reach her, but as they got closer to each other, Sarah disappeared into the darkened filthy room.

'It's a peach stone.' The voice spat at her. 'You loved my peaches, didn't you? Does it hurt very much? I really hope so. Oh dear, I'm sorry,' he snarled. 'Shout a bit louder. I remember you were very good at shouting.'

She tried another scream as the peach stone slid deeper into her throat, but her cry was weak. A shard of light from the filthy windows lit a raised hand. Something glinted and she saw a long, thick knife quivering over her head. It came down swift and heavy. She felt a blow to the side of her head. The pain had not yet reached her as she watched the hand rise high once more, hanging still in the air before swinging down again, this blow catching the other side of her head. Black clouds sped past in front of her as the pain ripped through her body. She wanted to scream, but couldn't. Raising her hands to the sides of her head, she felt blood spread through her fingers. She tried to scream again.

Pain she had never known before coursed through her as she slid further down through the grime on the floor. She tried to turn, but couldn't move. Lynn saw the large door opening before it swung shut again, with a devastating thud. She was now on her own. The fear and loneliness of the dark room tore at her soul, her body began to shake and uncontrollable soundless screams came from her throat.

She tried calling for her mother again, but the object now firmly lodged deep into her throat cut further into her flesh. No sound could escape.

She closed her hands tighter around her throat, pushing hard as she tried again to move the object stuck there. She was choking, and she couldn't breathe, her broken nails scratched uselessly at her neck. Air... the terrible pressure inside her lungs as she gulped and gurgled around the stone was unbearable. While the jagged thing in her throat felt as if it was on fire digging agonisingly ever deeper into her throat. This... was... She was dimly aware of thrashing around on the floor as she fought to breathe... She thought of Sarah... her mum... her dad... her whole life... And even as darkness hovered on the edge of her vision, suddenly she knew the voice ... the eyes ...the ... and the pain was no more.

CHAPTER SEVEN

Margaret Moore took her rubber gloves off having completed cleaning the oven. She stood for a few moments before turning to look at her husband. 'I'm starting to worry about Lynn, Robert. It's over a week since she's been in touch with us. I've spoken to Sarah and she hasn't heard from her either.' She took a handkerchief from the pocket of her dress. 'Although she did say that it's not unusual, Lynn is always so busy, and she sometimes takes a long time to answer her messages. Especially if they had had an argument, which was more often than not. She sounded very worried though, and asked me to call her if I heard from her.' She looked at her husband. 'Do you think it has anything to do with the argument they had when they were here last? You know how Lynn gets so angry at times.'

Robert Moore turned to see his wife almost in tears. 'I'm sure she's fine, love,' he said. 'You know how independent she is.'

'I just feel something is wrong. I think I should drop in to see her, just in case.' She looked appealingly at her husband. 'I know she's not good at telephoning us on a regular basis, but seven days without hearing from her is longer than normal.' She turned to look at the spotless cooker. 'Something's wrong, I just know it.'

'Are you sure you should drop into her flat, love? You know it's only just over a week. I'm sure she's just being her usual difficult self. You know how she can be.' He took his wife's hand and gave it a reassuring squeeze.

'I must go. I can't settle until I've heard from her, or have some clue as to where she is. She's never left it so long to get in touch, you know that.'

Her husband sighed and smiled at her. 'Okay, love, if it would help. I'm sure she's fine, though.' He rose from his chair. 'Come on let's get our coats. I'll drive.'

***

45

Margaret was cold as she got into the small car and shivered as her husband turned the key in the ignition. As the heater started to warm her, she recalled a conversation they'd had previously.

'Margaret, do you think that Lynn prefers girls? To boys … I mean?' Robert's expression had been earnest.

'I know exactly what you mean, and I've been waiting for the penny to drop for a long time.' She had waited for Robert to say something more, dreading the outburst.

'Is she happy? Is Sarah her … you know?'

'Her partner? Yes, she is, and yes, she's happy.'

'Good.'

No more was said.

They spoke very little on the drive, leading to the flats and Margaret began to focus on the task of finding out why her daughter had not been in touch as usual. Usual was two to three times a week at least, but mostly a quick call every day. None of her calls had been answered this week and none returned.

Reaching the door, she rang the bell twice, heard the sharp musical sound inside, and waited. After a few more seconds, she rang again. She turned to her husband. 'She's not in, is she? Do you think I should use the key?'

'I don't think we have a choice,' said Robert. 'Here, let me do it.'

Margaret passed the key to him. The door opened quietly, and they stepped into the warm, friendly, beautiful flat. The home of their daughter.

Margaret called out but didn't expect an answer. Moving cautiously further into the flat she looked for clues to Lynn's whereabouts but could see nothing that gave her any idea as to where her daughter might be.

Without thinking, she picked up the telephone and heard the dialling tone.

The sound stopped. 'You have seven messages,' said an unfriendly voice. 'Press one to listen to your messages.' *How can I intrude on my daughter's private life?* Margaret thought. *After all, it's only been just over a week.* Suppressing her guilt, she pressed one.

Messages one to four were either from friends requesting a meeting, or colleagues asking for case updates. Message five was from a man reminding her of a meeting that evening. Message six was from Sarah, cancelling a dinner arrangement for the next day, due to her mother being unwell. The last message was also from Sarah, asking for Lynn to call her back as soon as possible. Margaret held the phone in one hand. 'Robert, there's a message from Sarah, I think you need to know about this one.' She listened carefully again, before putting the phone back down.

'Robert ... Robert!' she called again. 'There's a message from Sarah, it was yesterday's date at three o'clock in the afternoon. She said she was concerned that Lynn hadn't returned her call, and that she hadn't heard from her for nearly a week and she was sorry that they'd had an argument. She asked Lynn to call her as soon as she got the message.'

Robert rushed from his investigation of the kitchen to his wife's side. 'How did she sound?' Robert said as he took his wife's hand.

'She sounded quite anxious. What on earth can we do, Robert?'

'Dial 1471. Someone else may have called and not left a message. But we could have a number to call back.'

Margaret dialled and listened to the same voice saying that a call had been received at ten hundred hours on 16 March, and to press three if she wanted to return it. Margaret pressed three and realised that it was her own unanswered call from two days before. This was followed by another unanswered call that she had made that day.

She put the phone down and turned to her husband. 'That last call was our number, I called her a couple of days ago, and earlier today.' She sank down onto the small chair by the telephone. 'Oh Robert, I'm sorry, but I can't help feeling worried.' She looked up at her husband and saw the deepening concern on his face.

'I think we should go home now, love, and call Lynn's work and try and speak with Sarah.' He decided not to mention talking to the police unless it became necessary, and gently pulled his wife to her feet, holding her close. 'I'm sure it'll be fine, Margaret. Let's get home as soon as possible, so I can make that call.' He helped his wife towards the open door.

'Yes, of course,' said Margaret. 'I'm sure we'll hear from her tomorrow ... but she's never left it so long before.'

CHAPTER EIGHT

A Summer Picnic

The sun was relentless and the heat tore through the soles of my new trainers, as I trudged behind my mother and father to the picnic ground they always came to have the dreaded picnic. There was nothing wrong with the place at the top of the hill leading to a beautiful stretch of wooded trees and grass, and of course a place for a picnic! My legs were aching, my feet sore. 'Thank God I won't have to put up with the ridiculous farce ever again,' I grumbled to myself. 'I hate it ... I hate it.' I spoke a little louder, but not loud enough for them to hear me. 'They're gonna hear how much I hate it soon.'

It was my mother's favourite picnic place and we went every year. I didn't know if it was my father's favourite place, I never bothered to ask him and he never said. Which was a nice change. My mood lifts normally. My anger getting worse and worse, I couldn't stop it.

I'd only had a few friends at Broomleigh, which had never bothered me. I must admit though, that the teaching had been good. I studied hard and reached the goal I had set myself, which was gaining a place at the University of Aberdeen. Just about as far away as I could get from my pathetic parents.

As we plodded closer to the stupid picnic spot I thought about my friend Wills. He had also gained a place at University, but at Leicester, so it was likely that I wouldn't be seeing much of him in future. It didn't worry me too much. I liked my own company and I hated having to be sociable. Still do. William was off to India on a three-month tour before going to Leicester. It was a gift from his parents for gaining a University place. And what did I get for getting straight A's? A bloody picnic with my parents! I wanted to scream at them as they continued walking just ahead of me. I clenched my fists to stop my hands shaking so much. I could feel the anger rippling through my body. One day... One day... I'll be free of you sodding pair of losers.

***

We reached the place of our picnics. A local beauty spot, with a Windmill in the background my mother insisted frequently that she had discovered it, and ridiculously called it 'Rose Lillian's Secret Garden'. My father and I never referred to the stupid name she had given it.

Rose Lillian was good at stupid names.

The picnic was always grand and this year was no different. A brilliant white cloth covered the rough, but very green grass and was held down at the corners by small glass weights, commandeered from my bedroom where they would normally be holding down important papers. Plastic cutlery, crockery and glasses were outlawed, on the assumption that it was so very cheap drinking and eating from such things. 'Not for people like us,' my mother had often said. Instead, there were Rose Lillian's best cut-glass glasses, Wedgwood crockery, and starched napkins matching the tablecloth. I hated it. I hated everything about this ridiculous picnic. I wanted to yell at them. Tell them how much I hated it, and their stupid airs and graces. But I didn't. My time would come. Soon.

The food was, as always, excellent. The main course was a Lobster salad with new potatoes, green salad and tomatoes, and pickles of every kind. There was fresh orange juice and normally there would be white wine, however, today was special, so there was champagne to congratulate their only son. The fact that no one liked champagne didn't stop Rose Lillian Smith from taking it to the picnic.

'He has obtained a place at one of the best universities in the country,' my mother boasted to anyone who was interested. Quite frankly, I don't think anyone was interested in what my mother had to say. 'Far better than Oxford or Cambridge,' she added with that sniff of hers, whenever she was trying to impress, which was all the time.

There were also peaches, six beautiful large ripe peaches. That was the best thing about the picnic, those lovely peaches.

During the meal, my mother stopped eating, patted her mouth with a stiff napkin and sat upright. 'Son, your father and I have decided that it would be a good idea if we bought, or rented, a townhouse just outside Aberdeen so that we could be with you during the week while you are studying. Just as we did when you went to Broomleigh. You can then come home to us at weekends.'

My father choked as he was placing a fork full of chicken into his mouth. 'We haven't decided anything yet, Rose.' My father's voice was louder than I'd ever heard it before. His face was red, and his hands were shaking as he waved them fiercely. 'You … you … just you … were saying that's what we could do. We haven't even discussed it with him yet! Nothing – nothing – has been discussed or agreed. Even when we moved to Bedford it was your idea, it was never discussed, and you made all the arrangements. It's always about you, isn't it?' He took a deep breath. 'It's always what you want, and what you want you to make sure you get.' He sat back and stared at my mother. 'I've just about had enough.' His face was full of rage as he rose and turned his back, his fists now balled, knuckles white. He stood for a few moments as his body began to relax. Then he turned to face my mother again. Chicken and spittle were spattered around his mouth. He looked like something out of a horror film. It was the first time I had ever seen my father so visibly angry with my mother.

About time, too, I thought. I looked at my parents, my mother's face was a deep shade of red as she tried to speak again.

'But I … but I …'

'There're no buts!' gasped my father, chicken now chewed and swallowed, and specks of the white meat visible on his tongue as he spoke.

Ugh!

'We're not going to Aberdeen or getting anything near Aberdeen!' He yelled. This final outburst, delivered at maximum volume and with bitter venom, seemed to take all the fight out of him. His sweaty face flushed so red it clashed with his sunburn, as he sat heavily on the ground.

He looked utterly stupid. In fact, they both looked bloody ridiculous. These were my parents, the people I was supposed to be grateful to for the rest of my life. I swallowed hard and rose, ready to leave, turning just once to face the two people who – apart from my tormentors at school – I hated most in the world. 'I shall be leaving for Scotland tomorrow, and I won't be coming home ever again, even if you do get a house or something near Aberdeen.

They stared at me, disbelief etched on their silly faces.

'I'm going for a walk now. When you've packed up everything, I'll come back home with you to get my things together.'

My father just stared at me, but as usual, said nothing. My mother was ready to weep her ugly wet crocodile tears.

'Don't go now, son, you haven't finished your picnic. Look, you haven't even eaten these nice peaches I brought for you. Please stay and have one, and we can talk about things.' Her voice was shaking as she passed a peach to me.

I took it and walked away without looking back.

✳✳✳

I tried to ignore the scream as I walked along the small path leading to a freshwater stream. It was my favourite place to disappear to on picnic days, and I had done so many times in the past. I could sit there for a long time and pretend I was someone else – anyone other than bloody Einstein Luther Smith.

I heard the scream again. I put my hands over my ears. 'What else will they do to get me to go back?' I said through gritted teeth. I turned and saw my father running towards me.

'Son … son! Please.' His voice was loud and breathless. 'Your mother … she's choking … she swallowed a peach stone and it's stuck and she can't get it out of her throat, please come, please it's hurting her so much. We need to get her to hospital and I can't move her on my own.'

We ran together to the picnic area. My mother was bent double on the ground at the side of the white tablecloth. Both her hands scratching at her throat. She tried to say something, but only a deep watery gurgle joined the saliva dribbling from her mouth, her eyes bulging. I could see she was pleading silently for help.

I knelt beside her as she squirmed from side to side. I put my fingers into her throat trying to release the stone, but her mouth closed around my fingers, gripping tightly. I pulled my fingers from my mother's mouth as she twisted up into a tight ball. Her eyes opened even wider and I felt her shudder. Blood spilled from her nose and fell down over her mouth and chin as her body fell still and quiet against mine. I let her down and removed my arms from underneath her body.

Rose Lillian Smith was dead.

My father staggered backwards, arms limp at his sides, mouth hanging open. He looked at me eyes wide. 'Is she?' He gasped. 'Is she …?'

'Yes,' I said. 'She's dead.'

My father started to shake. 'What are we going to do?' Tears formed and flowed down his face. 'What should we do, son?'

'There's not much we can do, except take her to the car and get her to the hospital.'

'Shouldn't we call the police?' My father looked like a scared rabbit.

'I don't know,' I said, and I truly didn't know. 'They'll tell us when we get there, come on, and let's get her to the car.'

Abandoning the picnic, we manoeuvred her body along the ground, rough with huge and swollen patches. The stones scattered throughout the whole of the long journey scratched and tore at our fingers. Finally, sweating and our bodies aching we reach the car and placed her gently onto the back seat. My father closed the door and moved into the driver's seat, and shakenly motioned for me to get in beside him.

'Did you try to get the stone out of her mouth?' I said.

'I did, but I couldn't. Not on my own, I just couldn't. I tried so hard before I came running to you for you to help. She was still breathing when I left her.' His voice was just a little sharper than it should have been.

Neither of us said anything more on the way to the hospital. But I had thoughts and questions running like the devil through my head. I had wanted many things to happen to my mother … but dead? I closed my eyes, trying not to think that it was my fault. And to ignore the fact that I didn't really care.

My father pulled up in the emergency car park at the front of the Accident and Emergency Unit of the hospital.

'You go and get someone, son, I'll wait for you here,' said my father.

I have to admit that I felt a bit sick as I ran into the hospital. I hated my mother … but dead?

Within a few minutes, two male nurses were rushing to the car, slowly dragging a large trolley with blankets loosely arranged on the top.

'What happened?' one of the nurses enquired, as they lifted Rose Lillian Smith carefully from the car onto a trolley and covered her body and legs with a white blanket. Her shocked face remained exposed, staring sightlessly at the sky.

'She swallowed a peach stone,' said my father quietly. 'She couldn't get it out of her throat. My son and I tried to move it but couldn't.' He was starting to cry again. 'She's dead.'

We followed the trolley through the doors and into the hospital.

'Please take a seat,' said one of the nurses pointing to a row of chairs. 'A doctor will be with you very soon.'

We sat in silence, staring after the trolley. After only a few minutes a doctor reached us.

'Good afternoon, I'm Doctor Richards. Come with me, please.' We were led along a small corridor to a room at the end. 'Please take a seat,' said the doctor, as he sat facing us. 'I'm so sorry to confirm that the woman is dead, is she a relation of yours?'

'She's my wife, Doctor and this is our son, Einstein.' The doctor gave me a strange look. I knew why. I had had that look many times before.

'What happened?' He asked looking at us each in turn.

My father related the dreary events of the picnic to the doctor, who seemed to be sympathetic.

I wonder if he believes him. I thought.

The doctor looked at me and raised his eyebrows, saying nothing, but demanding an answer. My version.

'I'd left the picnic and I heard my father calling. He told me that my mother had swallowed a peach stone and that she was choking. He said he'd tried to move it, but couldn't.'

'What did you do?'

'I also tried, but it had slipped so far down her throat I just couldn't reach it. She tried to take another breath, but only noise came out.' I looked down at my feet and shifted them together. 'My mother then fell further onto the ground and didn't move again.' I lifted my face to meet the doctor's calm enquiring gaze. 'There was blood coming from her nose and mouth.' I stared at the Doctor in front of me, my mind numb. I couldn't say anymore – I didn't know any more. I have had thoughts of my mother being dead. Thoughts of heavenly release from her stupid and selfish needs, thoughts I could not and would not share. But dead... now.

'I'm very sorry,' he said, turning to face my father again, 'but when we have a sudden death like this, we have to inform the police. 'Please wait here, I'll be back soon.'

Within a few minutes, he returned. 'An officer is on the way. It's usually just a formality but we can't carry out an autopsy until a coroner has agreed to it. I can get you a coffee or tea while you're waiting.'

'Thank you,' said my father, 'but I'm fine.' He looked at me. 'What about you, son?'

'I'm okay, thank you,' I said.

After a short wait, without any words passing between my father and me, two police officers arrived. They sat in chairs opposite us.

It was the tall one on the left who spoke. 'Dr Richards has told us your account of what happened to your wife, Mr Smith. However, we would like to hear it from you again, so we can make a report.'

My father repeated his account of the afternoon, as the officer on the right scribbled in a notebook.

'Had your wife had any trouble eating a peach, or any other food, before?'

'No, no trouble at all. Peaches were her favourite fruit and she always had them when they were in season.' My father's voice was shaking. Not for the first time that day I felt a mixture of sadness and anger at his weakness.

The same officer turned to me. 'And you, son, I believe you tried to help your mother.'

I also repeated what I had done. More scribbles from the silent partner, and then the notebook closed.

'As I said, we will need to make a report,' said the officer. If there are no further enquires we have to make, your wife's body will be released for the coroner to approve an autopsy. This may well take some time and we'll probably want to speak to you both again.'

The officers turned to leave the room. The taller of the two turned back to face us. 'I'm very sorry about your loss, Mr Smith, we'll be as quick as possible.' The door closed quietly behind them.

My father and I remained still, looking at the closed door.

'I'm sorry, Dad,' I said. 'I hope you don't mind, I'm still going to Scotland tomorrow. My plans haven't, and won't be, changed.'

'I didn't think they would, son,' was all he said.

My father looked at me, I could see the despair and sadness etched deeply on his face.

'I didn't think they would,' he repeated. 'You know, I did try to get the stone out of her throat.'

'I know,' I said, suddenly realising from the way he'd avoided my eyes that he'd done nothing of the sort. That he'd effectively killed her...

CHAPTER NINE

Peter joined the officer outside the hospital room where Mrs Williamson was recovering. Jenny had called him and asked him to go to the hospital immediately to talk to her, explaining that she'd been held up and urgently wanted Mrs Williamson interviewed.

'Has she said anything yet?' Peter asked the officer.

'Nothing at all, Sir.'

A young nurse approached the door. 'You can go in now, but I don't think you'll make much sense of what she's saying.' She moved aside to let him pass. 'Just a few minutes only, please, she's still very unwell.'

'Thank you,' said Peter, walking through the door and introducing himself.

Emma Williamson turned towards him, her face pale and drawn.

'Are you able to talk about it?' Peter looked sympathetically at her. 'We have nothing yet, that gives us any clues as to why your husband might have been killed in this way. Any information you can give us might help us to find the killer.'

She closed her eyes and sighed.

He waited a minute before prompting her again. I really need information from you now, Mrs Williamson. You must be aware that we want to find whoever did this to your husband as quickly as possible.' He thought he saw a flash of agreement in her eyes, and continued, 'When we spoke to you before, you mentioned that your husband deserved to die. Can you explain why you said that? You said you hated him. Can you also tell me what made you feel that way?'

Mrs Williamson opened her mouth just as the young nurse came into the room.

'I'm sorry, Detective, but your time is almost up. Her doctor was very specific about her not talking to anyone. I'm really sorry, Sir.'

Peter felt a touch of anger, although reluctantly accepting the apology and the Doctor's orders, even though he felt that Mrs Williamson might have been about to say something,

The nurse motioned for him to join her outside the room. 'To be honest, Detective, I don't think she will talk to you, I don't know for sure, but she doesn't seem to like men too much. She won't even let the male doctors touch her. Perhaps if a female detective could come you may have more luck.'

'Has she said anything at all to you?'

'No, she hasn't spoken a word to me, and even if she had I wouldn't be able to pass it on to you I'm afraid.'

'Thank you,' said Peter. He pulled his mobile from his top pocket and dialled Jenny's number.

'Hello, Peter, any luck?'

'That's what I'm calling about, Jenny. She won't talk to me, but from what one of the nurses have said she may talk to a woman.'

Jenny sighed. 'Okay, thanks for trying Peter. I've been called back to the station for now,' she said. 'There's been a report of a missing young woman. Everyone is getting excited about it. Let's hope we can find her soon.

'I'll meet you back there,' said Peter.

He turned to the officer outside of Mrs Williamson's room. 'Call me immediately if there's anything to report. Especially if she has any visitors. I'll get someone to relieve you as soon as possible, Officer.'

'Yes, of course, I will, Sir.'

CHAPTER TEN

There was a buzz at the station when Jenny arrived. Passing through the reception area, she saw a man and woman sitting quietly, their faces etched with worry. The woman rose as Jenny was about to pass them.

'My daughter is missing,' she said. Her face was full of anxiety, her hands clinging tightly onto her bag.

'Sit down, Margaret, love, they'll ask us questions when they're ready,' said the man.

'I'm so sorry to keep you waiting. We'll be with you very shortly. I will ask someone to get you a drink if you would like one,' said Jenny as she was about to pass the two people in front of her.

'Thank you, but we have just had one,' said Mr Moore quietly.

Peter was already in her office together with two of the detectives working on the Williamson case.

One of the officers opened his notebook and quoted the names of Robert and Margaret Moore as the parents of the missing person. 'Her name is Lynn Moore. Been missing for just over a week. Doesn't live with her parents, but in one of those posh new flats near Peirce's Wood.' He turned a page. 'Mr and Mrs Moore weren't worried until a short time ago, although they said it's unusual for their daughter not to be in touch at least two or three times a week. Mrs Moore said she visited her daughter's flat today and that she felt that it hadn't been lived in for some time. She said it "felt very empty".' He hesitated. 'Whatever that means? Heating was on a timer, so it was warm. She said that her daughter wouldn't have left the heating on if she'd planned to be away. He snapped his notebook shut. 'That's all I have, for now, Ma'am. Mr and Mrs Moore are in reception at the moment.'

'Somebody mentioned a connection with the Williamson murder, what is it?' enquired Jenny.

'Not sure it is a connection, Ma'am, but while in reception they saw the picture of James Williamson on the front page of the newspaper lying on the desk. Someone heard Mrs Moore say that she remembered her daughter had spoken about a James Williamson.'

'Did you enquire further?' said Jenny.

'I didn't have time before you arrived, Ma'am.'

'Well, it sounds interesting, officer. Take Mr and Mrs Moore to the interview room, I'll get someone to talk to them.'

'Yes, Ma'am.' He left the room. Jenny followed him to the reception and saw Alan Hughes standing close to Mr and Mrs Moore. She called him over.

'Alan, I've asked an officer to take Mr and Mrs Moore into the interview room. Give them time to settle, then I would like you to talk to them. It seems that Mrs Moore indicated that her daughter might have known James Williamson. DI Branden and I will be in the observation room.'

As Jenny stood by the observation window, she thought how austere, cold and unwelcoming police interview rooms were. It wasn't the first time she wished the rooms could be friendlier. Mr and Mrs Moore were seated on one side of the wooden table, DS Hughes on the other.

'I'm Detective Sergeant Alan Hughes,' he said, and he held out a hand towards the two people in front of him. 'I would like you to tell me about your daughter. Take your time, but please let me know anything that may help us find her.'

Mrs Moore took a huge breath. Taking a handkerchief from her handbag she slowly wiped her mouth. 'It's just that Lynn has never left it this long to contact us, and we can't get a reply from her phone at home.' Her voice was quiet and shaky, she glanced at her husband for support.

'She usually calls us at least three or four times a week,' continued Mr Moore, holding his wife's hand protectively. 'I've spoken with Sarah, her partner, and she hasn't heard from her either. To be honest we're really getting worried now. It's just not like her to leave it so long to get in touch with us. She's also not returning any calls, which is very unusual.'

DS Hughes turned to face Mrs Moore. 'Someone heard you say that Lynn might have known a James Williamson. Can you tell us about that?'

'Oh, that was such a long time ago,' she replied, her voice a little calmer. 'It's just … seeing the name of that poor man in the newspaper made me think of it, but it was years ago. I don't think he had anything at all to do with our daughter now. It's just that seeing his name made me remember that Lynn mentioned him many years ago.'

'Can you try and remember if she ever spoke about him to anyone?'

'No, I really can't remember. It's as I said. I saw his name in the paper out there.' She pointed past the door of the interview room. 'I just remembered Lynn talked about a James Williamson.' She turned to look at her husband. 'But, it was such a long time ago, officer, I may even have got the name wrong. It just seemed, well … you know … it just seemed to ring a bell.'

'Why are you asking us all this?' said Mr Moore. 'Are the questions relevant to finding my daughter? My wife and I are already extremely worried and upset and I would like to take her home as soon as possible.'

'I'm sorry, Mr Moore, we need as much information as possible to help find your daughter, and anything may be relevant, especially if it could link your daughter's apparent disappearance to a current case,' DS Hughes said. He looked at the two people in front of him. 'I hope you don't mind me saying this, Mr and Mrs Moore, but just over a week is not usually long enough to worry so much. Young people often go somewhere without telling loved ones where they are or what they're doing. Sometimes they just want to be alone or to do something on their own.' Her voice was sympathetic as he tried to lighten their mood.

Mrs Moore wiped a tear from her eyes again and looked directly at him. 'I understand that officer, but I know my Lynn wouldn't do that, I just know. I'm sorry, I will try not to worry and, of course, I'll help all I can. If I remember anything else about my daughter and James Williamson, I'll tell you immediately. We went to Lynn's flat. We have a key. Lynn always said we were welcome to go there at any time. Everything seemed normal. My daughter is very particular about her flat, she keeps it beautifully, and nothing was out of place – nothing. But as I said, it just didn't feel right.'

'Did you check the telephone?'

'Yes, I did, she had some missed calls.'

'Do you know who they were from?'

'The only one I recognised was from Sarah. The other calls were from her work.' She hesitated for a short time. 'Oh yes, I remember now, one was from someone reminding her of an appointment to view a property. My daughter and her partner were looking for a house to buy.'

'Did they give a name, or time and address?'

'No, he didn't. He just said he was looking forward to meeting her, or something like that.' Her eyes filled with tears again.

'Have you spoken to Sarah? asked Hughes.

'Not since she rang us to ask if we'd heard from Lynn. I just told her we hadn't and that we were very worried. We promised to call each other if we had any news. We really want to go home now, and want to be at home when she calls.' Mr Moore said.

'We'll do all we can to help find your daughter, Mr Moore. In the meantime, if you think of anything that may help, or if your daughter gets in touch with you, please contact us.' DS Hughes handed him a card.

'We will, of course,' said Mr Moore as he helped his wife through the open door. His wife hesitated and turned back to face DS Hughes.

'What's so important about … what we might know … about Mr Williamson?' She spoke quietly, her words broken as sobs took over again. 'I could easily have the wrong name.'

'Come on, love, we should get home now.' Mr Moore took his wife's arm and guided her through the door, not waiting for her question to be answered.

In the observation room, Jenny turned to Peter. 'I think we should go back into Williamson's background a bit more. Not much to go on, but the smallest clue at the moment is better than none. We also need to go to the offices of the bank he worked at, follow up on what we've found out so far about his working life. Get all the information you can, Peter, it should be logged by now and we can go later today or first thing in the morning.'

'Of course. What about getting the dogs out to search the woodlands at the back of the flats where Lynn Moore lived?' Peter said on his way out.

'Already organised.' She thought for a few seconds and then called him back. 'Peter, when you get chance, get Alan to go with you to Lynn Moore's flat, please. Go through the telephone calls again, especially the ones from the man about a property they should see. I'm sure that Mr Moore will let you have the key. Listen to the messages, there may be just something to give a clue as to her whereabouts. I need to do something first after which, I'll go to the hospital and see if I can gently persuade Mrs Williamson to talk a bit more to me.

CHAPTER ELEVEN

Jenny arrived at the hospital around two o'clock to discover that Mrs Williamson had left.

'How could she just leave?' asked Jenny.

'I'm sorry, I wasn't on duty when it happened,' the receptionist said defensively. 'They can give you more information if you go to the ward and speak to the sister in charge. She will be able to help you. Southdown Ward is on the second floor.' She pointed to her left. 'There're stairs on the right just along the corridor, or the lift is opposite the stairs if you prefer.'

Frustrated, Jenny strode down the corridor of the hospital towards the lift. Mrs Williamson had left the hospital and that she hadn't been told. *Someone's in for a rollicking,* she thought angrily.

As she reached Southdown Ward she saw two nurses at a large desk talking with what she assumed was a doctor. 'I'm enquiring about Mrs Williamson,' said Jenny, showing her badge. 'I believe she has left the hospital. Can you tell me if she went home and in exactly what circumstances?'

One of the nurses turned to speak to her. 'She left this morning, discharged herself.' Stopping briefly, she studied some notes. 'It was her sister who came and insisted she left with her. The doctor tried to stop her, but Mrs Williamson wouldn't listen. Her sister said she would be better in her own home. I'm sorry, that's all I have.'

'What about the police officer who was here?' Jenny worked hard to keep the anger from her voice.

'Oh, they both went with them. I believe one of them made a call to someone first.'

'Thank you.' Jenny turned and walked towards the lift and pressed the ground floor button. As she got in her car, she pulled her mobile from her pocket and called the station.

'DCI Trent here, put me through to someone in the duty office please.'

'Afternoon, Ma'am, I'm glad you've called, I was trying to contact you before you went to the hospital.'

Jenny instantly recognised Alan Hughes's voice. 'That's what I'm calling about, Alan.' She made no attempt to disguise her anger. 'How on earth was Mrs Williamson allowed to leave the hospital without my authority?'

Alan gave a nervous cough. 'The officers at the hospital apparently rang the station and said that Emma Williamson had her sister with her and that she was demanding that she be allowed to go home. It seems she was in a terrible state and just wouldn't take any notice of the doctors.'

'What is the duty office playing at? I should have been told. Thank you, Alan. If the super asks, tell him I'm going to the Williamson's house right now. I want to talk to Mrs Williamson,' she hesitated slightly. 'I would like you and DI Branden to go back Lynn Moore's flat to check everything again. Especially the phone messages. Report back as soon as possible. If anyone asks for me, you know where I'll be.'

'Before you go, Ma'am, I tried to contact you to tell you that DI Branden and I have already visited Mrs Williamson today. We've been waiting to see you so we could tell you what happened.'

'What do you mean you and Branden went to Mrs Williamson's house. Why wasn't I told what you were doing? And, how did you know she was home when nobody else did?'

'We didn't, Ma'am, it's just that we were visiting the people in Marden Close as you told us to, and after speaking to a Mr Collins, we just knocked on the Williamson's door on the off-chance there might be a cleaner or someone home, and Mrs Williamson opened it herself.'

'I see,' Jenny said, her mood calming a little. 'I want a full report on my desk within an hour, but in the meantime give me the bones of it and we'll catch up again after I've spoken to her myself.'

'Yes, Ma'am.'

After Alan had briefed her, Jenny replaced her phone in the holder. Notification of his missed call winked at her from the screen.

***

Arriving at Emma Williamson's house, Jenny was relieved to see a police officer was now on duty outside the front door.

'Afternoon, Ma'am.'

'Afternoon. Is anyone in the house?' said Jenny.

'Yes, Ma'am. Mrs Williamson, and another woman – I think it's her sister.

As she reached for the bell push, the door opened and a woman Jenny hadn't seen before, but who bore a remarkable resemblance to Emma Williamson, spoke, her tone sharp and clipped. 'Can I help you?' she said.

'Jenny introduced herself and held up her identification badge. 'I'd like to speak with Emma Williamson, please.'

'I'm sorry, she's not well enough to speak to anyone at the moment. She has already spoken to two of your people and she is very tired.' She began to close the door. Jenny moved closer.

'It's very important that I speak with her, either here or at the police station. We're investigating the murder of her husband and we believe she may be able to help us.'

A quiet, breathless voice from further inside the house said. 'Let the Chief Inspector in, Jill, it's okay now.'

The woman hesitated before opening the door just wide enough for Jenny to pass through.

Emma Williamson turned to face Jenny as she entered. 'Good afternoon, Chief Inspector, this is my sister, Jill. She is looking after me for a while, please sit down.'

'Do you want me to stay, Emma?' said Jill.

'I would prefer it if you did, please,' said Jenny. 'There may be information you can help us with.'

Jenny noticed the change in Mrs Williamson's appearance, her hair was well-groomed and her make up freshly applied. Before sitting, she walked towards her and offered her hand, which was shaken softly.

'As you know, Mrs Williamson, we are investigating the death of your husband, and I would like to ask you some questions which may help with our enquiries. You were, of course, extremely upset on the day your husband was killed. And then, just as I was leaving you screamed out that you were glad your husband was dead and that you hated him. Are you able to tell me what you meant by your comments?'

'I have already spoken to two of your officers who knocked at my door earlier. I don't think I can tell you any more than I told them.' She walked further in. followed by Jenny. 'I did hate my husband, Chief Inspector, and I am glad he's dead.'

'Please be careful what you say, Emma, darling,' said Jill. 'You know how things can be twisted and you're not really well yet.'

Jenny turned to face her. 'I appreciate your concern Jill, but we do need your sister to tell us everything so that she can be eliminated from our enquires.'

'Are you telling us that she's a suspect? Don't you think my sister has been through enough? And if she *is*, then I demand that a solicitor is here before anything else is said.'

'Of course I truly believe your sister has been through an awful lot, but I do need to set some answers and I am sorry, but your sister will hopefully be able to help us with that.

Emma Williamson touched her sister's arm. 'I'm fine, thank you, Jill. I'm just as interested as anyone to find out who killed him, and I'll give Chief Inspector Trent all the help I can.' She turned back to Jenny. 'I did not kill my husband, Chief Inspector. I can only repeat what I've already said – I'm glad he is dead.' Her voice shook. She looked straight into Jenny's eyes. 'You must decide for yourself, Chief Inspector, how much of what I'm about to tell you needs to go in your report. I, myself, cannot suffer further or feel any more embarrassed by what I allowed to happen.' Her fists clenched in her lap as she sat further back in her chair and breathed hard.

Jenny stayed silent, curiosity burning.

'I did not tell your two officers everything, Chief Inspector. Some things are just too hard to disclose to all and sundry. My husband, James Williamson, was a bully. He'd been a bully all his life. He wasn't just a bully, he was a sadistic bully.' She hesitated. 'And ... he was a nasty pervert who had the ability to get anyone to do exactly what he wanted.' She glanced at her sister who was sitting upright in her chair, eyes closed. 'He never hit me, and he didn't have to.' She shifted her feet nervously and moved uneasily in her chair. 'He used me for his own perverted needs.' Her eyes grew dark with anger, but her voice stayed strong. 'And,' she paused to look away. 'He felt no shame for what he did. I spent many nights on my own. It didn't bother him that I knew that he was with other women, he boasted about it. You see, Inspector sex, money and power were the most important things in my husband's life.' She looked away again. 'And he had plenty of them all.'

She stopped, apparently waiting for Jenny's reaction. But before Jenny could respond, she continued. 'We didn't have many friends, in fact, we never had *any* friends. But there were men who visited us often. I could hear them laughing for a while, then it would go quiet. I assumed they had gone through to the bar we have, Chief Inspector. The bar has a snooker and card tables. I hardly ever went to the room. Sometimes I would hear them leave, very late.' She shuddered, tears filling her eyes. 'He said we didn't need friends. What he didn't seem to realise, was that apart from his cronies and his tarts no one really liked him, or wanted to be friends.'

Jill's hand reached protectively for her sister's arm. 'Do you really want to continue, Emma? I'm sure Chief Inspector Trent will come back when you're feeling better.'

'No! I want to tell as much as I can.' Her voice heavy with emotion, her face determined. 'I feel ashamed that I didn't stop what he made me do and I will regret it all my life. I was weak and stupid, and I would like to find out who killed him.' She sighed quietly. 'And shake his, or her, hand.'

'Did you know any of the men he brought home?' Jenny said.

A short laugh came from Emma Williamson. 'Did I know them?' she repeated. 'My husband made sure I got to know them. They were nasty perverts too, Chief Inspector, I wish they were all dead. But they were strangers. I never knew their names, my husband said I didn't need to.'

Jill squeezed her sister's hand. 'That's enough for now, Emma, you must have a rest.'

'I'm fine,' said Emma, as she pulled her hand away from her sister's grasp. She looked across at Jenny. 'I'll tell you something of what went on, Chief Inspector, but I'd really rather no one else knew, please, if you can prevent it.' She sat back in the chair and took a handkerchief from her sister's outstretched hand.

'I'm so sorry, but everything you tell me will have to be recorded. This is a major enquiry and I am unable to sanction the suppression of any information you give me. What you tell me may well be used as evidence in a court of law. I hope you understand that,' Jenny said.

'Yes, of course, I do.' She coughed into the handkerchief and took a moment to compose herself.

'It started about five years ago, I had been in bed asleep for some time when my husband woke me, told me to get dressed and make myself look pretty. He said he wanted me to meet some very important clients, and that is was vital that I was with him. I had never seen any of the men who were standing around in the lounge. Every one of them was very smartly dressed, and they were all drinking.' She pulled roughly at the handkerchief in her hand. 'I wasn't sure how many they numbered but thought about six. I was introduced to them as his understanding wife.' She raised the handkerchief to her mouth and paused.

'I don't drink, Chief Inspector, but my husband insisted I should that night, to "be sociable". The men were very friendly, in fact, I thought they were being too friendly. I thought it was because of the drink. Later, when they'd gone, I asked James what he meant by describing me as his "understanding wife". He just sniggered and said "Work it out, sweetheart."' Emma Williamson's head dropped, and she stared at her fingers which were now pressed tightly into the palms of her hands.

Jill put a protective arm around her sister. 'Emma, would you like a break?'

'Yes, I would, thank you,' she said without looking up. 'Another cup of tea would be fine. I'm sure the Chief Inspector would like one.'

'No, thank you, I'm fine,' said Jenny. 'I would like to continue talking to your sister.'

Jill came back with a tray of fresh tea. 'I'm so sorry, Chief Inspector, but it might be better for my sister to have a rest until tomorrow, would you mind if we asked you to come back?'

'I've already asked the Chief Inspector to stay,' said Mrs Williamson, 'and I would like to say what I have to say, today. I'm perfectly alright and I want to get it over with.' She took a sip of tea and carefully put down her cup on the small table next to her.

'The next time James came home with clients I had gone to bed early. He woke me and asked me to join them again. This time he had bought expensive underwear and told me to put it on before I came down. I was shocked and angry. I asked him why he'd bought the underwear. I told him I wasn't going down to join his clients this time, and I threw the flimsy underwear across the room. I thought he would go away, but he didn't. He just stared at me and then grabbed my hair. He'd never done that before. For the first time, I felt frightened of him.' She took a big breath and wiped away the tears that had started to pool in the corners of her eyes.

'He told me that I would do as he said or things would change around here, and that, if I didn't understand what he meant, I would, soon enough. He grabbed my hair so hard that he had a handful of broken strands in his hand as he let go. He told me he would stay until I had changed and then I would come with him to meet his friends. He picked up the underwear and pressed it into my hands.'

Emma Williamson looked up at Jenny and then across to her sister. 'I didn't want to, but I was scared ... so I changed. When I'd finished he took my hand, I felt his nails digging into my wrists as he pulled me down the stairs.' She hesitated again. 'Downstairs a glass of champagne was waiting for me. I'd never drunk champagne before and wouldn't have known what it tasted like.' She sat upright in her chair and stared hard at the floor in front of her. 'I drank it. As soon as I'd finished my glass was filled again ... and again. I remember feeling warm and dizzy, and I started to giggle, and ...well ... I couldn't stop giggling, you know ... like a schoolgirl. I remember finding it difficult to walk and my husband holding me by the elbow, pushing me forward as two of the men walked towards me.' She stopped, and her sister moved closer to her.

'Emma, my love, please. No more, it's so distressing for you. Please, Emma,' said Jill.

'I'm sorry, but I must hear all that your sister has to say,' said Jenny.

'I've almost finished,' said Emma Williamson, ignoring her sister's pleas. She looked up at Jenny. 'I remember one of the men who was coming towards me. He was smiling and he put his arms around me. He undid my bra roughly ... he took his time because he was fumbling.' She sniffed quietly into her handkerchief. 'Even though he was pretty drunk I sensed he was embarrassed. I tried to stop him, but I couldn't, my legs felt like jelly. I just wanted to get away.'

Tears were running down her face, smearing her carefully applied make-up. 'It hurt so much.' And James, he ... just sat there staring at me, with a stupid sickly grin on his face. I'd never seen him look like that before, it was truly horrible. I wanted to shout at him to ask the man – to *tell* him – to stop, but he wasn't listening to me. Then suddenly, I wasn't hurting any more. Everything went … black.' She lifted her head to face Jenny. 'That's it. I don't know any more, I'm sorry if it's not enough.'

'What you have told me, Mrs Williamson is quite shocking. Your husband was abusing you. I have to ask why you didn't go to the police or get help of some kind.'

'Because I didn't want anyone to know, Chief Inspector, I was ashamed and scared.' Her face showed a remarkable change, gone was the frightened look, replaced by one of relieved determination. 'My life has taken a turn for the better. He's gone, and I'm glad and I am happy to answer any and all of your questions either here or at the police station if you wish.'

'I'm glad you're feeling better, Mrs Williamson, and there may well be more information we will need from you.'

She turned to face Jill. 'Did you know this was happening to your sister?'

'Emma only confided in me a few weeks ago, Chief Inspector. I was, of course, horrified, and I insisted she should go to the police and that I would go with her. But she said she was too embarrassed to do that, she didn't want anyone to know. She begged me not to tell a soul. I was due to come to see her later this week, to try and persuade her again to leave that truly dreadful man and go to the police.'

Emma Williamson rose from her chair. 'If you don't mind I would like to rest for a while, I'm sure Jill will show you out.' She walked slowly towards the open door. Jill moved towards her. Jenny could see the pain in her face. 'I'll come with you, Emma, love.' She turned to Jenny. 'Please, wait here, Chief Inspector. I'll settle Emma down and come back to you as soon as possible.'

On her own, Jenny began to reflect on what she had been told. How could any woman cope with that vile man?

'There's no more I can tell you, Chief Inspector,' said Jill when she returned shortly afterwards, her voice low. 'I knew nothing of this until just a week ago. I pleaded with her to let me go to the police, or for her to go to one of those women's protection places, but she just wouldn't listen to me. I'd already made up my mind to do something myself before I got the call telling me that her husband was dead. If that makes me a suspect as well, then, to be honest, I don't care, Chief Inspector. Why didn't she leave him? I don't know. I haven't asked her, and I won't. But I do know that she was terrified of him.' Jill moved towards the door. The talking was over.

'I'll see you out, Chief Inspector,' she said, then stopped. 'Just one more thing. You wanted to know why my sister reacted to his death the way she did, and now you know. Is there *any* way our conversation could be off the record? For Emma's sake.' It's just that she has had so much suffering and I so want it to get to a point when she can start to get her own life back to some kind of normality, as quickly as possible.'

As they reach the front door, Jenny turned to Jill. 'I can appreciate your request, Jill, but we will need the names of the people who visited this house. As I said to your sister, everything – *everything*,' she repeated, 'has to be recorded and,' she emphasised, '*nothing* can be off the record. As soon as your sister, to be honest, talk further with us we'll be asking a lot more questions. There's been a brutal murder and we need to catch the person responsible. There is, however, one question I would like to ask you, as you are obviously very close to your sister,' said Jenny.

'I know what you're going to ask, and no, Chief Inspector, I do not think my sister killed that dreadful man. I'm sure there are many people who will be glad he is dead and, like my sister, I'd also like to shake the hand of the person who did it. That's all. If anyone deserved to be killed, he did.'

The door closed quietly behind Jenny. She felt disturbed and horrified by what she'd just heard from Mrs Williams and wanted to get home. It had been quite a day, and doubtless, there was another waiting for her tomorrow.

CHAPTER TWELVE

Peter decided to move the car closer to Williamson's house, but not quite in front of the gate. It was bigger and grander than Collins' house. The garden was immaculate, with large shrubs already flowering in the spring sunshine. The area was now clear of the police cars and security units that had been hiding the opulence of the house on the day of his last visit when Williamson had been discovered.

'Phew!' was all he said, as he and Alan reached the double gates leading on to a large path.

The door to the entrance of the house looked like solid oak, with a small, stained glass window in the middle. There was no means on the door itself of alerting the household to the presence of visitors, but to the right, there was a shining circular brass bell push. Peter pressed it and deep chimes filled the air.

They waited, but heard no steps from inside the house and, as Peter was about to press the bell again, Emma Williamson opened the door.

Peter hid his shock well. 'Good afternoon, Mrs Williamson. DI Peter Branden – you may remember me from our initial investigation on the day of your husband's death?' He stopped, pointing at Alan. 'This is Sergeant Hughes. We'd like to ask you some more questions please.' They acknowledged the Family Liaison Officer, who had followed Mrs Williamson to the door.

'I'm not sure I can help any more,' she said, her voice so quiet, Alan had to lean forward to hear.

'I understand, Mrs Williamson,' said Peter, but we really need to ask you some questions about your husband. Would now be okay? Officer Spencer can stay with us.'

She hesitated, then sighed, and said 'Of course. Please come in.'

Following Emma Williamson, they reached the entrance to a large room. 'We can talk in here,' she said as she went through the door. 'Please, take a seat.'

Peter noticed how different Emma Williamson looked from the last time he had seen her. Although it was obvious that she was nervous, she seemed calm and bright, her blonde hair was held by an invisible band, strands floating around her face made her look small and vulnerable. She wore very little make-up, which emphasised her pale ivory skin, her blue eyes were bright and enquisitive. He suddenly felt he had looked too long and his eyes closed as he opened his notebook.

'How can I help?' she said.

After his experience at the hospital, Peter decided to keep his questioning factual and focused on her husband's work and social life. Jenny would want to talk to Mrs Williamson again anyway, and as a woman, she would probably have more luck getting through the apparent emotional block around the day of the murder itself. 'Mrs Williamson, we need to know more about your husband,' he said. 'What he did when he was not working if he had any hobbies, who his friends were?' He stopped, waiting for an answer from her.

She didn't move.

Peter continued. 'How did you get on with the neighbours? Did he, or both of you, socialise with them?'

'No, we did not!' Her voice raised in simmering anger. 'I sometimes spoke with the other wives.' She hesitated. 'Well, one or two of them anyway. They were very pleasant, but we never had a lot to do with them or their husbands. You see, Inspector, as I am sure you have been told by many people, my husband was not well-liked around here, so we were never invited to anything.'

'Why wasn't your husband liked by your neighbours, Mrs Williamson?' Alan looked up from his notebook.

'Because he was an arrogant bully, and everyone knew that.'

'What about Mr Collins a few doors away from you?' Did you or your husband have anything to do with him?'

'Mr Collins hated my husband. He blamed him for the breakup of his marriage, accused my husband of having an affair with his wife.'

'Was it true?' asked Peter.

'To be honest, I don't know, Inspector, but it probably was. My husband found a lot of women attractive and Mrs Collins is a very pretty woman.' She stood up and moved a few steps away from the chair, arms folded tight across her chest. 'I don't think I have anything else to say. I would like to rest now. Can I show you out?' Her voice was shaking. 'My husband is dead, Inspector, and he died in the most horrific way. I'm sorry I can't tell you more about his life, but I believe there are probably quite a few people who, like me, are glad he's dead. I can only tell you again, I have no idea who could have done it.'

'Mrs Williamson,' said Peter, 'I'm so sorry, and I know how hard it is, but I am afraid we need to know a lot more about your husband, please sit down. Unless we can find some answers soon, we're concerned that someone else may be hurt or even killed.'

Mrs Williamson took a breath, stepped back, and sat with resignation back down on the chair.

'After we have asked a few more questions, we would like to look around the house.' Without waiting for a response, Peter continued. 'Mr Collins said that your husband entertained people here quite a lot. Do you know anything about that?'

Mrs Williamson turned to look at Peter. Her expression was frightened and wary.

'I know that my husband brought friends here, but I was never involved with them.' Her voice shook. 'We have a games room in the house, Inspector. My husband had evenings when he brought people in to play cards, snooker, something like that, or just for drinks.'

'What did you do on these evenings?'

'My husband knew I wasn't interested so he suggested that I went and visited my sister.'

'How did you feel about that?'

'They were not my friends, Inspector. I didn't know who they were and I didn't want to. I was pleased to go.'

'Did any of the neighbours join in on these evenings?'

'I'm not sure, but I don't think so.'

'Had your husband always worked for the Standard Elite Bank in London?'

'For as long as I'd known him, yes.'

'You really didn't know very much about your husband, did you, Mrs Williamson?' Alan suddenly spoke again, his eyebrows raised a challenge as much as a question. 'How long were you married?'

Mrs Williamson shot a look at him. 'I knew as much as I wanted to, and we were married for just under twelve years.'

'We'd like to look at the games room, please,' said Peter and stood up without waiting for an answer. Alan and Mrs Williamson rose from their chairs together.

'Please come with me,' she said, pushing past them and leading them into the hall.

They followed Mrs Williamson, their shoes quiet on the thick-pile carpet, Spencer walking just behind them. They passed two highly polished oak doors on the right, and one on the left before coming to an open door leading to the kitchen.

The kitchen was expensively fitted with shining brilliant-white units and a large double cooker hob and oven. In the middle of the room was a generous island unit with matching cupboards underneath. Everything was immaculate.

'A lovely kitchen, Mrs Williamson,' said Alan. 'Do you do much cooking?'

'I used to, but not for a long time now. My husband was not one for home cooking, he preferred eating out.'

They continued past the kitchen into a small corridor. On the left was a door. Alan hesitated beside it. Seeing his hesitation, Mrs Williamson stepped forward to open the door and invited them into a spacious bathroom, with a large modern bath, shower area, toilet and bidet. Thick white towels hung from dedicated rails and the walls were fitted with gleaming chrome and glass shelves holding bath creams, soaps and perfumes. The floor shone with black glass tiles. Like the rest of the house, it was perfect, nothing out of place.

'You have a lovely house. 'It's unusual to have such a spacious bathroom on the ground floor, was that your idea?'

'No, it was my husband's wish. You see, when he had people in, he said they sometimes needed a shower or a bath before leaving and it was less intrusive to have facilities down here. To be honest, I've never used it, but I believe his guests did.'

'Did you not find it unusual that his guests, who after all, were just drinking and playing snooker, needed to have a bath before leaving?'

'It never bothered me to think that there was anything unusual about my husband's guests, Inspector. I wanted nothing to do with them. I am rather tired, Inspector. Do you have any more questions?'

'Your house is lovely, do you have someone to help you keep it this way?'

'Yes, I have, a cleaner she comes in once a week, and she spends all day here while I'm out. She was here yesterday, so no dust has had time to settle yet. It is a lovely house, Inspector, but as I disliked my husband intensely so I dislike this house. As soon as I can, I intend to sell it and move as far away as possible. That may sound shocking, Inspector, and I realise it may give you a reason to believe I could have killed my husband, but I didn't. I just hated him. And I am sure it's well documented that I said I was glad he was dead.' She pointed ahead of her. 'The games room is further down the corridor.'

She moved past the two men and they followed her to the end of the corridor, reaching another solid closed door. A security lock was fitted to the wall and Mrs Williamson tapped in five numbers. The door clicked and opened slowly.

The room was not as large as Peter had expected, but still sufficiently sizeable to contain a full-size snooker table, with snooker cues standing upright on a rack by the wall behind. There were two small card tables with packs of cards on them on the opposite side of the room, and two black leather settees facing each other in the middle. At the back of the room, there was a bar, fitted with an impressive range of spirits, wines and soft drinks. Next to the bar, a framed mirror took up almost half the wall, reflecting the whole room, giving it a much more spacious appearance. The room smelled of leather and expensive furnishing. *Very much a man's room* thought Peter.

'Does your cleaner come in here to clean?' said Alan.

'No, she doesn't. My husband didn't want women in here. He cleaned it himself, which accounts for the dust everywhere. I can't bring myself to ask my cleaner to clean it yet, and I can assure you that I don't want to do it myself.'

Peter walked around the room. Unlike the rest of the house, it felt cold and uninviting. He shivered.

'Thank you, Mrs Williamson, you've been very helpful. We may need to speak with again.'

'I'll see you out, Inspector.'

As she opened the front door to let them out, Peter turned to face her. 'We may need to speak with your cleaner, have you got her telephone number, please?'

'Yes, of course.' She went to a large table at the side of the hall, wrote on a small notepad and then handed Peter the folded page.

Alan turned just as he reached the door. 'Just one more thing, Mrs Williamson. You've told us how much you hated your husband and that you're glad that he's dead.'

'Yes, that's right, I have said that, and I meant it, sergeant. Why?'

'Why didn't you leave him?'

'What has that got to do with his death?'

'Nothing at the moment, Mrs Williamson, but it may have something to do with our ongoing enquires.'

'I'm afraid I can't answer that question, sergeant,' said Mrs Williamson. 'Because I am ashamed to say I don't know.'

Spencer was standing in the hall, close to the front door.

'Thank you for all your help, Mrs Williamson. Please call us if you need to, or if you're able to remember anything else that might help us to find out who killed your husband and why. Even the smallest detail may give us some important clues,' said Peter.

'Yes, of course, I will,' said Mrs Williamson. 'I can tell you now *why* he was killed, though. He was a horrible man, Inspector. Arrogant, selfish and quite nasty. As I have said before, a lot of people disliked him. A lot. I am also sure a lot of people are delighted he is dead.'

'I'm not convinced we know everything that went on in that house yet,' said Peter as he got into the car.

'No, we don't, and I believe Mrs Williamson could tell us a lot more if she wanted to,' said Alan.

CHAPTER THIRTEEN

Jenny opened the door to a joyful greeting from her beloved golden retriever, Honey, who, having heard the sound of her mistress's car, had searched for and found a toy to greet her with. The ritual usually lasted for about five minutes, ending with Honey happily munching her treat before joining her mistress on the large settee.

As she did every day, Jenny rose and went to the table next to the television where the last picture taken of her husband had been for the past three years. She still missed him, the emptiness inside her still so much a part of her life. She smiled at his handsome face. Kissing her fingers, she lifted the frame, touched his lips and placed it carefully back on the table. Jonathan had been dead for just over three years.

There hadn't been a day or night go by when she hadn't thought about the things they had done together. His loving kisses, his arms protectively around her, his strength when she needed support. He was her mentor, her lover, her friend. He had been the husband she adored.

After the diagnosis, his illness lasted just four short weeks. Because of the drugs, he suffered little, but the cancer killed him. Together they had planned to have two children, but they never came. Instead, she was presented with a small wriggly bundle of fur, which she called Honey.

'Come on, Hun, let's go out.' A ball of energy erupted, filling the space between Jenny and the settee with the grunts and squeals of an excited dog.

During the long walk, she thought about getting a Chinese takeaway from the nearby parade of shops. *I could do with just watching whatever's on the television and having an early night,* she thought. The day had been exhausting and long. It was hard not to think about what she'd been told about James Williamson.

✳✳✳

The phone on the bedside table let out its musical request to be answered. Its determination to get attention disturbed Jenny's deep sleep. She turned sleepily to look at the clock. It was 5.35 am. Propping herself on pillows she answered, 'Jenny Trent.'

'Jenny, its Peter. I'm so sorry to wake you so early, but Lynn Moore has been found.' His voice faltered, 'She's been murdered, and from the little I've heard, it sounds as brutal as the Williamson murder. Morgan-Jones is already at the station and wants you to go and see him before you go to the crime scene. Ben and Andrew were woken earlier and they're already on the way.'

'I'll be there straight away,' Jenny said. 'Tell the super I'll be about thirty minutes.' *No time for a hot refreshing bath,* she thought as she replaced the receiver.

Honey, unsettled by her movements, tried to get as close to her as she could, her wagging tail batting noisily on the side of the bed. 'I won't be long, Hun, promise,' she said, knowing that she was lying. 'Debbie will be here soon to take you out for a nice long walk.' She had realised a long time ago that she said the same thing every day when she had to go to work.

A quick, loving cuddle and she moved away to dress. In ten minutes she was ready to leave. Looking at her watch, Jenny realised that her estimate of thirty minutes was optimistic. She took a deep breath. Morgan-Jones would have to wait a little longer.

***

Peter greeted her just inside the double glass doors of the station.

'Glad you're here, Jenny. It was the second search in the woods that found her. The dogs got to an old derelict house on the north side. One of them got excited about something and wouldn't leave, so it was decided to investigate further. She was inside the house.' He paused. 'As I said, Morgan-Jones wants to see you right away, and I'll fill you in further after you've spoken with him and we're on the way.'

As she arrived at Morgan-Jones's office door it was opened before she could knock.

'Good, you're here at last,' he said. 'Come in,' gesturing her to a straight-backed leather chair. 'Take a seat. No doubt, Peter has told you that Lynn Moore's body has been found. I want you to go to the crime scene immediately. Ben and Andrew can talk you through the details. It looks very much like the previous murder.' He hesitated, before picking up a pen and jabbing it hard on the desk. 'We have no clues, Jenny, the press are going to have a field day if we can't come up with something soon.' He threw the pen onto the desk. 'I want to know if any of the neighbours at either place know anything at all. Report back to me with all the information as soon as you can.'

'Yes, Sir.' Jenny rose from the chair.

'Before you go …' he motioned with his hand for her to remain seated. 'You were speaking with Mrs Williamson yesterday, I understand she is the prime suspect. What did you find out?'

'I did speak to her and her sister and my report will be with you very soon. From what they told me, she is still a suspect, but there is room for doubt. An officer is still with her.'

'No doubt you've written up the conversation and the reason for coming to that conclusion,' he said. 'However, I'd like to form my own.'

'You'll have my report tomorrow, Sir.'

'Why do you believe she may not be a suspect?'

'I don't believe it yet, Sir, but as I said, from the conversation I had with her and her sister, I'd like to keep my thoughts on that open for a bit longer.'

Jenny stood up and took a step closer to Morgan-Jones. 'Although Emma Williamson is still a suspect, there's a lot more to find out about her husband. She claims she was abused by him, and the details are very disturbing. If what she says is true, then I understand why she said 'I'm glad he's dead.' I will, of course, ensure a full report is lodged. You'll have it by tomorrow.' She held his gaze. 'I believe Emma Williamson had a good reason to dislike her husband. We need more time to find out if she did kill him, or organised someone else to do it.' She raised her voice. 'Or if she had nothing to do with his death at all.'

Morgan-Jones rose from his chair, walked to the window and gazed out for what seemed a long time. 'I'll look forward to the report.' He turned quickly away from the window. 'Good. In the meantime, continue your investigations into the murder of Lynn Moore too'

Just as the door was closing, she heard her name called. Turning, she pushed the door open again.

'Jenny, my head is on the block on this. We need some answers. Soon.' She could almost taste his desperation. Jenny could feel his deep concern, matching her own.

'I understand, Sir. All our resources have been made available and the whole team is working hard. We'll have something soon, I'm sure.'

The door closed behind her as she left.

Peter was walking towards her.

'Did you find anything of interest in Lynn Moore's flat, Peter?'

"Fraid not, Jenny, There was nothing at all that Mr and Mrs Moore hadn't already told us. And no more phone messages, sorry.'

'Have the arrangements been made for the neighbours to be further interrogated? Someone has to know more about Williamson, otherwise, he wouldn't have been so disliked.'

'That's already being organised,' said Peter.

'Persistence and a fresh face could bring forward that little nugget of information we need to open things up.'

'How was the Super?' Peter said.

'Well,' Jenny hesitated. 'Like us all, he's looking for answers. And we're not giving him any yet. So, yes … he's fed up and I don't blame him. We must have another team briefing, Peter. I want to know much more about the neighbours on Marden Close. Once all the reports are in we'll arrange it. Why did they dislike him so much? I'll check with Ben and Andrew first to see what they can let us have regarding Lynn Moore. Can you see how the photographs are getting on? We'll need those too.'

'I'll make sure they're ready.'

'Before that,' said Jenny. 'We need to get to the new crime scene ourselves. Scientific support is already there, let's go and see what they've got so far.'

***

They drove in silence on narrow unkempt roads, the trees brushing the car as they weaved around bends and across small junctions.

Suddenly the area became alive, police cars with blue lights flashing, an ambulance and other unmarked police vehicles parked untidily along the narrow road either side of the entrance to the house they were approaching. Jenny noticed Ben's Ford Capri close to what appeared to be the front gate of the property.

The house looked as though it had been abandoned for years, disappearing behind ivy, unattended shrubs and trees planted long ago. The wood that once framed the windows, now crushed by the spreading tentacles of ivy in their endless search for more sunlight.

Nature can be relentless and cruel, thought Jenny. She shuddered, turning to Peter. 'See what you can find out from the officers, I'll find Ben and Andrew.'

Peter was already out of the car walking towards the scene.

Blue protection overalls on, she reached the front of the house and saw Ben by the door.

'Hello, Jenny.' He took her hand without shaking it. 'Come with me, but be very careful, everything is falling to pieces around here. Here, hold on to my hand.'

She held Ben's gloved hand willingly as he guided along a huge hallway with a broken staircase in the centre. *It looks like it could fall at any time,* she thought.

'It's the room at the end on the right,' Ben said, still leading her carefully. 'It was one of your dogs that found her. Apparently, the door was locked with a large bolt from the outside. Be careful when you go in, we've set up lights, but it's still pretty dark in there and the floors are slippery. Andrew's still there. Don't disturb a thing.' He released her hand as he walked forward into the room.

Jenny was wishing she could be anywhere but in this wild, dying house. She took a careful step into the dark room where Lynn Moore's body lay.

She had prepared herself for the shock as she walked in. The body was lying face up, hands at the sides of her head. As Jenny moved forward the musty smell of the room collided with the distinctive odour of blood. She reached the body and raised her hands to her face.

Andrew's voice was gentle. 'Here, take this.' He handed her a large white tissue taken from the inside of his blue overalls. 'The victim's ears have been sliced off. At a quick glance, it could have been done in a similar way to how James Williamson's feet were cut off, we'll have to confirm that later.'

'Was that what killed her?' said Jenny.

'We're not sure yet,' said Ben. 'We haven't touched the body. I need to take a closer look so we can see more. Once my team have finished in here, I'll get her moved to the lab.'

Jenny forced herself to look around the room. It was filthy, with a damp acrid smell, she shivered, wanting to leave, but needing to know more about the dying house. *Who owns it? Why did they just leave it? Why did Lynn Moore come here? Did she know her killer? Who is her killer?*

She left Ben in the room leaning over the dead woman's body. Andrew walked with her, guiding her away from broken woods and sharp edges.

'Nice to see you again, Chief Inspector Trent,' said Andrew. 'It's a shame we keep meeting in such awful surroundings. Perhaps you'll let me make up for it soon?' He smiled broadly as he let go of her hand. 'I think you'll be safe now.' They were at the front door. He turned away from Jenny as her hand slipped from his grasp. 'Take care, please,' he said.

Jenny felt a warm flush run swiftly through her body. 'Of course, I will.' she smiled.

Peter was walking towards her. 'Not much more than we know already. Nobody else was around when the dogs got excited, expect the handlers. What are Ben and Andrew making of it?'

'At the moment it looks very similar to the murder of Williamson, but they're keeping their opinions wide open for now. Stay here and see if you can find out anything else.'

Her mind was working hard on the way back to the station. Something was wrong, things were not slipping into place as quickly as they usually did. The killer was ahead of them. The whole team were working on this and no one had come up with anything yet. Morgan-Jones was entitled to be anxious and stroppy. There must be a connection between the two murders. She tried to put the thoughts out of her mind. She was dreading the imminent, but necessary visit to Lynn's parents.

When Jenny arrived back at the station, PC Spencer was waiting for her.

'Not looking forward to this, Ma'am.'

'Is this your first one?'

'Yes, Ma'am'

Jenny touched the young Officer arm. 'We never get used to it Officer, but time helps.'

CHAPTER FOURTEEN

Margaret Moore saw Jenny and PC Spencer approaching the front door as she was closing the bedroom window. She called to her husband, who was in the garden busy cutting down an unruly hedge.

'It's the police at the door, love, can you open it? There may be some news about Lynn.'

'Right, I won't be a minute,' he said, moving quickly to the back door and removing his hands from thick gardening gloves. He walked the few steps to open the door just as Jenny pushed the doorbell.

'Hello, Chief Inspector. Have you any more news about our daughter? She still hasn't got in touch with us.' He opened the door wider. 'Please, come in.'

Good morning, Mr Moore. This is PC Spencer, I've asked her to join me today.'

Robert Moore acknowledged the PC with a smile. 'Please, do take a seat, my wife will be here shortly.'

Margaret Moore arrived in the lounge just as they sat down, she looked nervously at her husband.

They know, thought Jenny. They mostly do.

'Have you found our daughter, Chief Inspector?' Mrs Moore's spoke quietly. 'I do hope so, we've been sick with worry.'

Her husband moved cautiously towards her. 'Sit down, Margaret, love.'

'Yes, we have found your daughter, Mrs Moore.' She hesitated and took a deep breath.

Mrs Moore gasped as Jenny moved closer to her and took her hand. 'I am very sorry to have to tell you that your daughter is dead.'

Margaret Moore was quiet for a few seconds. She looked up at her husband, then she screamed as he put his arm around her, his eyes filling with tears.

'It's not true … it's not true. Please, tell us it's not true.' Her eyes were wide, she looked terrified. 'How? How? You must be wrong. My Lynn isn't dead, she can't be.'

'We don't know what happened yet, Mrs Moore,' said Jenny, her voice soft. She stopped and looked at Mr Moore, his eyes were closed as he held tightly onto his wife.

'I am so sorry. I also have to tell you that it appears your daughter has been murdered.' She stopped as Mrs Moore looked at her, disbelief and shock in her voice as she spoke.

'Murdered? Murdered!' Mrs Moore fell against her husband. 'Who would do that to our daughter? You must be wrong, Chief Inspector, she can't have been murdered. No one would do that.' She cast an appealing look at her husband. 'Would they?' Her husband held her tighter.

Jenny turned to PC Spencer. 'Can you get Mr and Mrs Moore a drink of water, please?'

'Do you have anyone who can be with you? We can contact them,' said Jenny.

'My wife has a brother, I'll call him, he'll come immediately, I'm sure,' said Mr Moore. 'Oh my God, love, we have to tell Sarah.' He groaned. 'How on earth are we going to do that?'

'One of my officers can do that for you, Mr Moore,' said Jenny. 'I understand that your daughter was close to Sarah. Have you got her address, please?' She handed Mr Moore her notebook and pen. With a shaking hand, he wrote slowly and handed the book back to Jenny.

'When you last saw your daughter and Sarah together, how were they?' Jenny looked at each of Mr and Mrs Moore in turn.

'As far as I know, they were fine, Chief Inspector. Like everyone, they had little tiffs,' Mr Moore said. He looked at his wife. 'They were alright, weren't they, love?'

'They loved each other very much,' said Mrs Moore. 'I know they were looking to buy a house together. I only ever heard them have one bad argument, and that was a few days before we last saw Lynn.'

'Do you know what that was about?' said Jenny. 'Was it a serious argument?'

'I don't know what it was about,' said Mrs Moore. She turned towards Jenny, her face twisted in grief, her body shuddering, wracked with sobs. 'Why? … Why do you want to know what it was about?'

Mr Moore put a protective arm around his wife again. 'I don't think my wife can take any more, Chief Inspector. I was here when they had the argument, I think it was something to do with the property they wanted to buy. Lynn got a bit angry.' He looked at his wife before saying, 'Our daughter was a really lovely person.' He tried a smile. 'She did have a bit of a temper, which could upset us, but she always made up for it. I'm sure you know what it's like, Chief Inspector. Why do you want to know all this? As you can see, my wife is upset enough, I don't think she can answer any more questions.'

'I'm so sorry, Mr Moore. It's just important for us to get as much information from everyone as possible so that we can find out who murdered your daughter.'

'I understand,' said Mr Moore. 'Is it possible for you to come back? I really need some time to take all this in and help my wife as much as possible.' Tears were brimming as he hugged Mrs Moore even closer into him.

'Of course,' said Jenny. If there's anything that you are your wife remember that might help, please do contact us.' She handed Mr Moore a small card. 'My direct telephone number is there, you'll come straight through to me.'

Jenny pointed at the officer standing directly behind her. 'PC Spencer is your Family Liaison Officer, Mr Moore. She will stay with you for now. As I said, if there is anything you or your wife can remember that might help our enquiries, or if there is anything we can help you with, please let me know immediately. If you're unable to reach me, PC Spencer will know exactly what to do.'

'Spencer, I would like you to stay with Mr and Mrs Moore for a while. Help them to contact Mrs Moore's brother, and when he arrives, call the station.'

'Yes, Ma'am.'

'We'll need someone to identify the body, I'm afraid,' said Jenny, looking at Mr Moore. He nodded without answering her. 'When we have more information we will, of course, speak with you again.' She looked at the two shattered people in front of her. 'I'm so very sorry. There are people that can help in such awful situations, Mr Moore.

Mr Moore held up his hand. 'Thank you but for the moment we just need each other and family.'

She closed the front door gently, the sobs echoing from the room occupied by two very distraught people. She opened the note Mr Moore had given her containing Sarah's contact details. 'The day's not over yet.' she murmured to herself, before lifting her phone to call Peter.

CHAPTER FIFTEEN

Jenny realised that it was mid-afternoon and she was hungry, she pulled in at a local newsagent to buy a sandwich.

Arriving at the station, she parked the car at the front and ran up the steps and into the reception area. She was anxious to have her sandwich and get on with the day. She walked swiftly to her office, ignoring the people she passed on the way.

A young officer made a tentative approach as she reached the door. 'Excuse me, Ma'am, I thought you should know that the super knows you're here. He said to tell you that he would like to see you immediately. He doesn't sound very happy.' He gave a sympathetic grin.

'Thank you. I'll go and see him now.'

Jenny pulled herself up straight and walked briskly along the spartan corridor to Morgan-Jones's office. Before she could knock, his booming voice invited her in. He was sitting behind his desk with his back to her. 'Sit down, Jenny.' From the tone of his voice, she knew it was not going to be a good meeting and felt her mood turn defensive as she sat on the chair facing him.

The superintendent's chair spun round. He looked straight at her and threw a newspaper onto his desk. The headline was big, black and bold,

WOMAN FOUND BRUTALLY MURDERED
POLICE CLUELESS AGAIN

'No doubt you've already seen this?' He didn't wait for a reply. 'What's going on with your team?' His voice raised his eyes.

Jenny picked up the paper. 'No, I haven't seen any papers this morning, Sir. I've been to see Mr and Mrs Moore. I wanted to tell them that their daughter had been murdered.' She read the paper. The headline seemed to scream at her, she wanted to tear the paper in shreds. *Whoever is carrying out these vicious attacks will love this,* she thought angrily as she raised her head to look at the man in front of her, his black glare a mirror of her own frustrated feelings.

'Jenny, I want some answers and I want them quickly. The press are saying we're not up to the job, and from what I can see I'm beginning to question whether we have the right team working on this one.'

She met his glare. 'I've just returned from the scene of the second murder, after which I went directly to see the parents of the murdered woman, Sir. My team are working hard. SOCO are still at the crime scene looking for anything they can find that will help our enquires. I've not yet fully read the report in the newspaper, so I am not aware of what they're saying. I can assure you that we have the best team working on this. You only have to look at our record to know that,' she said defiantly. 'When I left, Dr Seldon was working with Dr Baines to get the body back to the lab. As soon as I hear from him, I'll know more.'

'Well, you'd better get on with it,' he snapped. 'Find the killer. Find him, or her, before another statement is made.' He stood up, his knuckles resting heavily on the table.

'I don't like this force being called clueless by the press. If you're not up to the job, let me know, before I let you know.' He sat down and swung his chair back round to face the window.

Fighting the urge to fire back an angry response, Jenny walked out into the empty corridor and moved quickly past the open-plan office, relieved that it was unusually quiet. As she reached her office her phone rang. She took the phone from her pocket and recognised Peter's number.

'Hello, Peter,' she said. Any new information?'

'The body's been taken to pathology. Ben will do the post-mortem tomorrow, early. He said he hopes to have some answers by mid-morning.'

'That's great, Peter, thanks.'

'Just one thing, Jenny,' said Peter. 'When Ben turned the body over, he was able to see that she had a something stuck in her throat, the same way that Williamson had.'

Jenny took a deep breath. 'Was it a peach stone?'

'Not sure yet, and Ben was giving nothing away. Probably won't know until he's removed whatever it is. I can't help feeling it will be, though.'

'I bet it will be too,' Jenny muttered. 'As soon as we have the information from Ben I want a briefing in the incident room. Make the preparations, aim for tomorrow afternoon. I want everyone there. I want the new photos ready before the meeting and I'd like to know the neighbours' reactions to Williamson's death, and … I want to know why he was so despised.'

'I'm going there right away.'

'Peter,' she said, 'this is getting a bit tough. Morgan-Jones is very touchy, and I can't really blame him. Your help and determination is very much appreciated, as always. Thank you for your support. Oh, and by the way, did you see the headline in the paper today?'

'Yes, I did.' He sighed and quietly swore.

'Yes – I think we're all thinking the same thing. Take care, Peter,' said Jenny, and she closed her phone and replaced it in her pocket.

Sudden tiredness brought on an unexpected soft yawn. Seeing the unopened sandwich on her desk, she realised she still hadn't eaten. She had a yearning to feel Honey's soft silky fur. The dog was her rock, and the bond between them made her daily homecoming to an empty house bearable. But that would have to wait – the day was far from over.

CHAPTER SIXTEEN

Jenny walked through the autopsy lab and saw Andrew bending over the body of a woman, he looked up as he heard her.

'Morning, Jenny. As you can see it's me. Ben had an urgent call about the death of a child. Almost finished here. I think Peter told you there was something caught in her throat? It's over there.' He pointed to a large metal bowl with a peach stone in the middle. You'll see there're spots of blood congealed on it, just like the other one.'

'Was it the stone that caused her to die?' said Jenny.

'Well,' Andrew paused. 'She certainly choked to death.' He stopped what he was doing and came around to where Jenny was standing. 'Some doctors believe that there is a basis for the so-called "frightened-to-death" syndrome. If there's an inkling of truth in it, then your victim was frightened to death. The distortion of the face as rigor mortis was setting in can easily be seen in the photos that DI Branden has. Like the previous victim, she looks absolutely terrified.'

Jenny's voice was quiet, hiding the emotion she felt. 'I have a full briefing to give this afternoon, Andrew. Should I mention what you've just told me?'

'Good Lord, no!' he said, his voice raised slightly. 'Your lot would have a field day at my expense, not to mention Ben's response.' He smiled warmly at Jenny. 'So keep it to yourself.' He removed his glasses and cleaned them with the corner of his white coat. 'In the Arthur Conan Doyle's *The Hound of the Baskervilles* Sir Charles Baskerville dies from a heart attack brought on by extreme psychological stress. Findings come by research shared in a new medical article by sociologist David Phillips at the University of California, San Diego, suggest that people can indeed be scared to death, both in fact as well as in fiction. As I said, some doctors are starting to believe it, but at the moment they wouldn't want anyone to know that, and there are a lot of eminent doctors challenging it.'

'The briefing is at three-thirty this afternoon, Andrew, will you be there?' said Jenny.

'Yes, I will. Ben also mentioned it and didn't think he could attend. And, the best bit is that I'll see you again. Looking forward to it.' He smiled.

Before getting into her car Jenny rang Peter. 'Andrew Baines will be at the briefing this afternoon in place of Ben, is everything ready?'

'As ready as it can be. Mason has a report on his meeting in London where James Williamson worked. I haven't been through it with him yet, but from what Mason has told me, it seems Williamson really was quite an unpleasant character.'

'I think that's already been well established,' said Jenny. 'But there may be something we're missing. Tell him I want to see him half an hour before the briefing to go through it with him. As soon as the briefing is over, I want you to go to Marden Close yourself and speak to some of the neighbours again.'

'Of course. I'll ring Maggie and tell her that it's going to be another late one.'

$$***$$

Detective Constable Mason knocked on Jenny's half-open door.

'Come in, Martin, thanks for coming. What did you find out about Williamson?'

With eager steps he entered the room, and sat down opposite Jenny, opening his notebook. 'As we already know, Williamson was an investment banker with Standard Elite Bank at their headquarters in London. Been with them for the past ten years. I spoke to quite a few people there, all of who said he was very good at his job and that his skill had helped the bank to become the fourth largest on the London Stock Exchange, he made millions, some said billions, for them.'

'Was he liked?' said Jenny, aware of what the answer would be.

'No, Ma'am, he was not. I spoke with a chap called Ewan Payne whose job it was to ensure Williamson had every bit of information about shares, acquisitions, venture capital investments, that sort of thing.' He looked up from his notebook. 'According to Mr Payne, he was an arrogant …' he coughed, and raised a hand to cover his mouth, 'shit, and he also confessed that he disliked him – intensely.'

'Did you speak with anyone else? What about his boss?'

'His boss wasn't there, somewhere in the States, I believe. But I did speak with a female banker.' He turned a page in his notebook. 'Name, Harriett Gillow. She didn't want to speak to me at first, but eventually, she admitted to having had a short fling with him. It seems he had a reputation of being one for the ladies, although none of them lasted long.' He looked at Jenny and waited a few seconds. 'At first, Harriett Gillow said, he was the ideal boyfriend, expensive gifts, top-class restaurants.' His right hand moved to his mouth again as he coughed. 'Apparently, he was very good in bed.'

'Did she explain why the affair didn't last long?'

'Well, Harriett wasn't all that explicit, but she told me his sexual needs became more and more demanding, and that he was a "nasty pervert".' He looked up at Jenny. 'Not my words, but hers, she hated him, said he deserved to die.' He closed his notebook. 'She wouldn't tell me what she meant by a nasty pervert. Just said, 'You're a man – work it out.'

'Do you think Harriett Gillow could have killed him, Martin?'

'I am afraid I can't answer that, Ma'am. I got the feeling she was frightened of him. I sensed most of the other people in that office were, too.'

'Thank you, well done,' Jenny said.

Martin got up to leave and then sat down again. 'Ma'am, there's just one thing I'm not sure if it's relevant, but there was one person there who seemed very quiet and nervous. He certainly didn't want to speak to me. In fact, as I approached him to ask him something, he rushed out of the door. I asked who he was and when he would be back. His name is Rhys Mason, but no one could tell me how long he'd be gone. I think we should go back and speak with him, Ma'am?'

'I think that would be a good idea. But I'll go, Martin, and I'll take the DI – unannounced. You've done a great job, now let's shake them up a bit and see what else comes up.'

'Very good, Ma'am,' said Martin as he closed the door.

∗∗∗

She arrived at the incident room and found Peter placing the new photos on the whiteboard. A photo of Lynn Moore's face was next to a similar one of James Williamson's. The same terrified expression on both. She was reminded of Andrew's 'frightened to death' comments at the autopsy lab earlier.

The room started to fill, voices buzzing with anticipation. She rose from her chair by the side of the whiteboard and, as she did so, she saw Morgan-Jones at the back of the room, sitting next to Andrew Baines.

She held up the front page of the previous day's newspaper,

WOMAN FOUND BRUTALLY MURDERED
POLICE CLUELESS AGAIN

A groan of acknowledgement vibrated around the room. 'I knew that was coming,' said a voice from somewhere in the middle.

Jenny held up her hand to quieten the disappointed grumblings. 'Unless we get something out of this briefing,' she said, looking around the room, 'it would seem that we *are* clueless. And, I know that is categorically untrue.' She waited just long enough for everyone to take in the urgency in her voice. 'So far we have very little to go on.' She turned to look at the whiteboard and continued. 'It seems almost certain that both victims were killed by the same person. The murdered woman also had a peach stone pushed down her throat. And both had parts of their bodies cut off by someone who seems to know what they're doing.' She looked at Andrew Baines, who had raised his hand.

'Please carry on, Dr Baines.'

'Thank you.' We can now confirm that it was the peach stone pushed into her throat that killed her, before her other injuries had the chance to do so, as with Mr Williamson. She choked to death. It's quite clear from the autopsy carried out by Dr Seldon and myself, that whoever killed James Williamson also killed the woman.'

'Thank you for that, Dr Baines,' Jenny said.

She turned her attention to the team in front of her. 'It's been suggested that Williamson and Moore knew each other and that before they died they were terrified. 'Any questions so far?'

A hand went up in the middle of the room. 'Do we know how they knew each other?'

'No, we don't yet, but we hope to know a lot more very quickly. A good question, thank you,' Jenny said.

'Is there any news from the dead woman's parents? Wasn't it the mother who thought her daughter knew Williamson?' The question came from the back of the room.

'Yes, she did say that,' said Jenny. 'We'll be getting further details from the Moores soon. Moving on, we have other information that might help.' She looked at Martin Jones. 'DC Jones will share the findings of his visit to James Williamson's office in London.'

Peter made notes on the whiteboard, writing the names of Harriett Gillow, Ewan Payne and Rhys Mason with an arrow joining them to Williamson's photo.

'If they were so frightened of him, why didn't they tell his boss what a bully he was?' The question came from a female officer at the front.

'Because he was making a fortune for the bank and everyone knew it. They were all convinced that nothing would be done about it,' said Martin. He turned to Jenny. 'That's all I have, Ma'am.'

'Thank you, Martin,' she said.

'Has anyone spoken to Lynn Moore's friend, Sarah?' someone asked with a snigger.

Jenny caught a grin on the face of a young officer in the middle of the room.

'You,' she glared at him. 'Stand up! Who are you?'

'DC Jack Stone, Ma'am'

'And what is so funny, Detective Stone?' she demanded angrily.

'Well ... well,' he shifted his feet, passing his hand across his mouth as he coughed. 'They were lesbians,' he said, his face flushing.

'And? Detective Stone, if you think it's funny that two people have been brutally murdered, and if you think it's funny that so far we have no idea who has committed the murders, then perhaps you should not be doing the job you're doing! When we've finished here,' she continued, 'you can go with an officer from uniform, and find Lynn Moore's partner, Sarah, and talk to her. She's yet to be informed of the death. Find out more about their relationship, find out when they last met, where they went, find out everything about them, and her. Her address is in the records.'

Stone looked appealingly at her. 'But, Ma'am, I'm due to go off duty in an hour.'

'In this job, Stone you can forget about time and going off duty, especially when we have no suspects yet. Or perhaps you are in the wrong job? Just get on with it.'

Stone sat down heavily. 'Yes, Ma'am.'

Peter pointed to a photo of Williamson's house. 'Apologies for taking a step back to Williamson's murder, but I think it's important to note that there was no sign of a break-in. The killer must either have been invited in or had a key,' he looked around the room. 'However ... it's unlikely that he, or she, was invited in as both Mr and Mrs Williamson were in bed, although in different rooms.

A voice came from the middle of the room. 'DC Eddie Callam, Sir. Mrs Williamson could've got up and let him in.'

Peter looked at Eddie Callam, new to the team from the Brighton force.

'Carry on, Eddie,' Peter said.

'Well, she hated him, right? Said she was glad he was dead. Seems to me she had a pretty good motive for getting someone to kill him.'

Jenny stood up. 'You're quite right, Eddie, it does seem that way. We need to speak to her again. 'I want you to come with me and talk to her.' She caught the new DC's eye. 'Mrs Williamson will likely insist that her sister is with her, but don't consent to go back any other time, even if her sister isn't there.'

'Yes, Ma'am.'

Peter moved again to the whiteboard, pointing at the wild, dilapidated house. 'Let's move on now. Lynn Moore was discovered in a room in this house.' He stopped, turning his gaze back to the intense group in front of him, still pointing at the house. 'There's no sign of her being dragged into the house or to the room, so we have to believe that she went there of her own free will and was murdered in the room where she was found.'

'Is there any information as to why she went there?' The question came from the middle of the room again.

'DS Hughes is interviewing her parents right now, and DC Stone will be talking to Lynn's partner, Sarah Coombes. Once we hear from them we may be able to answer that.' He looked around the room. 'That's all we have at the moment. Does anyone have any questions?' There were no replies. 'Right, let's get on with it then.' The room emptied quickly.

As Jenny began putting away her notes, she noticed that Morgan-Jones was still at the back of the room talking with Andrew Baines. Finally, she heard him say, 'I'll just be a few minutes, Andrew.' He managed a smile as he approached Jenny. 'Well done, Jenny, you managed to get them moving. Are you coming for a drink in a bit?'

'Yes, I think I will,' she said.

'Just one thing, Jenny.' Morgan-Jones held up his hand. 'Make sure you know who everyone is in your team. Having to ask who someone is doesn't exactly make you look like you're in charge, does it?' He turned and walked through the door.

✳✳✳

The pub was noisy, mostly with staff from the station, everyone enjoying a late afternoon post-shift drink. Morgan-Jones's rebuke was still in her thoughts. She noticed that Andrew Baines and Morgan-Jones were together again at the front of the bar, drinks already in their hands.

'What will you have?' said Peter, calling her to the other end of the bar. 'I won't be able to stay long, but a bit later can't make it much worse. 'I'm not drinking. I want to go to have another chat with the Marden Close neighbours, just here for a few minutes to be sociable.'

'I'll have a glass of wine, please, Peter.' The mood of the pub calming her. 'Are things still not good at home?'

'Worse than ever,' said Peter, with a wry smile, but despair in his voice. 'Maggie says she can't go on like this anymore.' He stopped to order drinks. 'But I don't think it's just my work. I'm sure she's met someone else. The signs are pretty strong, and in this job, you get to know about signs.' His voice was shaky. 'I guess I'm just waiting for her to tell me.' He handed Jenny her wine.

In a few minutes, he was ready to go. 'It was a good briefing. The team are fired up, they don't want to let you down.'

'I know,' said Jenny. I have you Peter and I have a great team.'

She watched him leave and wished more than ever she could help him. The best she could do was be there when he needed her.

Andrew Baines brushed past her, looked back and returned to her side. 'I was hoping you'd make it, Jenny.' His gaze was intense and it unsettled her, in a good way. 'I'm not one for drinking a lot, and the Fancy Coffee shop is still open, would you like to join me?' he sounded hesitant. 'No shop talk, though.'

Jenny looked around the busy room. 'I'd like that,' she said, trying not to sound too pleased.

CHAPTER SEVENTEEN

'Okay, 'you're in charge,' said Peter. DCI Trent thinks this will give you something to work on. But … I promise I will step in if the needs arise. Ring the bell.'

Jack pushed the button and within a short time the door opened. An attractive young woman said, 'Hello.'

'Are you Sarah Coombes?' Jack said.

'Who wants to know?' the young woman said.

'I'm DC Stone and this is DI Branden. Both held identification badges in front of her. 'We would like to come in, please.'

'I'm sorry, yes, please come in,' she opened the door wider for them to enter, and then closed it behind them.

'Can you please confirm that you are Sarah Coombes?' Jack said as he took a few steps into the hall. He saw the hesitation in the woman in front of him and was about to ask again.

'Yes, I am. Are you here about Lynn?' Her voice was shaky and breaking up. 'I've been trying to get hold of her for a few days now and she's just not answering her phone. I called her mother and she hasn't been able to talk to her either.' She pointed to a small room on the left. 'Please, come in and take a seat.' As they sat down, Peter could see her trembling slightly. 'Do you know where she is?' said Sarah.

'What was your relationship with Lynn Moore?' Jack asked.

'We're partners and are about to move in together. Why do you ask that?'

'I'm afraid we have some very bad news, Miss Coombes. I am so sorry to have to tell you that Lynn Moore is dead.'

Sarah put her hand to her mouth. She stood up. Her eyes widened as she looked at the two men in front of her.

'What did you say?' Her voice was little more than a whisper. 'What did you say? Dead ...' she shook her head. 'Dead ... She can't be, you ... you must be wrong. You must have the wrong person.' Her eyes looked from one man to the other. 'We're going to buy a house together. We're going to live together. She can't be dead.' The volume of her voice was rising. 'Please ... Please tell me you have the wrong person, please.'

Peter carefully placed his hand on the trembling woman's arm. 'Sit down, Miss Coombes.'

'No, no, I don't want to sit down, I want to know why you're saying this to me.' She stared at them, the pleading clear in her eyes, which were now full of tears.

'I am so sorry,' said Peter, and he moved closer to the stricken woman in front of him. 'I am afraid it's true. Lynn has been found dead.'

Sarah sat sharply down, releasing his hand. 'How ... how ... did she die and when did it happen? It's been nearly a week since I spoke to her.' She stopped, her head dropping as quiet sobs released the tears to run down her face. 'It's not true, you must be mistaken. You must be.' She looked up at Peter. 'How did she die? She was a very good driver and has never had an accident. Whose fault was it? Who was it? Please tell me what happened. Did anyone else die?'

Peter sat down next to her. 'I'm so sorry, it wasn't an accident.' He took a deep breath. 'I am so sorry to tell you, Miss Coombes, but Lynn was murdered.'

Sarah jumped up again, her body shaking, her eyes wild. 'Murdered? She can't have been. No one would have any reason at all to murder my lovely Lynn. Everyone loved her.' Her hands folded tightly together and she held them to her chest. 'Please, please don't say that.' Her words began to run into each other as she sat once more, her sobs loud and frantic. She tried to say something, but the words didn't come.

'I'm so sorry, Sarah,' said Peter. 'I'm afraid we're unable to tell you any more at the moment as our investigation is ongoing. Are you able to answer a few questions?'

'Questions, questions. Why do you want to ask me some questions? You can't surely think I had anything to do with Lynn's death.' She looked at Jack and Peter in turn, her eyes wide, tears now drying on her face. 'What on earth can I tell you that will help you find who killed my Lynn?'

'At the moment we're asking everyone questions, Miss Coombes,' said Peter, 'which is why anything you can tell us might help. Anything you can tell us, anything at all, might help us find the person who killed your partner.'

'Yes, I'm sorry,' said Sarah, and she sniffed into a handkerchief pulled from a pocket of her trousers. 'What do you want to know?' Her head bowed as she began to weep again. I don't know if I can tell you anything. I just can't ...'

'Is there anyone who can be with you, Miss Coombes? We can get someone here very quickly, but it's really important that we have some answers now,' said Jack.

'No, I don't know anyone who can come now,' Sarah said quietly. 'I'll try and answer your questions.'

'Thank you,' said Jack. 'We'll be as quick as possible.' He checked to see that Peter had his notebook open. 'Why did you not make enquiries as to where Lynn was before we came here, Miss Coombes?' he said. 'After all, it's been over a week now, you must have wanted to know where she was.'

'Of course, I did, but I was angry. We'd had an argument when we were last at her parents' house. I didn't want to make the first move and, to be honest, I thought she'd gone off somewhere on her own. She's done that once or twice before when we've had an argument or something. But she's never been away more than a few days.' She stopped to wipe a tear from her face. 'As a matter of fact, I called her parents to see if they knew where she might have gone – they didn't, and we agreed to leave it a while and let each other know if we heard anything. I suppose I would have gone the police eventually, but she's a grown woman, I wanted to give her some space.'

'How long have you known Lynn and her parents?' asked Peter.

Sarah bent her head. 'About five months. We met at a friend's party. We fell in love very quickly.' She looked up again. 'That's why we were moving in together, Inspector.'

'The argument you had at Lynn's parents' house – what was that about?' said Peter.

Sarah blinked. 'What do you mean what was it about? Everyone has arguments.

'I'd still like you to try and recall what it was about, please, purely because it was just before Mr and Mrs Moore couldn't get in touch with her,' said Peter ignoring her question.

'Neither could I,' said Sarah, her voice raised. 'I already told you that.'

'We'd still like to know what it was about please, Miss Coombes,' said Jack his voice noticeably hard and also raised.

Sarah sighed, and her shoulders dropped. 'Lynn was a lovely person and I loved her a lot, but she had a bad temper and quite honestly she could get a bit nasty when things didn't go her way, or if she didn't like someone. I think even her mum and dad got a bit frightened of her sometimes. Like me, they loved her a lot and forgave her all the time.' She hesitated. 'Just the same as me,' she repeated.

'How do you get on with her parents?' said Jack.

'We get on very well, they're really nice people. Her mum's especially nice and kind to me. I think her father's unsure of me though.'

'So what was the argument about, then?' Jack asked again. 'We really need to know, Miss Coombes.' He saw a flicker of anger cross her face. 'You must realise how important everything little thing is in an investigation of this sort.

'It wasn't very much really. Lynn was in a bad mood because someone had accused her of bullying at work and she'd been asked to attend a disciplinary meeting. I wasn't joking when I said she could be a bit nasty sometimes. She asked me about it, and I gave a flippant answer that she didn't want to hear. She just flew at me, told me to go away and that she never wanted to see me again. I knew she didn't mean it, but I didn't react very well to her telling me to go away, so I told her a few more things about herself. To be honest, it was the worst argument we've ever had. I was deeply angry with her. I told her to forget buying a house and I walked away.' She looked at Jack. 'I was so angry with her, but I love her and I wanted to put it right. But I couldn't get hold of her.' She sighed heavily. 'But you already know that.'

'Where did you go when you left her?' said Jack.

Sarah started to cry again. 'I don't know, I can't remember. I can't answer any more of your questions, detective, I just can't.' Her sobs were now relentless as she covered her face with her hands. 'Please, just leave me alone.'

'I can see this is distressing for you, Miss Coombes, but I shall want to ask you more about your relationship with Lynn Moore, either here or at the station. We'll let you know when, but it'll be soon. Please don't make any arrangements to go anywhere until we're completely sure we have every bit of information from you that could help us. I'm sure that's what you want as well, Miss Coombes.'

'You can't believe that I had anything to do with Lynn's death. It was just a silly argument that got a bit out of hand. That's all.'

'Can you think of anyone who could be with you right now, Miss Coombes? It may help you feel better if you're not on your own.'

Sarah didn't answer but nodded.

'We'll leave now,' said Jack. 'If you feel you need to tell us something please let us know immediately.' He handed her a card with a telephone number on it. 'Ring the number shown here.'

Without looking up, she took the card.

As they walked to the car, Jack spoke quietly. 'She seemed very defensive. I think we probably have enough to consider her as one of our prime suspects.'

'Yes, of course, she's a suspect, Jack,' said Peter, 'but we don't have enough to charge her with. There's a lot more to find out yet about the relationship between the two women, and the connection between Moore and Williamson. There's a lot of work to do, and we need to get on with it. For DCI Trent's sake. That argument Sarah and Lynn had sounded like more than just a silly row. And it would appear from the information we got from Lynn's parents that she wasn't really a very nice person at all. But they loved her. She was their daughter. So, no one appeared to like Williamson, and now it seems that Lynn Moore might have been hard to like as well. These aren't just random victims, Jack. They're connected in some way. I am sure of that.' Peter walked faster as they got closer to the car. 'We need to speak to Mr and Mrs Moore again.'

'Miss Coombes was so upset,' said Jack. 'Quite frankly, distraught.'

'You would be too if you'd just killed someone, especially bearing in mind the viciousness of the murder.' He stopped. 'Jack, did you think there was anything strange about Sarah Coombes' questions?'

'Not that I can think of. Why?'

'If you'd just heard that the person you loved probably most in the world had been murdered, then apart from who did it, what else would be important to you?'

Jack looked upwards, his eyes closed for a short time. 'Got it! I'd want to know how she was murdered. Strangled, stabbed, shot … or whatever. Of course, I would. And where. She never asked anything like that.'

Peter nodded, his expression grim. 'You have to remember though, she is and will be very very distressed and not thinking about what she should or should not have asked.'

CHAPTER EIGHTEEN

Jenny was in her office early. As she was about to open up her computer, she was surprised by a knock on her door.

'Come in, Peter. Why so early?'

'I've got a report on our interview with Sarah Coombes.'

'Great, let's have it then.'

'She was very upset, of course, so it was hard to get much out of her, but it appears that they were thinking about buying a house together. She knows Lynn's parents a little, and it feels like she has a decent enough relationship with them. She said that she had called them when she started to get concerned about Sarah.'

'Did you ask her when she last spoke to Sarah?'

'Yes, I did, and she indicated it was that argument they had at Lynn's parents' house and she had walked out. They were due to have dinner together a few days after that, but Sarah had to cancel as her mother was ill.'

'Did you ask her if Lynn had told her she was viewing a property?' said Jenny.

'Yes, I did. She said that Lynn hadn't told her about it, but that she'd missed a call from her and it may have been about that.' He closed his notebook. 'As we were speaking with her, she became more and more upset.' He stopped and fidgeted with the top button of his open jacket. 'I didn't think I could get any more information from her, so I agreed to go back again another time. I asked her if there was anyone who could be with her, and she said she had someone she could call, and that it was okay for us to leave.'

Jenny felt the need to encourage him. 'Well done, Peter, good work. Go and have a short break and we'll be off to London.'

'As soon as you're ready we can go.'

'I'll be with you in fifteen minutes.'

He returned as promised. 'We'll take your car,' Jenny said.

'Have you told James Williamson's boss we're coming to see him today?' said Peter once they were on the way.

'No, but I had one of the team make a general enquiry call, and apparently, he's in meetings all day, so I know that he'll be in the office somewhere. I don't want him to make any preparation regarding our visit. I want to surprise him.'

✲✲✲

They arrived at the headquarters of Standard Elite Bank at eleven o'clock. As they neared the visitor's parking area, a uniformed officer standing close to the barrier stopped them. 'Do you have an appointment?' he demanded as he held up his hand.

'No, but we would like to see Mr Richard Poole,' said Jenny, showing her badge.

'I'll tell him you're here,' said the officer, sounding a little unsure. He put his mobile to his ear. 'Hello, Jill, I've got two police officers here who want to talk with your boss. Shall I send them up?' He looked at Peter and indicated that she was going to ask if it was okay.

In less than a minute, he had his answer. 'You can go up, his secretary will meet you on the fourth floor.'

When they arrived, they were met by an attractive young woman, smartly dressed, with a security tag around her neck announcing her name as *Jane Green – Standard Elite Bank*.

'Mr Poole needs just a few minutes before he can see you. Please come with me,' she said.

They approached an expensively furnished room, with large leather chairs and settees, walls covered with thick velvet paper, and gleaming photos of office buildings identified by the Standard Elite Bank name and the country where each office was located. In between the pictures, gleaming chandelier lights were all lit, the glass reflecting the colours of the room.

'Please take a seat. Can I get you a coffee or tea while you're waiting?'

'No, thank you, we're fine,' said Jenny.

Within minutes, the secretary returned. 'Mr Poole is free now, sorry for keeping you waiting.'

Richard Poole stood to greet them as they walked across his spacious office towards him. 'Good morning, please sit down.' His voice was warm, although not friendly.

'Good morning,' said Jenny. 'I'm Detective Chief Inspector Trent and this is my colleague Detective Inspector Branden. We've come about the murder of James Williamson, I understand he was a member of your staff.'

Poole held up his hand as Jenny spoke.

'He was not one of my staff, Chief Inspector, and was not employed by us. He was completely freelance. I've already given that information to one of your people.'

'But you knew him well enough?' Jenny responded quickly. 'He worked with your bank for a long time.'

'Yes, about ten years I think.'

'What can you tell us about him, Mr Poole? We would like to know how he came to work for your bank. We know from a previous visit by one of our officers that he was not very popular, can you tell us more about that?'

'We don't take references up for freelance people, Chief Inspector, but he had an excellent CV and came very highly recommended.'

'Recommended by who?' said Jenny.

'From the American side of our organisation, Chief Inspector. He did some good work for them, and ...' he hesitated. 'Before I go much further, I must tell you that he did an excellent job for us too.' His expression hardened as he looked at Jenny. 'He created a lot of new business, brought in many new clients, and made a lot of money for them.' He turned away from Jenny's enquiring stare. 'He did the same for this bank, Chief Inspector. He's a great loss to our business.'

'Why was he so unpopular with everyone? If he made plenty of money for your clients and your bank, you would have thought he'd be very popular.'

'I don't know where you got that from. He wasn't unpopular. There were many people who looked up to him and who liked him very much.

There were some people who were jealous of his success, it's just the way it is in this business.'

'Bit of a ladies' man, I understand.' Peter spoke without looking up from his notebook.

'How on earth would I know that?' said Poole his back straightening. 'If he was, that was his business, I can't see what it has to do with me or your enquiry.'

'Mr Poole,' said Jenny, leaning forward in her chair, hardly controlling her anger. 'James Williamson was murdered, and if you've read the newspapers you will know that it was a very brutal murder.' She stopped to allow him to take in her mood. 'It's extremely possible that he knew his killer and that he was terrified. Any questions we ask are relevant to the investigation. You knew him, Mr Poole, you may even be a suspect.' She stopped, as she saw a look of shock spread over Richard Poole's face.

He stared at her. 'You can ask me whatever you like, but I can assure you, Chief Inspector Trent, that I did not kill James. I had no reason to, and as I have already said, his death is a great loss to the bank.' Pushing back his large chair, he rose. 'Now, I'm a busy man, if there is anything else you want, please let me know quickly.'

'Please sit down, Mr Poole, we haven't finished yet,' said Jenny.

Poole sat and swivelled in his chair to meet Jenny's gaze.

'Did you socialise with James?'

Poole was quiet and thoughtful. 'Not really, we used to have a few beers now and again,' he shifted, a little uneasy.

'Did you ever meet his wife?'

Poole's eyes closed with frustration. 'What the hell has that got to do with this?'

Jenny put her hand up and stopped him. 'Did you meet his wife?'

'Once or twice, that's all.'

'Would his wife know you, if she met you again, Mr Poole?' said Jenny.

'Of course, she would.'

'I'm sure she would, Mr Poole.' Jenny rose, looking him directly in the eye.

'Rhys Mason. I'd like to speak with him as well, Mr Poole. Would you ask your secretary to get him, please?'

'Why? What's Rhys got to do with this?' His voice was now shaking with anger.

'I'll find out when I speak to him, Mr Poole.'

'I'm not sure if he's in today, Chief Inspector. Rhys also works freelance. I'm not always aware of his movements.'

'Perhaps you would be good enough to find out. It's important that I speak with him as soon as possible,' Jenny said.

Poole picked up the telephone. 'Jane, can you please find out if Rhys is in his office.'

'When you met Mrs Williamson, was it at her house or somewhere else?' Jenny spoke quietly as she sat down.

Poole shifted in his chair, his face flushing a deep uneven pink, and when he finally spoke his voice was angry, but cautious.

'Mostly we met at James's house.' He stopped, turning slightly to meet Jenny's stare. 'Where are we going with this, Chief Inspector? If you think I had anything to do with James's death, you are very wrong. He was a valuable part of this business and a friend. If this goes on much longer I shall have to insist I have my solicitor with me.'

The telephone rang, breaking the tension.

'Thank you, Jane' he replaced the receiver.

'I'm sorry, Rhys Mason is not in today.'

'When will he be, Mr Poole?' said Jenny.

'I understand he is with a client in Worcester and will be back on Tuesday next week.

'We'll be back on Tuesday next week, Mr Poole, please make sure that he's here when we arrive.' She rose from her chair. 'Just one more thing, Mr Poole. Do you know if he socialised with James?'

'You'll have to ask him that, Chief Inspector.'

As Jenny reached to open the door she turned to face Richard Poole. 'Are you married, Mr Poole?'

'Yes, but what's that got to do with anything?'

'Not much, at the moment. Thank you for your help, we'll be back on Tuesday to speak with Rhys Mason. If for any reason, we need to speak with him before that we'll let you know. Perhaps you can ensure you have details of where he is and how we can contact him. We may want to speak with you again too. So don't go visiting anywhere without letting us know, Mr Poole.'

Richard Poole shifted in his chair, and as the door closed Jenny saw him place his elbows on the desk, bringing his hands up to hold his head.

✲✲✲

The journey back to the station was quiet. Jenny was not sure if it was because Peter was concentrating on the traffic or if something else was on his mind. She was inclined to think it was the latter, and made a mental note to speak with him soon.

Although it was late when they arrived back, Jenny went to her office to check her mail before going home. She was tired and needed a long hot bath. Peter came up behind her.

'Jenny, before I go. I think Emma Williamson must have thought about killing her husband. Anyone who lived with a monster like him must have wanted him out of the way and may have thought about getting someone to kill him.'

'I'm sure they would, but with the evidence, we have so far it's pretty obvious that the two murders have been committed by the same person. Both had peach stones pushed into their throats and both bodies were brutally mutilated. Emma Williamson may have had a motive in getting her husband killed, but surely not someone else as well? We need to know more about the victims. Once we do, we'll know what the motive for the murders is.'

'We should get more from the neighbours, once I've spoken to them again.' Peter said. 'I'm sure they're hiding something. The only thing that seems consistent is that nobody liked him. There must be a reason for it.'

That's enough for now, you're tired. You should be having a couple of days off. Go home and rest. If anything urgent comes up I'll call you.

'I think I'll go to the neighbours first. I've got a hunch.' He grinned.

CHAPTER NINETEEN

Jenny thought about her coffee meeting with Andrew Baines. He was easy to talk to. They had laughed at silly things and, after three coffees and two sticky buns, she had felt lightheaded and happy. When they parted, she realised that she knew very little about him, and ... that she liked him. A lot.

As she called Honey for her Sunday walk, she wondered if she should telephone Andrew and return the invitation for coffee. 'I'll think about later,' she said softly to herself.

Honey bounded towards the front door, waiting for it to open onto the freedom and the joyous smells of a journey to the park. As the door opened, she burst through and Jenny decided that she would, after all, call Andrew sooner, rather than later.

The walk to the park was hampered only by the wait for three trains to pass at the railway crossing. Honey sat patiently, then moved urgently forward as the gates began their slow, noisy movement upwards. It was a lovely warm early-spring day and, having made the decision to call Andrew, Jenny felt calm and relaxed. She ran slowly with Honey towards the wider open space of the park, which was already busy with children playing football and other dog walkers avoiding the young footballers and their yelling dads.

Honey bounded off towards the bushes, only once looking back to make sure Jenny was visible.

Jenny walked towards the children's play area, and couldn't help but think about Emma Williamson. Could she have killed her husband? She had hated him and wanted him dead. She was an obvious suspect. What about her sister? She also had a good reason for killing her brother-in-law. Then there were the similarities with Lynn Moore's murder. Why would Emma Williamson or her sister want to kill her? Did either of them even *know* Lynn Moore?

She sighed. There was still so much more to find out, her mood darkened. She turned to see if Honey had finished investigating the bushes. She wasn't behind her, so she carried on walking around the play area towards a break in the fencing, leading to a small wooded area.

Honey was still nowhere to be seen. It was unusual, the wooded area was one of her favourite places, mostly because of her endless quest to catch a squirrel, or one of the diving birds that consistently teased her by seeing how close she would let them get to her, before squawking off to join the squirrels, safely at home in the heart of the big trees.

Jenny called, 'Come on, Honey. Let's see what we can find in the woods now.'

There was no response to her call and Jenny retraced her steps. As she got to the edge of the park she called for Honey again but there was still no sign of her.

A young man, one of the regular walkers, with a large German shepherd walked past and smiled at her. 'She won't be far away,' he said reassuringly.

Loud, excited shouts were coming from the young footballers. Someone had scored and the whoops and delighted cries from proud dads and smiling mums drowned out the sound of congratulations from the other players.

There was still no sign of Honey and Jenny felt anxiety creeping over her already tense body. Honey never went anywhere without ensuring Jenny was within sight. Once, she had teased her and hidden behind a large tree. Honey became frantic looking for her and she had felt guilty as she saw Honey' frantically looking for her.

Jenny began to run towards the bushes, calling for Honey. A woman she regularly chatted to on their walk asked if she could help.

'It's Honey, she seems to have disappeared, and she never runs off,' said Jenny.

'I'll help look for her. You go over there,' the woman said, pointing to the left side of the park. 'I'll carry on here.'

'Thank you,' said Jenny. She thought how frightened Honey would be if she were lost.

Jenny began beating the bushes on her side of the park, calling for Honey. Her mind was in turmoil. How could she lose the thing that had become most precious to her since her husband had died? Honey couldn't just disappear without a trace.

She heard the excitement from the players and families as someone scored another goal, the clapping was loud again, and she wanted it to stop so she could hear if the woman called.

Jenny continued pushing the bushes away, her hands becoming covered in long deep scratches which she didn't feel, or notice. She stood to take a deep breath, as she began to move aside more bushes she heard a boys voice.

Dad! Come 'ere there's a big dog, I think he's dead he's covered in blood. Dad! Dad! Quick, quick. It's a dog and he's dead.'

Jenny's breath caught in her throat.

'Dad! Dad!' The boy's voice was getting louder and more urgent. 'A dead dog's 'ere and there's blood everywhere. Quick ... please, Dad.'

Jenny called to the child. 'Wait, wait I'm coming, stay there, please!'

She raced towards the boy, who was still shouting for his Dad, who, having heard his son's frantic calls, was also hurrying towards him.

Other people in the crowd had heard the commotion and were joining the movement towards the boy shouting in the bushes. Children were clustered in the clearing. A little girl was crying.

Jenny took a sharp breath as she saw Honey lying down. Blood was falling in a steady trickle from a large open wound on her side, just above her front legs. Jenny knelt down, putting her hand on Honey's head, her other hand pressed firmly over the wound in an attempt to stop the bleeding. As she did, Honey lifted her paw and placed it on Jenny's arm, claws digging deep into her flesh, something she had always done when she wanted attention or just a loving stroke.

'She's not dead, she's not dead,' said Jenny.

'Rory, go and get Mrs Richards,' said the boy's father. 'She's a first-aider and may be able to help.' His son sprinted towards the middle of the field, calling for Mrs Richards.

Jenny pulled at her phone and passed it to the boy's father. 'Grove Lodge vets have an emergency vet on duty on Sundays. The number's on my phone, please try and get someone here as soon as possible.'

Jenny was grateful for her own first-aid training. Although it had not been for an animal, she hoped the processes were similar. She pressed harder on the wound, trying to stop the flow of blood.

Mrs Richards arrived. 'Move away, everyone, let me get in.' She was a big woman and everyone shifted to make room for her.

'Has anyone called a vet?' she demanded.

'I'm trying to get Grove Lodge now,' said the boy's father.

Honey was panting quietly, claws still deep into Jenny's arm.

'Hold on, girl,' was all Jenny could say. Her stomach ached with anxiety as she blinked away tears.

Mrs Richards began studying Honey. 'That's a nasty deep cut on her side, and it looks like she's had a knock on her head too, which is probably why she's not trying to get up.' She looked up at the boy's father. 'Have you got them, yet?'

'They can't get anyone to come here. We have to take the dog there.'

'Great. It's a heavy dog. How on earth are we going to do that?' said Mrs Richards.

Jenny looked at the boy's father. 'Do you have a car with you?'

'I've got a van, I'll go and get it.'

He handed Jenny's phone back to her and took off his coat. 'Here, take this – you can put your dog on it before we lift her into the van.

Mrs Richards spread the coat out and called for someone to help lift Honey onto it. Two young men volunteered and, with Jenny's help, moved the injured dog carefully onto the coat. Honey's panting got faster as she was moved. Jenny stooped down to comfort her and Honey placed a paw on her arm again, the claws digging even deeper than before.

Jenny stroked the head of the dog she loved with all her heart. 'We just want you to get well,' she said, unashamed of talking to her dog, and oblivious to the onlookers.

The boy's father arrived with the van. He opened the back doors and cleared a space, and between them, they picked up Honey and carefully placed her into the vehicle.

Jenny pulled her hand away from Honey, who seemed too weak to object. Her eyes closed and for a moment and Jenny felt a shiver of panic. She touched Honey for reassurance, she was still breathing.

The woman who had helped look for Honey took Jenny's hand. 'I'm sure she'll be fine.' Her eyes were damp with tears. 'My name's Patricia. I don't think we exchanged names before.'

Jenny hugged her. 'Thank you for all your help. I'm Jenny,' she said. 'You've been very kind. I know I'll see you again when Honey's well and back in the park.'

The van's engine roared into life and Jenny ran to the front. The boy was already in the middle seat and Jenny jumped in beside him.

'It won't take us long to get to the vets. I'm sure your dog will be fine,' said the boy's father. 'By the way, my name's Rob, and this is my son, Rory.

A tall man dressed in a white coat met them as the van stopped at the entrance to the vet's surgery. He wheeled a large trolley to the back of the van, and with Rob's help moved Honey onto it.

'If you don't need us any more, we'll go back to the park,' Rob said. 'But if you'd like us to stay, we'd be quite happy to until you know more about how your dog's doing? Wouldn't we Rory?'

'I'd love to stay Dad, Can I? Please, Dad … Can I?

'That's so kind of you, but I think I'd rather stay on my own now,' Jenny said. 'Thank you so much for all you've done, I'm very grateful. Please leave your address and number at the desk and I'll have your coat cleaned and returned to you.' She turned to Rory. 'And thank you, too, for finding her.'

'Can't I stay?' Rory looked appealingly at his dad.

'No, Rory, you can't, but I'm sure we'll know how Honey gets on, won't we?' he looked at Jenny.

'Yes, of course,' said Jenny. 'I'll call you. And we'll be back in the park on Sundays as soon as Honey is well.' Rory beamed.

The trolley with Honey on it was pushed past the open doors of the building and into a small room on the left of the reception area. Jenny followed the trolley into the room. The tall man in white turned to Jenny.

'Good morning, I'm Stephen Wade. On duty over the weekend.'

'My name's Jenny Trent, and this is Honey, she's registered here.'

'What happened?' Stephen said as he began his inspection of the wounded dog.

Jenny took a deep breath, the words sticking in her throat as she held back the need to cry. 'I'm not sure, she went missing on our walk in the park, and the young boy who was with us found her.' She stopped, her head lowered, as she looked at Honey, so quiet in front of her. 'I really don't know what happened.' She swallowed hard. 'Will she be alright?'

Stephen straightened his back. 'She's not going to die, but she's had a nasty knock on her head and a very deep deliberate cut has been made in her side. She'll need surgery for the wound, and will need to be here for a few days.'

'What do you mean by a deliberate cut?'

'Well, someone has cut her with a very sharp knife or weapon of some sort. That's the only way she could have sustained this sort of wound. Whoever did it, hit her head to stop her moving away. And whoever did it,' he repeated, 'didn't want to kill her. The nature and depth of the cut seem very precise. For some reason, it looks as if they just wanted to hurt her.'

He removed the collar from Honey's neck, passing it to Jenny without turning, concentrating on the injured dog lying motionless on the large trolley. 'I need to get on with this now. There's no reception cover today, but if you leave your telephone number at the desk I'll call you once I know how she's getting on.'

'Thank you,' said Jenny.

She retrieved Rob's details from the notepad at the desk and replaced them with her own, then ran home without stopping. The warmth from the sun had now gone and she shivered as she opened her front door. She walked into the hall, and found herself leaning against the wall, she cried with loud uncontrollable sobs. Why would someone want to hurt Honey?

Moving into the kitchen, she forgot her grasp on Honey's collar and it dropped to the floor. Oblivious to either the action or the sound, she put the kettle to boil and moved like an automaton around the kitchen, preparing her drink.

Hot tea helped her calm down. She missed Honey excitedly pushing a toy towards her, her paw reaching out for attention. She rose from the chair she had slumped into with tea in hand. As she walked slowly towards the lounge, she saw Honey's collar on the floor and bent to pick it up. The nametag was loose and she made a mental note to get a new one before Honey was ready to come home.

As she sat down, she saw that the slip of paper that held her contact details on Honey's collar was poking out of the small chamber which contained it. She pulled it out. There was something different about it. She had written on white paper, this was blue. She opened up the curled strip.

YOU REALLY ARE NO TRYING HARD ENOUGH DETECTIVE CHIEF INSPECTOR JENNY TRENT

NOT HARD ENOUGH AT ALL.

OH DEAR!

The words on the small piece of paper were black, large and accusing. What did it mean? What was it she wasn't trying hard enough at? Why would someone want to hurt her dog, why?

She took another sip of tea before the realisation hit her. Whoever had done it didn't care a jot about hurting Honey. They wanted to hurt her.

CHAPTER TWENTY

Jenny woke a full hour before her alarm sounded. She was angry with herself, she had let herself become lost in her grief about Honey. She dressed quickly and skipped breakfast.

She arrived at the station early with the blue note in her hand.

Peter was at his desk. '

Good morning peter. I want a full incident briefing this morning, Peter, can you make sure everyone is there. Honey was attacked in the park yesterday, it was nasty and it was personal.' She handed him the blue piece of paper, already bagged ready to send to forensic 'This was hanging from her identity tag. I didn't find it until I got home.'

Peter quickly read the words the paper. 'What does it mean?'

'There has to be a reason why they chose to hurt Honey. They know more about me than I feel comfortable with.'

'I'm sorry,' said Peter. 'How is she?'

'She's been badly cut and was hit over the head, but the vet says she will be fine in a few days.'

Jenny was aware that she hadn't asked Peter about his problem at home and made a mental note to talk to him as soon as possible. They were due to revisit the offices of Standard Elite Bank the next day and she would have time to talk to him on the way.

'If Alan Hughes is in, Peter, please ask him to come in and see me. I want him to go back to Williamson's neighbours with you. Something is going on there, and we still don't know what.'

Almost before she had time to sit down at her desk, Hughes knocked on and opened the door to her office.

'You wanted to see me, Ma'am?'

'Yes Alan, have you got anything from the Williamsons' neighbours?' Jenny said.

'Not much, Ma'am, nobody really wanted to say anything. One or two of them said that he wasn't a very nice person, and one even said he deserved to die.'

'Did you enquire further about that? It's a pretty nasty thing to say about someone who has just died in such a pretty awful way.'

Hughes looked a little unsure of himself. 'I tried to, but he made it very clear by his attitude that he had no intention of saying anything else. It is very strange,' he said. 'There's a weird feeling about the place.'

He paused before opening his notebook. 'As I said, no one wanted to say much. They either knew very little about the Williamsons or didn't want to. I spoke with a Mr Collins two houses along and he seemed more than anxious – angry, even – he just said that he wasn't sorry he was dead and closed the door on me.'

Closing his notebook, he looked at Jenny. 'There was a sense of fear around the place, and no one seemed to feel at all sorry for Williamson's death.'

'At the briefing this morning,' said Jenny 'I want you to update everyone on what you've told me. Then, I'd like you and Peter to go back to the neighbours, but this time I want you to make some threatening noises. Tell them that if they're not more talkative, warrants will be requested to search some of the houses. Speak to Mrs Williamson, as well, also, in particular, see Mr Collins again – there's something he's not telling us. If necessary, threaten them with a trip to the station. Remind them all that this is a murder enquiry and they could well be on the list of suspects.'

'Yes, Ma'am,' said Hughes, and he left the room.

Peter had organised the briefing for ten o'clock. The room was almost full when Jenny arrived. Most were drinking out of plastic cups. Morgan-Jones was standing at the back of the room.

'Good morning, everyone,' she Jenny. There was a murmured reply.

She turned to the whiteboard and pinned a white piece of paper with the words found on the note from Honey's collar in the space under the photos of James Williamson and Lynn Moore. 'I don't intend this briefing to last long,' she said, looking around the room. 'Yesterday, my dog was attacked in Victoria Park, she was cut badly and hit over the head, by someone who deliberately wanted to harm her. Whoever did it left a note for me.'

She pointed at the piece of paper pinned on the board and read out the message. "This is not the actual piece of paper with the message on it, that's with forensic looking for fingerprints"

'At this stage, I'm not sure if this has anything to do with the Williamson and Moore murders.' She looked around at the enquiring glances. 'But, it doesn't take much to work out that the attack on my dog was meant as a message to me. Right now I don't know why, but we will find out.'

'Is your dog alright?' The question came from PC Spencer.

'Yes, she'll be fine in a few days, but she needs surgery for her wounds. I want a SOCO Officer to report to me as soon as we've finished here so that we can go to the park where my dog was hurt and look for evidence. There may be nothing left to find, but anything is worth a try.'

She turned to Hughes. 'Alan, please give us your report on your visit to the Williamsons' neighbours.'

He rose and repeated what he had told Jenny earlier.

Jenny returned to the front of the room. 'There's something going on in that neighbourhood.' She paused. 'Something that has made a lot of people very wary of talking. Alan, I want you to go back to the Williamsons' neighbours with DI Branden. Get a search warrant for the Williamsons' house, and I want the others to know that their houses may be searched too, I want to know their reactions.' She turned to face the board.

'Now, let's think about Lynn Moore, the second victim.' Jenny allowed herself a glance at Morgan-Jones, who was sitting now with his arms crossed, she was unable to guess his mood.

She looked around the room for DC Callam. 'Detective Callam, I want you to visit Lynn Moore's parents again. The mother made a comment that she thought she'd heard their daughter mention James Williamson's name at some point. Find out more about that. There was also a voice message on Lynn Moore's answerphone from someone regarding an appointment, find out about that too. You will need to go to her flat, The Moores have the keys, I am sure they will give them to you.'

'Any questions?' She looked around the room. No one responded. 'It's been almost a week since James Williamson's murder and we need something to go on. Right, let's get on with it. I want to hear from anyone with something to say, no matter what time of day or night it is.

Morgan-Jones rose slowly from his chair and walked towards Jenny who was gathering a notebook and pens from the table.

'Jenny,' his voice was quieter than usual. 'I'm so sorry about your dog, I know how much she means to you.' He reached the front of the table. 'You said the attack on your dog was personal?' He paused, waiting for a response. 'I mean, do you think there is somehow a connection between you and the other murders, other than the fact you're investigating them?'

Jenny looked directly at Morgan-Jones. 'I've thought about it, and to be honest I can't answer that question yet. Once we find out more about the two victims I hope I'll be able to. But, I do think the message was meant to frighten me.'

'Jenny,' Morgan-Jones reached out and touched her shoulder. 'Don't put yourself in any danger. The moment you feel you are in any sort of trouble, tell me. Please.'

She excused herself. 'Thank you, Sir. I will, of course.'

CHAPTER TWENTY-ONE

Peter and Alan arrived at Marden Close just after noon. They pulled up two doors away from the Williamson's house. Alan opened the black iron gate and they walked up to the front door.

'You'd need a lot of dosh to live here,' said Alan. He shivered, even though it was warm in the early spring sunshine. 'Everything's a bit cold and uninviting,' he grumbled. He raised the huge, brass, lion-head and knocked. Receiving no response after a second, harder knock, they turned to leave but hesitated upon hearing footsteps slowly coming to the door, which then opened halfway.

'Good morning, Mr Collins,' said Alan. 'DS Hughes. I spoke with you about James Williamson's death a few days ago.' The door started to close, and Alan wedged his foot into the opening. 'Sorry, Mr Collins, it's very important we speak with you again.' He turned his head towards Peter. 'This is Inspector Branden.' Peter held his badge close for Collins to see.

'We need to talk to you again about Mr Williamson's murder. Can we come in, please?' said Peter. The man in front of them stared but said nothing. 'I'm afraid you have no choice, sir, it's either here or at the station,' said Peter, waiting for a reaction. 'It's your choice, Mr Collins.'

'Not much of a choice, is it?' He said as he opened the door fully. 'You'd better come in then. I've already told him,' he said, jabbing a finger towards Alan, 'that I didn't know Williamson very well. What else can I tell you? Bloody nuisance he was killed, I suppose, but no one liked him. Nasty piece of work. Got what he deserved, if you ask me.'

They followed him through a large hall to the kitchen. 'His wife's nice, though,' said Collins. 'Always looked sad. I felt sorry for her really, having to live with that obnoxious man.'

He pulled out two chairs from the kitchen table. 'Take a seat,' he said. 'What exactly do you want to know that I haven't already told you?' He sat down in the chair facing both detectives.

'First of all, said Peter. 'Was it you who said he'd got what he deserved, outside the Williamson's house when we were first there investigating what had happened?'

Collins shrugged his shoulders. 'I think a lot of people might have said it.'

'I asked if you said it, Mr Collins,'

'If I didn't say it I would have certainly thought it,' Collins said. 'I'm sorry, detective, but I just don't remember.'

'Do you live here alone, Mr Collins?' said Peter.

'Now I do. I chucked my wife out a year ago. She was having it off with him.' He used his thumb to indicate the direction of the Williamson's house. 'When he got fed up with her she thought I'd forget it and make out nothing had happened.' He was quiet for a few moments, his head lowered. 'I thought they were going to go off together, but as I said, he got fed up with her and dumped her. Same as he did with all of them. Well, I can tell you,' he sniffed, 'I didn't want anything to do with her after that, and I let her know it.'

He looked up swiftly and stared at Peter. 'No, I didn't harm her, Inspector, I just couldn't be in the same place as her, and yes, I still loved her, and probably still do, but that's another story.' He turned away from the detectives' enquiring eyes. 'I provided her with a nice house near Brighton and I give her a reasonable allowance.' He gave a short laugh. 'She's a very attractive woman, Inspector, a bit younger than me, so I hope she finds someone to make her happy. Thank God we had no children.' He got up from the chair and Peter saw a broken, unhappy man.

'Do you work, Mr Collins?' asked Alan, without looking up from his notes.

'Yes, I'm an architect, and before you ask, I work mostly at home. I also have an office in town and a girl who looks after my admin needs, but I meet my clients here. I have a workroom with everything I need. It's upstairs if you want to see it.'

'Thank you, we would like to, later,' said Alan.

'We need more information on Mr Williamson,' said Peter. 'No one seems to have liked him much and we know his wife was frightened of him. There has to be a reason.' He stopped Collins as he was about to speak. 'Before you answer, Mr Collins, I'm sure you will know that another murder took place soon after that of Mr Williamson and that we believe it was carried out by the same person. Any information we can get on both victims will help us to catch the culprit before another person is attacked.'

'I know about the woman who was killed. It was in the paper, which wasn't too impressed with the way you lot are dealing with it.' Collins allowed himself a little smile as he looked Peter in the eye.

'No, they were not, which is why we need some answers from you, and we need them quick,' said Peter.

'I'll tell you everything I know,' said Collins, 'which as I said before is very little. Williamson was an investment banker. He had a lot of money and threw it around a bit. Occasionally gave grand parties. Some of the neighbours went, but I was never asked.'

He glanced at Alan writing notes. 'I was never one of his cronies and didn't want to be. He was a nasty, arrogant piece of shit, Inspector, and I make no apologies for the language.'

'Did he have other visitors, people who weren't neighbours?' said Peter.

'What, apart from my wife, you mean?' His voice was quiet and sarcastic. 'Yes, he did. There were lots of men who came quite frequently, mostly in the evenings.' He stopped, his eyes closed in thought. 'They had big flashy cars. Sometimes there were young women with them. Most times they stayed all night, leaving very early in the morning, I guess. A nasty-looking bunch.'

'Was Mrs Williamson there during these visits?' said Peter.

'Wouldn't know, Inspector. No one ever saw her much, you'll have to ask her.'

'Did any of the neighbours who were invited to his parties join the other people on those evenings?'

'I did see the bloke who lives opposite them go once or twice, but I don't know his name and have never spoken to him.' Collins rose from his chair. 'I really don't think there is anything more I can tell you, Inspector. If I think of anything else I'll call you immediately if you give me your card.'

'Please do,' said Peter, taking a card from his inside pocket and handing it to Collins. 'Before we go, can we see your office upstairs?'

'Of course, follow me.'

Upstairs was just as grand as the downstairs, with solid oak doors and thick dark-red carpets. At the end of a long corridor, they came to a double door. Collins pressed a switch on a side panel and the doors opened. They followed him into a large, beautifully furnished room. The walls were fitted with shelves filled with books. A polished table with eight leather-upholstered chairs took up a lot of space at the end of the room. A four-seater black leather chesterfield sat under a large curtained window, matching black armchairs placed neatly to each side. In a corner behind the table, there was a tall cocktail unit. Glasses gleaming and a large variety of spirits and wines on display. To the left of the room, there was an architect's drafting table, holding unfinished drawings held down with an array of technical implements and a huge electric magnifying lamp. And there was still enough space for a magnificent, highly polished desk and a green leather captain's chair. Taking centre stage on the desk were two large monitors, the screens side by side.

'Do you meet all your clients here, Mr Collins?' Peter said.

'Mostly. I do a lot of work for local councils and I have clients looking for designs for extensive new buildings in London.' He turned to look at the two detectives. 'I find it easier here to guide some people into not making silly mistakes with buildings.' He stopped, a small smile lit up his eyes. 'You'd be surprised how many young, enthusiastic council officers think they should have a Gherkin in the middle of a seaside town.' He moved further into the huge room. 'Is there anything else you would like to see, Inspector? I should be getting down to work as soon as I can.'

'No, not for the moment. Thank you for your cooperation, Mr Collins, if we need to speak with you again we'll be in touch.'

Peter and Alan made their way to the car and sat quietly for a moment.

'Quite a decent chap, I think,' said Alan, thoughtfully. 'What do you make of the people visiting Williamson's house?'

'Not sure,' said Peter, 'but we'll find out. As a suspect, he's gone up the pole. He's obviously pretty upset about Williamson and his wife. In fact, I think he's only just coming round from being a broken man. But. He hides it well.'

'He would have a good reason to want him dead,' said Alan. 'Should we report this to the DCI immediately?'

'We report everything to the DCI, 'said Peter. 'Just remember that at all times. First, let's see if Emma Williamson's in,' said Peter. 'We might get some answers before we speak to the bloke opposite Williamson's house, it's number 15.'

CHAPTER TWENTY-TWO

Andrew Baines joined Jenny and PC Spencer at the park. Jenny tried hard to hide the pleasure she felt in his company and thought again about a return coffee invitation.

Under Jenny's instructions, the area had remained cordoned off, but light rain had washed a lot of the disturbance away.

The bushes had already been searched, looking for fabric that might have been torn away from clothing. The ground was covered in smudged footprints, which Andrew painstakingly measured and photographed. He scooped up a sample of earth containing traces of Honey's blood and secured it in a plastic bag.

After two more hours examining bushes, muddy earth and stones on the ground, Andrew said that he didn't feel there was any more they could find, and with Jenny's agreement they decided to return to the station.

'I'm really sorry about your dog, Jenny,' he said. 'I know she means a lot to you. I'm sure she'll be fine. When do you pick her up?'

'In a few days, I hope,' said Jenny. 'She appears to be recovering well, and I'm looking forward to having her home again.'

'As soon as I've studied what I have here I'll let you know if there's anything that might help with the investigation,' said Andrew, holding up several plastic bags. His smile almost encouraged Jenny to make her invitation for coffee there and then, but she didn't.

∗∗∗

Back at the station, Jenny found Peter waiting for her. She motioned for him to join her in her office.

'Alan and I have spoken with Emma Williamson and her neighbour Mr Collins this morning. Collins was quite helpful this time. It seems his wife had an affair with Williamson, so he kicked her out. I think it was deeply upsetting for him at the time, and it's pretty clear that he's still traumatised and an indication of why he hated Williamson so much.' He paused as the telephone rang on Jenny's desk.

'Good morning, Sir,' said Jenny. 'Yes, I'm getting reports now and will call you with an update as soon as I have all the information.' She gave Peter an exasperated look as she put the phone down.

'Still on about getting some answers? We certainly need some,' said Peter.

'Yes he is, and yes we do.' Jenny's voice was edgy. 'Did you learn anything else from Collins?'

'Yes, he was quite talkative. He said that Williamson had people visiting his house quite a lot, mostly men, several at a time. Sometimes one or two young women were with them.'

'What sort of people were they?' asked Jenny, hoping for a description of Richard Poole.

'He just said they were …' he thought for a second. '"A nasty-looking bunch."'

'Did he say if he knew any of them?'

He saw the bloke who lives opposite the Williamsons go there, other than that he didn't know any of them,' said Peter.

'Did you speak with the man opposite?'

'No, we haven't yet, but we spent some time with Emma Williamson. She certainly seems to have got over her husband's death and looked remarkably settled compared with the last time saw her. She showed us the games room again, where her husband spent some time with his visitors. I told her I wanted another look.' He stopped, his face clouded. 'There's something funny about that room.' He hesitated to take a sip of coffee. 'Can't quite put my finger on it, but my initial feeling was that it was smaller than I thought it was going to be, and I got the same sense today.'

He stopped suddenly, his eyes flashing. 'That's it, Jenny, it *is* smaller, not by much, but it's smaller. And it shouldn't be. The house is bigger than Collins's property, yet his office – on the first floor in the same part of the house as the games room in Williamson's place – feels bigger.' He stood facing Jenny. 'I'm going back and I need a warrant to search the place.'

'When you have the warrant come back here. Take Alan with you again and two other officers, I'll finish here. I need to update Morgan-Jones.'

***

Morgan-Jones sat quietly listing to Jenny's update.

'Peter is applying for a warrant now. As soon as he has it he'll go back to search the house,' she said.

'Do you still think Mrs Williamson has nothing to do with her husband's murder, Jenny? I can only say again that she seems to have a very good motive … and … have you considered the fact that she may have paid someone to do it?' said Morgan-Jones.

Jenny hesitated. 'I have thought about that, yes, but it would have been a clean, precise murder, not such a brutal one. And the murder of Lynn Moore in such a similar way doesn't really add up to a contract killing.'

'I hear what you say, Jenny, but in my book, and until we have more to go on, she's still a suspect.'

CHAPTER TWENTY-THREE

Peter and Alan arrived at Williamson's house and ordered the uniformed officers to wait by the car. They walked to the front door and rang the bell. Within seconds Mrs Williamson opened the door.

'We have a warrant to search your house, Mrs Williamson,' said Peter, showing the document.

'But I've already shown you everything, Inspector, what more can you be looking for?'

'We need to take a look at the games room again, Mrs Williamson.'

She shrugged. 'Come in,' her voice showed no sign of alarm. 'I'll show you the way again. Do you want me to stay with you?'

'Yes, please,' said Peter. He motioned to the two uniformed officers to join them, and they followed him into the hall. 'I'd like you two to take a careful look in the rooms here,' he said. 'Careful means careful – I don't want anything broken or anything thrown around.'

They nodded and walked into a room, pulling on gloves as they went.

Mrs Williamson entered the code to the games room and the door opened. The room was exactly as before, cold and unwelcoming.

Peter and Alan moved to the far end of the room. Peter looked closely at the vast framed mirror that took up almost half of the wall space. To its left, was the well-stocked bar and to the right an oak-shelved bookcase. Nothing appeared to have been moved or touched since their last visit. 'Is there anything behind this wall, Mrs Williamson?' said Peter, turning to look at her.

She looked puzzled. 'Of course not, Inspector, the wall and mirror have always been there.'

'They may have been, but we have reason to believe that this room should be larger than it appears and that there might be a concealed space behind them,' Peter said.

His hands moved slowly along the top of the mirror, down its sides and along the bottom. Wiping his hands, he moved to the bookcase, feeling every line of the shelves, moving the books backwards and forwards as he went. The top shelf held just four books and two large expensive looking vases. He moved the books to one side, feeling the back of the bookcase and the surface of the shelves. He moved a vase away from its place, feeling below and behind and then replacing it. He stepped back and looked hard at the bookshelf. Nothing had changed, he felt disappointed and moved on to the bar.

Alan had also decided to investigate the mirror, moving his fingers over the frame again, but finding nothing that gave a hint of anything unusual.

'I'll check the bookcase again,' he called out to Peter.

'Fine,' Peter acknowledged, passing his hand under the counter of the bar. 'The opening must be on this wall somewhere.' His exasperation was beginning to show.

Alan had reached the top shelf with the two large vases. He used both hands and moved them together, placing them carefully side by side in the middle of the shelf.

'What on earth is happening? 'Mrs Williamson walked hesitantly into the room. Her eyes wide, looking past them. She looked frightened and opened her mouth to speak again, but nothing came out.

Both men turned to follow her gaze and saw the bookcase swinging silently open. As it came to a stop, they were able to see what looked like a large, white, painted door that had been completely hidden behind it.

'Moving both vases at the same time must have triggered a movement,' said Alan.

'What is it?' said Mrs Williamson quietly. 'I know nothing about it, I never came into this room, and my husband never wanted me to.' She was close to tears. 'Is there another room? … Can we go in?' Her voice was shaking, and tears began to fall lightly down her face. Then, 'No. No. I don't want to go in,' she whispered.

Peter moved towards her. 'We need to bring some more people in here, Mrs Williamson. I suggest that you go back to the lounge and stay there, we may need to talk to you again soon. Alan, please go with Mrs Williamson. I'll call Chief Inspector Trent.'

He reached Jenny quickly. 'Jenny, can you get here with some help immediately? I know why the games room looked so small. There's another room at the back. We can see a door, which is most likely locked. We will need the means to break the door down.

'I'll be there, Peter.' She ordered an incident car and several officers to join her. Everyone moved fast, cars filled up, blue flashing lights lit up the exit from the station car park. She located her mobile and called Morgan-Jones. There was no reply so she left a short message to update him.

Three police cars pulled up outside the Williamson's house. Jenny was out of the first car almost before it had come to a stop. She ran inside and called for Peter.

Glancing to the left, she saw Mrs Williamson in the lounge, sitting in an armchair. Standing next to her was a uniformed officer. Passing along the hallway she saw that the door to the games room was already wide open and Peter and a police officer were standing in the middle of the room.

'Thanks for coming so quickly, Jenny. No one's been near the hidden room yet,' Peter said.

'So your hunch was right. Well done. Peter.' Jenny paused, before walking towards the door that had been revealed by the bookcase. 'Did Mrs Williamson know it was here?'

'I'm pretty sure she didn't, she was very shocked when she saw it.'

'How was the bookcase door opened?'

'When Alan moved the vases together it must have triggered something. It swung open. It was so quiet that neither of us noticed it until we heard a sound from Mrs Williamson behind us. She saw it open and was obviously shocked. I believe that both vases had to be moved simultaneously in order to release the mechanism.'

They turned their attention to the white door, searching for something that might open it. They could find nothing like buttons or switches.

'We can't wait any longer,' said Jenny. 'Get some photographs taken and then I want the door knocked down.'

Morgan-Jones met Peter as he was going through the kitchen to get help. Peter quickly explained about the door, and Jenny's order to have it photographed and broken down.

'Excellent,' Morgan-Jones said. He joined Jenny in the corridor leading to the games room. 'They'll be here shortly with the ram, Jenny. You'd better get out of the way.'

Jenny moved past him into the games room. An officer arrived with a camera and quickly took several shots of the closed door.

Three police officers then hurried in with a battering ram, their heads covered with helmets and goggles.

It took three minutes for the door to give in to the onslaught, before crashing to the floor in the inside of the room it was protecting.

'Jenny, you, Inspector Branden and two officers will come in with me.' Morgan-Jones ordered.

They passed carefully over the broken door. Darkness hid the way forward. Peter found a light switch. He pressed it down, and lights came on revealing a carpeted staircase leading down to a polished oak door at the bottom. They walked slowly down. As they reached the door the lights began to dim, making the stairway look darker, but everything was still just visible. Peter reached the door first and pushed gently. Feeling it move, he pushed harder and the door swung easily open into a room. He fumbled for a light switch and the group moved forward into the dimly lit space. The air around them felt damp and sticky, and there was a strong smell of stale perfume.

One of the police officers gave a slow whistle and others just stood there in silence, waiting for someone else to speak.

'Bloody hell,' came from the entrance to the room. 'What the ...?'

Most of the walls were covered with large black hooks, hanging from which were whips, gas masks, wooden bars, handcuffs, and shackles of various sizes. At the far end of the room were bondage chairs with straps, straitjackets, sex toys, gimp masks and more shackles, cattle prods, and car batteries. In the middle of the room, two long tables were covered in black leather. Large mirrors hung over the tables reflecting the black leather beneath them.

'What we have here is a fully functioning sex dungeon.' Morgan-Jones spoke quietly. 'Would someone fetch Mrs Williamson? I want to know what she knows about this.'

One of the uniformed officers left the room.

Jenny squinted into the gloom, then walked to the opposite side of the dungeon, finding a narrow door with a padlock in the corner of the back wall. She held up her hand quickly.

'Please, shush! I can hear something.'

'It's probably a rat or something like that,' said one of the PCs. Jenny waved her hand for silence. She heard the sound again, it was a scratching, but very weak.

'Something's behind this door, Sir, I'm sure of it.'

Peter moved to her side. 'The padlock's open, we can go in.' He took the open lock out of its loop and slowly pulled the door open. The scuffling became louder as Jenny and Peter moved forward.

'No! No! Please, please! No more.' The words were followed by a throaty scream. 'Please ... leave me, go away, go away ...'

The words, weak and hardly audible came from a corner. Jenny moved towards the sound and stopped. 'Some light here please, quickly, there's someone here and I can't see properly.' Someone handed her a large torch. Jenny shone it towards the sound.

'Oh my God!' Her voice shook at the sight in front of her.

The girl looked no older than her early teens. She had thick, matted black hair. Her eyes were dark with a terrifying stare. Her body filthy and covered in bruises. What little clothes she wore were dirty and torn, exposing her young breasts. As the light found her face again, a loud piercing animal scream filled the room.

Jenny moved a little closer, but the girl tried to move away.

'Jo ... Jo Ju lutem!' The words spilled from the young girl in front of her, her voice broken, each word becoming more and more agitated and incomprehensible. She tried to pull away, and as she did, Jenny heard the sound of metal scratching at the walls. Shining the torch slightly away from the girl she saw that her right wrist was handcuffed to the wall, the iron cutting into her flesh. Blood, now dried brown, had poured down her thin arm. It took all of Jenny's determination to stay put, and not retreat from the frightened, injured girl in front of her.

Jenny looked at Peter, she touched his arm. 'Get someone to call an ambulance immediately.'

She turned to Morgan-Jones. 'Sir, please get everyone out of this room until the girl has been seen by a doctor and taken to hospital.'

'We need to get the handcuffs off,' he said, his voice shaking.

'I don't think we should do anything until a doctor arrives,' said Jenny. 'I think she'll need to be sedated before she'll allow anyone to touch her.' Jenny removed her coat and placed it gently over the shaking girl.

'Get more light in here,' she demanded.

Additional torches were passed through and more light revealed the rest of the gruesome room. There was a dirty toilet, a small washbasin and a table with boxes of food and bottles of water. Half-eaten food and empty water bottles lay around the edges of a narrow bed. There was no natural light and the walls were covered in what looked like thick metal sheeting.

Jenny moved further into the room, and let out a muffled scream at the sight of another girl lying on a second filthy bed. She looked even younger than the first girl. Jenny felt her knees crumble and she sank to the floor. The young girl in front of her was dead.

'Jenny, are you alright?' Peter said anxiously from behind her.

'Yes, I am, but what on earth has been going on here?' She looked at him, not expecting an answer.

They both turned towards the door where Morgan-Jones was now standing, a loud commotion disturbing their thoughts of the events that might have taken place in the dreadful room.

'Sir, Mrs Williamson is here.' The officer shouted loud enough for Morgan-Jones to hear.

'Keep her out there.' demanded Morgan-Jones, but Emma Williamson had already pushed her way through the dungeon and into the hellhole beyond.

She stopped just inside the room and took in the sight in front of her. She looked around, her face strained and white as she tried to say something.

'Take her out of here!' Morgan-Jones shouted angrily at the officer by the door. 'What part of "keep her out" don't you understand?'

As Emma Williamson was led from the room she let out a long deep scream.

Jenny heard the urgent sound of the ambulance. Once inside the house, the paramedics moved swiftly to the staircase at the back of the games room. Only Jenny and Morgan-Jones were with the girl when they arrived. They showed no shock as they set about the business of sedating her.

'We have SOCO outside,' said Morgan-Jones. He turned to the open door. 'Get them in here immediately,' he shouted. Within seconds two officers were in the room.

'We need you to get started on this,' said Morgan-Jones, his voice shaking.

'There's another girl at the other end of the room,' said Jenny, but I'm afraid she's dead.'

Jenny followed the paramedic out of the dungeon room and joined Morgan-Jones, who was standing straight, hands held tightly at his back. His face showed an emotion Jenny had never seen before.

'Can we get out of here?' She tried to keep the chaos of her mind out of her voice.

'Let's go into the kitchen,' he said. 'We need to contact the National Crime Agency to let them know what's been going on here. I'm afraid this situation might be one the UK Human Trafficking unit will want to take over.'

By the time they reached the kitchen, he had already taken his phone out and was talking, outlining the details of their find.

'They're on their way.' He hesitated and turned to look at Jenny. 'Take a seat, Jenny. You need to rest for a minute. I'll check with DI Branden to ensure everything is cordoned off.'

Left on her own, Jenny was able to think about Emma Williamson. She felt sure she'd had no idea about the two rooms under the house. She was still just as sure that Emma hadn't killed her husband. She was also sure that Morgan-Jones did not share her view.

A few minutes later, she joined her boss in the hall.

'We need to contact Ben Seldon, Sir, and get his team here to investigate the death of the young girl. I'll get onto it right away.'

'Do that, Jenny, I have to get back to the station. The chief superintendent will need to know what's happening here. Keep me informed.'

He didn't wait for an answer.

***

Ben Seldon answered his phone immediately Jenny's name appeared.

'Hi, Jenny, what can I do for you?'

'Ben, I need you and your team to get to 6 Marden Close as soon as possible, there's been another death in the same house where Williamson was killed.'

'I'm on my way, Jenny. Is it similar to the Williamson death?' said Ben.

'No, not at all, but the circumstances are just as grim. I'll fill you in as soon as you get here.'

'Before you go, Jenny, I was about to call you to let you know that there was a footprint at the place your dog was hurt that matches one from the garden of the Williamson's house. No doubt Andrew will tell you later.'

'Thank you, Ben, at least we can now be absolutely sure that there's a connection with everything that's going on.'

Jenny found Peter with Emma Williamson in the lounge. He looked concerned as he turned to greet her.

'I think she's in shock, she can't talk,' he said quietly.

'Call Joe Barton again, let him know what's happened here.' She looked at Emma Williamson. She appeared broken and shattered. 'I'm worried that Morgan-Jones might come down heavily on her, so we need a report from Joe as soon as possible.'

She heard the unmistakable sound of Ben's car outside the house. 'As soon as you've spoken with Joe, get a PC to stay with her and join Ben and me so that we can update him together.'

As she walked towards Ben's car, other members of his forensics team were arriving.

'Afternoon, Jenny. I see that the boys have arrived. Let's get moving. Update me as we walk.' Seeing Andrew Baines get out of a car, Ben called him and another of the forensics team to join them. Peter followed them into the kitchen.

'PC Spencer is with Mrs Williamson and Joe is on his way.'

'Good,' Jenny felt a small sense of relief.

They reached the games room and passed over the broken door into the dungeon.

'Bloody hell!' said one of the blue-suited forensics team. 'What on earth …?'

'There's worse to come,' said Jenny, as she stopped outside the door of the room where the body of the young girl was. She picked up the torch as she entered the room, and pointed out the area where the girl had been chained to the wall on a filthy bed. 'There was a young girl held captive here, she was just alive and very frightened, we had to get help for her as quickly as possible, she's on the way to the hospital now.'

Ben moved in front of her. 'I hope not too much was disturbed.'

'Unfortunately,' said Jenny, ignoring his question, 'there's another young girl at the other end of the room.' She turned on the torch and asked everyone to follow her. 'I'm afraid, she's dead. The first girl was able to reach some food and water. This girl was unable to get anything.'

'She's only a kid!' said someone from behind.

Ben's voice was unusually quiet as he turned to Andrew Baines. 'Let's get started, Andrew, make sure no one else comes through to these rooms.' He thought for a minute and turned to Jenny. 'It looks like a lot's been going on here. I'll let you know more as soon as I can.'

'Thanks, Ben, we'll leave you to it.' Jenny felt glad to leave the room and, looking at Peter, she could see that he felt the same.

As they arrived at the front of the house they met Joe Barton.

'I'm glad you're here, Joe,' said Jenny. 'Mrs Williamson has had rather a shock again and she's in pretty bad shape. Spencer's with her now, I'll come with you.'

In the lounge, PC Spencer was trying to stop an officer from UKHT from talking to Mrs Williamson.

Joe walked quickly towards the small group. 'I'm Dr Joe Barton from Sussex Police HQ. I'm afraid she's not well enough to talk to anyone at present. I need to help this woman and will let you know as soon as she is able to talk to you.'

'Thank you,' said the UKHT officer. 'We will need to speak with her as soon as possible.' He turned abruptly and walked past Jenny without a word.

Joe was already arranging for an ambulance to take Mrs Williamson to hospital.

'We'll leave you now, Joe,' said Jenny. 'I need to talk to whoever is in charge here now and then get back to the station.'

As Jenny and Peter reached the outside of the house, they saw that two uniformed officers from the NCA were talking to Mr Collins, helmets, batons, torches, restraints and taser equipment hanging heavily from their belts. Another two were escorting a man from the house opposite to an unmarked police van. Most of Marden Close was cordoned off with blue and white police tape.

Some of Ben Seldon's forensics team were scattered around the garden of the Williamson's house, their head-to-toe blue suits stark against the gentle fresh spring green of the foliage. The area had a surreal look, and in spite of the heavy police presence, it was bewilderingly quiet.

'Chief Inspector Trent?' The question came from a tall plain-clothed man walking up the long garden path from the gate towards Jenny and Peter.

'That's me,' said Jenny holding out her hand, 'and this is Detective Inspector Peter Branden.'

'Good afternoon, Chief Inspector. He acknowledged Peter. I'm Michael Davies, chief superintendent from the National Crime Agency.' He paused, as both acknowledged him.

'I'm afraid it's pretty obvious that we have a serious crime here,' he said. 'One that looks as though it could involve human trafficking at its nastiest. I've spoken with your superintendent and he's agreed that we will take over the investigation regarding these young girls. He will fill you in with the details as soon as you arrive back at the station.'

***

Jenny and Peter spoke little on the way back to the station. It was turning into another long day.

There was a message for Jenny saying that Morgan-Jones was in his office and she was to see him immediately.

'I'd better go, Peter. You go home, and I'll call you as soon as I can.'

'I won't go yet, I'll wait for you here. And I could do with a cup of coffee.'

Jenny knocked on the door of Morgan-Jones's office. 'Come in, Jenny, take a seat. I've already outlined our investigation of the Williamson and Moore murders to Michael Davies, of the NCA, and he has suggested that the Williamson and Moore cases could be to do with a revenge attack. Human trafficking tends to attract a lot more than just your average undesirable people. Traffickers are ruthless and violent.' he thought for a moment. 'They would think nothing of chopping someone up into a million pieces, Jenny.'

'I think we should keep an open mind about that, Sir. After all, Richard Poole from the Standard Elite Bank was a visitor at the Williamson's house, he could have been involved in both incidents. The NCA has told me that they'll be visiting Standard Elite,' said Jenny.

Morgan-Jones looked enquiringly at her. 'I understand that you were intending to go back again yourself.'

'Yes, I was, Sir.'

'They want Richard Poole and Rhys Mason arrested on suspicion of human trafficking,' said Morgan-Jones. He thought for a second before adding. 'And with causing the death of that poor young girl. I'd like you to go with them and arrest them yourself.'

For a moment Jenny was silent as she thought of her previous meeting with Poole.

'I'd very much like to do that, Sir, as long as the NCA are informed about me going.'

'I've spoken with them and they're more than happy for you to make the arrest. They're waiting for you outside now.'

He returned to his chair, turning to face the window. 'We need more information on the connection between Williamson and Moore. We have to solve this and we have to solve it quickly. The chief's on my back and, quite frankly, I don't blame him.' He rose and walked around the desk to face Jenny. 'It seems to me that the hidden room might have been found sooner. Obviously, a thorough search was not made. Had it been, then we may just have got there before the other girl died.'

'Yes, Sir,' said Jenny. 'I'll arrange a briefing for tomorrow. DC Callam should have some information from his meeting with Lynn Moore's parents by then.'

'Thank you. Please keep me informed, no matter what time of day,' he hesitated, 'or night.'

Jenny returned to Peter in the main office. 'Just got a bit of a rollicking for not finding the room earlier, otherwise, I just might be having one of the best days of my life. We're off to the Standard Elite Bank, sorry, you can't go home yet. We also need a PC to come with us. Can you arrange that Peter quickly Peter?

She acknowledged the two officers from NCA who were waiting for them outside. 'Let's go. We should get to the bank before anyone lets them know we're on the way.'

CHAPTER TWENTY-FOUR

As Jenny, Peter and the NCA officers reached the steps of the Standard Elite Bank a uniformed security guard approached them.

Jenny and Peter pulled their badges. Jenny's voice was quiet but firm. 'DCI Trent and DI Branden, we're here to see Mr Poole and we would like you to come with us.'

'I should let Mr Poole know you're here.'

'No, we would rather you didn't. Please come with us.'

The guard started to object, looked warily at the NCA officers, and then muttered his agreement.

The sun glinted on the tall glass building, sealed windows reflecting the afternoon brightness. They walked into the large atrium reception, which was expensively furnished with polished white glass walls, and large black leather seats around gleaming glass tables. The floor was covered in black mirror tiles.

'Can I help you?' An attractive young woman enquired as she gave them a frosty, enquiring stare. Her name badge introduced her as 'Masie Brown – Reception and Visitors.'

'I believe Richard Poole's office is on the fourth floor,' said Jenny, waiting just long enough to get a reply.

'Yes, but …' exclaimed Masie, looking cautiously at each of the strangers in front of her. 'I need to tell him that you're here.'

'I'm sorry Miss Brown but you don't – and please don't call him,' said Jenny. 'We know where he is.' She turned to the two NCA officers. Constable, please stay with Masie and the security guard, while we find Mr Poole.'

'Yes Ma'am'

As they reach the lift the door opened immediately and they travelled swiftly and silently to the fourth floor. As the doors opened, Jenny recognised Sarah Green walking towards them.

'Good afternoon, Chief Inspector. I didn't know you were coming today. Does Mr Poole know you're here?'

'He will do soon,' said Jenny. 'I know where his office is, thank you.'

'But, I need to …' She stopped as the visitors and the security guards walked swiftly past her.

Unlike their previous visit, the staff stopped what they were doing and stared at the unannounced visitors. One smartly dressed young man walked towards them as they approached the restricted area outside Poole's private office.

'Can I help you? I know Mr Poole is very busy.'

'No, thank you, we have all the help we need,' said Peter as he walked past him.

'Peter, knock at Mr Poole's door,' said Jenny, trying hard to hide the pleasure she felt of Poole's impending shock when he would see her and the officers walk through the door.

'With pleasure.' He knocked twice.

'Come in, come in.'

As they opened the door, Richard Poole saw Jenny and stood up.

'Good God! What the bloody hell are you doing here? I told you everything I know about James Williamson.'

He glared at Jenny, before noticing the two uniformed officers.

'And what are they doing here?'

He saw the bank's security guard. 'Why didn't you let me know these people were coming to see me?' Without waiting for an answer, he turned back to Jenny. 'These are private offices and I'm asking you to leave now.' His hand went to the phone on his desk.

'I wouldn't do that, Mr Poole, we're not here about Mr Williamson's death.' She moved closer to the centre of the room. 'But we would like to know more about the activities that took place at the house.'

She ignored the angry stare from Poole as he replaced the telephone on its receiver. 'You visited the house many times, I understand,' said Jenny.

Poole's eyes half closed, as he regarded her. 'Not that many, I can assure you,' he said. 'And what James did in his own time was his own affair, I only cared about his work for the bank.' His stare hardened. 'I believe we have already discussed this Inspector.'

He sat down at his desk, hands sweeping non-existent dust from the surface. 'Now, if you don't mind I have a lot of work to do. If there is any more information you need you can speak to my solicitor. My secretary will give you his number.'

Jenny moved around the desk and close to the side of Poole's chair. 'It doesn't quite work like that, Mr Poole, and you may like to contact your solicitor yourself so that you can speak to him at the police station.'

'What the hell are you talking about?' he said. 'I've already told you, I didn't have anything to do with what went on in that house!' He stopped his mouth open. 'I mean …' he groaned, sinking back into his chair.

'Richard Poole, I'm arresting you on suspicion of human trafficking and rape. Oh, yes,' she said, hesitating just slightly, 'and murder.' You do not have to say anything, but it may harm your defence if you do not mention when questioned something which you later rely on in court. Anything you do say may be given in evidence. Do you understand, Mr Poole?'

Poole looked at Jenny, his face turning a deep angry red, hatred in his eyes.

'Do I understand? Do I understand? What sort of stupid question is that?' he bellowed. 'Of course, I understand. And believe me, when this is sorted, you, DCI Trent, will understand just how much I can make you suffer.' He stood up, his back straight, his eyes blazing, staring directly into Jenny's face. 'Your career will be ruined!'

'You can walk out of this office between my colleague and the uniformed officers, or you can walk out handcuffed to one of us, Mr Poole. It's up to you.'

'Do you have to do,' he snarled.

'Before we go, Mr Poole, please ask your secretary to bring Rhys Mason here.'

'Get him yourself,' he said through gritted teeth.

'Wait!' Jenny demanded, and she walked to the desk and picked up the phone.

It was answered immediately. 'Yes, Mr Poole?' Jenny recognised Sarah Green's voice.

'Please ask Mr Mason to come to Mr Poole's office immediately. Let me know when he's here, and ask him to wait outside.'

'I'm not sure if he's in the office,' said Sarah Green.

'He is,' said Jenny. 'Get him now, please.'

Jenny led the party with Poole, attached to Peter by handcuffs, through the door into the main office. All eyes were immediately focused on Richard Poole and the party surrounding him.

Someone clapped, quietly at first, then others joined in as the clapping grew faster and louder.

'Caught up with him at last,' came a shout from the back of the room.

A door at the side of the room opened and Jenny saw Sarah Green come through with a tall good-looking man dressed in an expensive, dark, single-breasted suit.

'You asked to see Mr Mason, Chief Inspector,' said Sarah.

'What's going on?' Rhys Mason turned to Sarah. 'Why have you brought me here? What on earth is this all about?' He stopped as he saw his boss in the middle of the group.

'We would like you to come with us, Mr Mason.'

Rhys Mason recognised the demand in Jenny's voice and looked at Poole for support. Poole just stared past him.

'Whatever he's done it has nothing to do with me,' Mason said, his eyes darting from one face to another in the group.

'Shut up, you fool,' Poole shouted. He turned, looking for his secretary. 'Sarah ... Sarah,' he shouted. 'Get my solicitor immediately, tell him to get here, right now!'

Sarah walked slowly across the room to stand facing her boss. She swiftly pulled earrings from her ears and released a gold necklace from her throat. Holding them in one hand, she threw them at the man she had worked for over the past five years.

'Do it yourself, sir.' She gave him a wide smile, her eyes twinkling. 'Or ... perhaps I can telephone your wife and get her to do it for you!' She turned her back on him and stalked off, just as Poole tried to take a step towards her.

As the doors of the office closed behind the group, Peter handed Richard Poole and Rhys Mason over to the NCA officers, who quickly handcuffed them together. 'We'll take over now, Ma'am,' said the senior officer as he shook Jenny's hand firmly. It's been a pleasure working with you.'

***

'You enjoyed that!' said Peter as he got into the car with Jenny for the drive back to Sussex.

'You'll never know how much,' said Jenny, smiling.

'What will happen to the girl we found in Williamson's house?'

Jenny thought for a moment, as Peter drove the car safely away from the bank.

'Well, once she's received medical treatment and she's well enough to leave the hospital, I imagine she'll be taken into care until her family can be traced in her home country.' Jenny was thoughtful. 'I know there are organisations that investigate in these situations, Peter. I'll see what I can find out about her progress. I need to put my mind at rest over this too.'

'That poor girl, she'll need a lot of support,' said Peter, his mind drifting back to the scene in the room where she was found. 'If she lives.'

Jenny felt his anguish and decided to lighten the mood a little. 'Everyone will be in the pub when we get back. It was a good result, and the NCA have now taken over. Why don't you go and celebrate? I'll be picking up Honey on the way home so I won't be joining you,' she said.

'No, I won't go either this time,' said Peter. 'I need to think about Maggie and Josh, I'm not quite sure what's happening. Maggie's with her mother for a few days.'

'Peter, I'm so sorry. It's been so hectic recently that I haven't had time to talk with you.' She stopped him from answering. 'Why don't you come over to mine this evening? I'll make supper and we can talk. It can be about Maggie or work. Whatever turns up?'

'Thanks, said Peter. 'I'd like that.' He thought carefully for a few seconds, 'I'll bring in fish and chips. I've heard about your cooking!'

He managed a soft laugh. Jenny relaxed.

CHAPTER TWENTY-FIVE

Jenny pulled up at Grove Lodge. It had been a distressing few days, made only slightly better by the arrest of Poole. She had missed Honey so much and couldn't wait to see her.

She walked swiftly up the few steps and through to the reception desk. 'Good evening, I'm Jenny Trent and I've come to pick up Honey,' she said in response to the enquiring glance from the uniformed girl behind the desk.

'Take a seat. We won't keep you long, but as you can see we're rather busy.'

As Jenny sat down, a German shepherd strained at his leash towards her but was pulled sharply back by its owner. 'No! Brutus ... Stay.'

Brutus stayed.

'Hello, Jenny, come with me please.' She was pleased to see Stephen Wade, the vet who initially dealt with Honey.

'Honey has recovered well, she's eating and should be back to full health soon.'

Jenny followed the vet into a small room filled with large cages. She heard a soft whimper and saw Honey lying in the last cage. Stephen opened the cage and Honey stood up and walked slowly out, her tail wagging gently.

Jenny ran to her and knelt down, wrapping her arms around her head. 'Honey, Honey, I'm so pleased to see you.' Honey tried unsuccessfully to jump onto her lap. The effort was too much for her, so instead, she sat panting in front of Jenny, a paw resting possessively on her knee.

'She was hurt quite badly, and the wound was very deep,' said the vet. He stopped, waiting for Jenny's full attention.

'Whoever did it used a very sharp object and cut deep. In those circumstances, she would normally have died. It's now obvious to me that they didn't want to kill her. The person who harmed your dog knew exactly what they were doing. Have you found out anything more?'

'We're working on it, Stephen,' Jenny said, and then stopped, anxious to change to subject. 'Thank you so much for all you've done for her.'

Stephen smiled at Jenny. 'She's a very lucky dog,' he said, passing her a small box. 'Make sure she has one of these with every meal. She still has some pain and they'll help. I'll need to give her another check in about a week, and she'll need to stay overnight so that I can check the wound thoroughly. I'll need to anaesthetise her to do it. Check at reception and they'll book her in.'

Honey stood up as Jenny put her collar and lead on her. 'Come on, girl, let's get home.' Honey responded with an excited but shaky yelp. She lay on the back seat on the short ride home, only once looking up to make sure Jenny was with her.

Jenny drew the car into the parking bay outside of her house. She opened the car door, just as Honey sat upright. 'Come on Hun, let's get you inside.' Honey followed, head down, tail wagging cautiously.

As Jenny sank into the comfort of her settee, Honey hesitated but managed the short jump up to join her.

It had been a busy day and Jenny felt her eyes closing with the inevitable comfort of rest and warmth. Honey let out a deep sigh and closed her eyes as she rested her head on Jenny's lap.

The doorbell woke both of them. Jenny rose sharply, remembering her invitation to Peter. She went to the door, leaving Honey on the settee, neither moving nor offering her usual growling bark as a warning to Jenny of visitors.

Jenny opened the door to see Peter standing with a parcel of fish and chips. He smiled. 'You've been asleep.'

'I have,' she confessed. 'And I haven't even warmed the plates. Come in, Peter.' She waved him to the lounge where Honey had reached the floor and was moving slowly forward to welcome him.

'I tell you what,' said Peter, bending to give Honey a soft stroke. 'Why don't we eat out of the paper? It's clean and saves washing-up. You don't look as though you need any dirty dishes right now.'

'Suits me, I'll get the wine.'

They ate mostly in silence, a bottle of cooled wine washing the fish and chips down. Neither of them had realised how hungry they were.

'I haven't done that for a long time, Peter, thanks, that was great.' She took the greasy paper and screwed it into a ball. Honey followed her into the kitchen, ready for her own meal.

'I know you're having a rough time at the moment, Peter,' she called from the kitchen. 'Do you want to talk about it?'

'Not much to say really.' He settled further back into his chair as Jenny joined him again. 'Maggie's gone to her mother's with Josh. Says she want time to think about things. I've been working so much she feels ignored and says that I should understand the time has come for her to think about going back to work. She says we've drifted apart and I hadn't even noticed.'

He took his wine glass from the coffee table in front of him and sipped slowly.

'I don't quite know how to handle it, Jenny.' He shifted forward, his arms resting on his legs. 'Truth is, she's right. I haven't been at home as much as I should've been. Maggie's a clever girl and had a very good job before Josh came along. We had long discussions before he was born about her going back to work when he was old enough, and me working less. To be honest, she would probably earn more than me, so it seemed to make sense at the time.'

'I'm guilty of putting my head in the sand. For a long time now I've been guiding Maggie away from the subject, and for a long time it seems she's tried to speak to me about it but I haven't been listening.' He gave a soft laugh. 'You could say we're both as bad as one another, I guess. But poor Maggie hasn't had the chance to do what we agreed so long ago, and I feel bad about that.'

'A little while ago you mentioned that you thought she had someone else. Do you still think that now?' said Jenny.

Peter was quiet for a short time. 'Not sure to be honest, and I can't bring myself to ask. Maggie is a very honest person and whatever she said would be the truth.' He took a long look at his friend in the chair in front of him. 'If she has got someone else I don't know how I'd be able to take it. She's the most loving person I know and I've ignored her needs for a long time. To be honest, Jenny, I'm rather frightened of the truth right now.'

'What do you want to do, Peter?' said Jenny. 'If you want time off I can get someone to cover you, just let me know.'

'What I want right now is to catch the bastard who's killing people on our patch. I know that the NCA are working on the human trafficking business, but the rest ...' he stopped for a few seconds. 'I'm pretty damn sure the murders of James Williamson and Lynn Moore are connected. Until we have all the questions satisfactorily resolved, and the murderer, or murderers, locked up, I won't take time off. I can't.' He was quiet for a few moments. 'I know Maggie would want me to finish this, I just have to talk to her about it. After that, I'll take time off and we'll make plans that I hope will suit us both. I love Maggie so much, Jenny. Let's hope she loves me enough to just bear with me a little longer.'

With a resigned sigh, he stood. 'I'm pretty sure she does!' he said, with a forced smile. 'I'd best be off.' He walked towards the front door ahead of Jenny. As he reached to open the door he turned to face her.

'I'll go and see Lynn Moore's parents again tomorrow. They have to remember some link between their daughter and Williamson. From what I hear Callum hasn't spent time with them yet, which is very frustrating, not sure if he's going to make it, we'll give him a bit longer to prove himself.

As he reached the gate at the end of the path he turned to wave. 'Goodnight, Jenny, I have work to do.'

Jenny waved back and smiled at her friend. She could see the gritty determination in his face.

CHAPTER TWENTY-SIX

Jonnie French looked at his watch for the fourth time in an hour. *Thank God it's time to go. I've had enough for today. Bloody spoilt women and hyper kids, It's the worst part of this job,* he thought.

He picked up a thick white towel from the floor and threw it into a plastic laundry bag neatly placed on the wall near the door leading to the reception. 'They think I'm a bloody servant!' he said through gritted teeth.

He stood by the door to reception and hesitated. He was supposed to do one more check of the pool areas to make sure no one had locked themselves in the dressing rooms or toilets. Today, he couldn't be bothered. *If they're stupid enough to lock themselves in, that's their lookout and they can stay there.*

The phone on the reception desk burst into action and he felt a pang of irritation, just as he was about to go home.

'French.'

'Oh, Mr French, I'm so glad you're still there.' The voice sounded excited and relieved. 'I'm afraid my daughter has left her bag in the changing rooms. Is it possible I can come and get it?'

'I'm sorry, we're just closing, sir. Can you come tomorrow and we'll have it ready for you in reception?' French managed to keep the growing anger he felt from his voice.

'My daughter is bereft, Mr French, her cuddly dog is in the bag and she won't sleep without it. I would be willing to pay you for your extra time. I really would be most grateful. I'm not far away.'

French looked again at his watch, another quarter of an hour gone, he was late already. *Another ten minutes won't make that much difference,* he thought, and he fought to keep his voice level. 'I'll leave the main door unlocked while I go and fetch the bag. What dressing room was your daughter using?'

'Number twelve, I think.'

'We don't have a number twelve,' French replied sharply. 'They have names, and they are all small cubicles allowing for one child and a parent.'

The voice on the phone was quiet for a few seconds.

'I'm not sure then. Perhaps when I get to there we can look together. I'm very sorry about this. My daughter is not with me at the moment, and it's so important that she has her bag today.'

'Look,' said French, making no attempt to hide his anger now. 'I'll go and check in the cubicles. When you arrive, just stay in reception and wait for me.' Without waiting for a reply, he slammed the phone down. As it touched the wood it slid towards the edge. He looked on helplessly as it tumbled to the hard floor, splitting into three pieces.

'Just what I fucking needed.' The words spat from his mouth as he kicked the broken phone towards the wall and watched it splinter into several more pieces.

Glancing at the main entrance door he noted that it was still open and turned back towards the door leading to the changing rooms.

Jonnie French didn't hear the main door ease open as he left the reception. He was too angry to notice the sound of the door being locked or hear the footsteps walking past the desk. He just wanted to find that stupid girl's bag and get out. He was hungry and not in the mood for hide-and-seek. He would charge the girl's father a tidy sum, enough to pay for a good meal and a drink, or two. *Why shouldn't he pay? It's not my fault that his spoilt brat has been careless. And what about my bloody phone? That's his fault too. Another thing he can pay for.*

Searching three of the individual dressing rooms, he could find nothing resembling a child's bag. He moved on to the next three dressing rooms, and stopped abruptly, hearing a scuffling sound from the room opposite.

'Who's there? What are you doing? You should've been gone a long time ago. Come on, get out. You're bloody lucky I'm still here or you'd have been locked in.' The movement from inside the dressing room stopped. His voice grew to a shout. 'Come on … come on! I'm not in the mood for playing games.'

He reached the door, the name 'Bluebell' painted on the front. All the rooms had the names of flowers, voted for by the female senior staff, much to his disgust. Numbers were much easier to handle, he'd reminded his boss many times, only to be told, 'Names are much more appropriate for our fitness rooms. After all, we want to encourage a warm, friendly atmosphere, especially with mothers and their children.'

He pushed the door. 'Come on out, whoever you are.' There was no sound or movement.

'Look,' he spat out angrily, 'I'm getting fed up with this game. If you're not out within the next minute I'll come in and get you, and don't think I won't call the police.'

He waited. Taking a deep breath, he pushed the door. Before he could get further inside the small room, he was pulled roughly through the door. As he tried to see who was in there, he received a heavy punch to his back. He cried out in pain, coughed and dropped to the floor.

'Wha ... What the hell?' he spluttered as another blow, this time to his head, forced him even further down, and his arms were pulled behind his back, pressure from a heavy knee rendering them immobile. He was powerless to move. 'What's going on, who you are?' he said, his voice thick with fear.

No one answered.

He felt an arm snake around his throat, pulling his head back, and suddenly he couldn't breathe. As he opened his mouth to gasp something fell into his throat, scratching at the sides. His head dropped, and he closed his mouth and moved the sharp object with his tongue, managing to spit it out, heaving and coughing. Small slithers of blood mixed with spittle formed a pool on the floor next to his face. Another hard punch to his back made him feel sick, and he retched.

'Oh dear! Oh dear! We can't have that, can we? You love peaches, I know you do, and now you've spoilt my little game.'

'Who are you? What do you want?' French tried screaming but only managed a whimper as the arm closed tighter around his neck again.

'I'll have to come back with another peach. You don't mind, do you?' The voice loud and snarling. 'Of course, you don't. After all, you love peaches, you stupid man. Now I'll have to go to the trouble of getting another perfect one. You've ruined my day and you'll pay for it. Believe me, you will pay for it.'

The arm loosened its grip around his throat, but French still couldn't move.

'Oh, by the way, Jonnie French,' the voice whispered softly in his ear. 'Don't tell anyone about my little visit. You see, I know what you do, Jonnie French. 'Oh yes, I know what you do!'

The arm slid away from French's throat, and his arms were released as the attacker stood and delivered a vicious kick to his body, making him wrench violently. He rolled onto his side, bringing up his knees to his aching stomach as he tried to look at his assailant. Lifting his head, he saw only the man's feet as he left and the door closed behind him.

French tried to move, but the pain prevented any swift movement. He rolled towards one of the padded benches. Arms aching, he pulled himself up. As he reached a sitting position he heard a scream, so loud it sounded like a frightened animal knowing it was about to be slaughtered. He held his hands to his ears, the scream reverberated around the walls of the swimming pool, a scream of manic anger and desperation.

'Jonnie French! … Jonnie French! … Stupid Man! …Stupid Man!'

The sound of his name rebounded off the walls as he pressed his hands tighter over his ears in an attempt to lessen the pain and terror burning through him.

The sound abated, and he collapsed in relief as he heard the door to reception open, and then close. He coughed again, spitting blood. His throat was sore and he tried to swear, but the pain of torn flesh stopped any words spilling from his mouth. He wanted to cry, but more than anything he wanted to get out of the place. He wanted to go home.

His body was aching and his stomach threatened to release his lunch as he grabbed a mop to clean the floor in the small dressing room. The mop found the peach stone resting just under the bench, he picked it up and wiped it on his trousers. So that's what it was, a bloody peach stone, bloody sharp too. Christ, no wonder it had hurt. He threw it into the mop bucket, the sound hurting his ears again as it hit the metal side. *Forget looking for that spoilt brat's bag. They can sack me if they want. I'm getting out of here,* he thought.

Only as he locked the heavy front doors did he begin to wonder why anyone would want to attack him. He shivered, the pain in his throat reminding him of the peach stone that had been pushed into his mouth. *What the bloody hell was that all about?* He tried to speak, but still, no words could come from his mouth. *Some bloody drunk deciding to burgle the spa,* he decided.

Then he stopped, and fear rippled through him. *No, he knew my name. He knows me! That bastard knows me, how? How?*

He walked slowly to his car, his body aching as he sank into the driver's seat. He sniffed as he held back angry tears.

I've fucking pissed too many people off! A tear rolled down his face as he turned the ignition key.

CHAPTER TWENTY-SEVEN

Peter knocked at the Moore's house. A Family Liaison Officer was with him. He wasn't looking forward to asking them more questions. He felt sure they would both be still in a state of shock.

Mrs Moore opened the door. She looked more drawn and pale than when he had last seen her and he felt a pang of sympathy, knowing that the body of her daughter hadn't yet been released.

'Hello, Inspector, please come in.' She guided the two men into their lounge.

'Hello, Mrs Moore,' said Peter, he turned to the uniformed officer with him. 'This is George, your new Family Liaison Officer. He's here to offer any help or guidance you may need, as PC Spencer did before.' He heard movement coming from the kitchen. Mr Moore walked into the lounge carrying a tray of tea.

'Good morning, Inspector,' said Mr Moore, his hands shaking as he placed the tray on a small table.

He looks ten years older, thought Peter.

'My brother is still here, Inspector,' said Mrs Moore. 'Do you want him to join us?'

'No, there's no need, thank you. Unless you'd like him to be with you.'

Mrs Moore looked at her husband. 'I think I'd like Bryan here please.'

A middle-aged man dressed in casual but smart clothes came in.

'I heard Margaret ask for me, I was just outside. I'm her brother,' he said as he offered his hand to Peter.

'It's nice to meet you, sir,' said Peter. He introduced the officer with him and turned to Mr and Mrs Moore again. 'I wonder if I can ask you a few more questions that might help us find the person who killed your daughter.'

'Yes, of course,' said Mr Moore, taking a deep breath. 'Please, sit down.'

'You said that there was a message on your daughter's home phone reminding her of an appointment. Do you have any idea who that may have been from?'

Mrs Moore raised a handkerchief to her eyes. 'I really don't know. Sarah and Lynn were looking for a house to buy. The call said something about an appointment.' She turned to her husband. 'Robert, I ...'

'She's very upset, and can't remember much at all,' said Mr Moore. 'It's difficult to understand why this has happened, Inspector.' He sighed. 'Lynn had no enemies, she was a lovely person. We just can't understand who would do such a terrible thing to our daughter.' His eyes filled with tears, and he took his wife's hand. 'Why can't they release her body so that we can bury her and move on?' He took a sharp breath raising his hand to stop his own tears from falling.

'I'm so sorry, Mr Moore,' said Peter. As soon as the body can be released we will let you know.' He hesitated, adjusting his notebook. 'When you were at the station before we found your daughter, you said that you recognised the name of James Williamson. Have you remembered anything more about that since then?'

'My wife is so upset, Inspector. I don't think she's able to remember very much at all.'

His wife placed a hand on his arm. 'I'm alright, dear, I'd like to help all I can.' She looked at Peter. 'I'm not sure, but I think she mentioned his name years ago when she was at school.' She sat thinking, her eyes darting from the floor to her husband. 'I'm sorry love, I just don't know. Perhaps I'm wrong, she knew so many people. She had many friends, Inspector, she was a very popular girl.'

'What school did she go to?' Peter asked the question and waited patiently for Mrs Moore to reply.

'Her first school was the local primary. She was thought of as a very bright little girl so we used our savings to send her to a private school when she was eleven, where she boarded until she got a place at Cambridge. We were so proud of her.'

Her husband held up his hand. 'I'm sorry, Inspector, this is really too hard for us. Perhaps you could come back some other time. My wife really needs to rest now.'

'Just one more question, please, Mr Moore.' said Peter. 'What was the name of the boarding school that Lynn went to?'

'Oh, it was a really good school, worth every penny. Lynn did so well there, didn't she, love?' He gently squeezed his wife's shoulders.

'What was the name of the school?' Peter gently pushed for an answer.

'It was Broomleigh House School, Inspector. We only saw her during the holidays and missed her very much, but she was very happy there. Wasn't she, love?' he looked to his wife for support.

'I really don't think my sister and is able to help any more at this stage, Inspector,' interrupted Mrs Moore's brother. 'If I think of anything that may help at all I will, of course, let you know.' He moved a few steps towards Peter, who rose in response. 'I'll see you out, Inspector.' He handed Peter a slip of paper. 'This is my telephone number. Would you mind giving me a call if you need to come again? I really would like to be with my sister.'

'Of course, and if you hear anything that you think may be of interest perhaps you would be good enough to call me.' Peter handed Mrs Moore's brother his card.

'I will call you immediately,' he said. 'Thank you.'

'In the meantime,' Peter turned to the Family Liaison Officer, 'James will be your immediate contact should you need any help or support. He can be with you at very short notice. He handed Mr Moore another card. 'Here is his number. You can call at any time, night or day.'

✳✳✳

As she turned to leave her phone burst into action as it requested her urgent attention.

'Hi, Peter, any luck with the Moores?'

'Well, it was difficult getting anything out of them, but I think the connection might come from a school their daughter attended. I'm on my way back to the station, I can give you a full report then.'

Peter arrived and knocked on his boss's door and, without waiting for an answer, went in. Jenny was on the phone.

'Peter is here now, as soon as I've spoken with him I'll let you have his report.' She was silent, listening. 'Thank you, Sir.' She replaced the phone. 'You can guess who that was. He's getting a bit anxious. The Chief Constable is visiting tomorrow and he's hoping we've got some news.' She looked up at Peter. 'How did it go with the Moores? I don't expect it was easy.'

'No, they're still in a bad way. But they did tell me a few more things.' He opened his notebook. 'Lynn Moore and her partner had intended to buy a house together. Do you remember there was an untraceable telephone call reminding Lynn of an appointment? Well, from what her mother said that they were looking to buy a house together, but that they hadn't viewed anywhere yet or even made any appointments to view anything. But the call was to remind their daughter of an appointment, so it could have been to view the house we found her in.'

'What about a possible connection with the Williamsons?'

'Ah, well, we may have something there,' he closed his notebook. 'Mrs Moore couldn't remember anything at first, but her husband said it was probably a very long time ago. I pushed harder, trying to get her to remember any friends or acquaintances from schools, etc.'

'Did you ask her what schools their daughter went to?' said Jenny.

'Yes, I did, and this is where it got interesting. Her first school was the local primary. It appears she was very bright and her parents saved for her to go to a private school in Bedford, called Broomleigh House.'

Jenny took a quick breath and stood up, pushing back her chair. 'What did you say it was it called?'

'Broomleigh House, I think it might be the link.'

Jenny felt a rush of adrenalin. 'It certainly is, Peter. That's the school I went to before going to university.'

She sat down again, putting her hands to her head. She remained still and quiet for a few moments before lowering her arms and looking up at Peter. 'Now I know why I'm on his radar too.' Her voice quiet and thoughtful. 'He hurt Honey to warn me.' She rose from her chair. 'At last, I think we're getting somewhere.'

Peter was about to speak but she stopped him. 'Trouble is, I think we've got as far as he wants us to at the moment, no more, no less. He's still playing with us, Peter. Get as many of the team to the incident room as possible this afternoon for a briefing, and give them an update of the information about the connection with the Broomleigh House School. I'll see Morgan-Jones and give him the news.'

'Any particular time?'

'No, just let me know when you've spoken to them. But as soon as possible. We have to visit Broomleigh House School. Let's hope they've kept good records.'

***

Morgan-Jones was leaving his office as Jenny arrived.

'Have you got anything that will help with my meeting with the CC?'

Jenny didn't miss the sarcasm.

'I think so, Sir.'

'You'd better come in then. My lunch can wait.'

'We've discovered the connection between James Williamson and Lynn Moore. They went to the same school together. In fact, I went there as well,' said Jenny.

Morgan-Jones's eyes met hers. 'Did you not remember either of the names?'

'No. I think they were in the same year together. I didn't make the connection and I don't remember either of their names. It wasn't a big school, just over four hundred pupils.'

She stopped, waiting for a response from Morgan-Jones, who remained silent.

'What I *do* think,' she continued, 'is that the killer will know by now that we've discovered the link, and exactly where we've got to in the investigation.'

There was still no reaction from Morgan-Jones.

'I intend to visit Broomleigh as soon as I've briefed the team.'

'Do you think you're implicated?' said Morgan-Jones. 'If so, it may frustrate the investigation in some way.' Jenny was surprised to note a little concern in his voice.

'Since I went to the same school as the two victims, I believe I should go and find out what happened there. I intend to see this one through, Sir. I know the school well, I know what questions to ask and I'll find the killer, I can assure you.'

'Good work, Jenny.' Morgan-Jones breathed a sigh of relief. 'At last, we may be getting somewhere.'

Jenny followed him to the door.

'Just one more thing, Jenny,' he opened the door ushering her though. 'I must repeat my warning, if at any time you think you're in danger, you must let someone know, whatever the time of day.'

He placed a hand on her shoulder. 'Or night,' he added.

***

The data recovery unit was located on the lower ground floor. The room was small and only two people worked there. A large part of their responsibilities was to search the National Archives for information on past criminal court findings when required. They were not often seen anywhere else, except when a success was being celebrated in the Red Bull. The two young men were totally committed to their work and good-naturedly boasted that without them, the success rate of the station wouldn't have improved so much over the last ten years. No one could bear to tell them they were probably right.

The work that Mickey Jones and Sam Willis did with computers and data stored locally at the station, together with the information held in the National Archives, often enabled them to analyse and extract critical evidence, even if it had been hidden, forgotten, or seemingly destroyed.

'Afternoon, Mickey. Can we take up a little of your time?' Jenny gave him a warm smile as she entered.

'Hi, Jenny, nice to see, how can we help?' Mickey acknowledged Peter with a short wave.

'We need to know if you can do an enhanced database search on a private school in Bedford, called Broomleigh House,' said Jenny.

'What exactly do you need to know?'

'Everything, Mickey, but especially, if you can find out if there were any scandals surrounding the school going back to the early nineties. Also anything about outstanding or underachieving pupils, teachers, and headteachers. Just about everything, there is, Mickey.'

'When do you want it?'

'Don't know quite how to say this, Mickey, but DI Branden and I want to visit the school tomorrow.' She gave him an apologetic grin.

'Tough call, Jenny, but we'll do our best. We often get leads from the Disclosure and Barring Service checks, but they're usually for individuals, and you need their consent to access the data. Anyway, I'll see if we can locate anything. There may well be other stuff lurking in the files that the DBS wouldn't necessarily pick up.'

'Thanks, Mickey, please do what you can.'

CHAPTER TWENTY-EIGHT

Another Mistake

He stared at the wall, his eyes unblinking, his thoughts were muddled and angry. Jonnie French should be dead. *He should be dead,* he repeated to himself. Another stupid mistake. He opened his mouth and shouted. 'You fool! You bloody fool, you've made another mistake.' He stopped, his mouth twisting into a snarl. 'And you won't make any more.' The words spat from his mouth and he used his arm to wipe away the spittle running down his chin.

'I'm just going to have to find another perfect stone now,' he said, as he picked up the peach stone lying on the table by his chair. 'Not you. You are for someone much more important.'

He held it tight in his hand, feeling the sharp edges dig into his palm. 'Yes, much more important than that petty criminal, Jonnie French. He doesn't deserve you.'

After carefully wrapping the stone in soft tissue, he rose from his chair and placed the stone back on the table. 'I have to work quickly now, time is running out and the best is yet to come,' he said quietly.

Pulling his coat off the hook in the hall, he checked for his car keys and left his house to buy more peaches. *I'd better go further away this time, can't risk some silly woman wanting to know who I'm buying the fruit for.* He caught his breath. *If only she knew.* He laughed as he pushed the key into the ignition.

✳✳✳

It took him most of the day to buy six peaches from three different shops. On the drive home, they lay on the passenger seat. He caressed them, trying to feel which one might be perfect for the job, his anger subsiding as he touched each new fruit.

Back home he ate hungrily, already planning the next visit to Jonnie French. He would need to eat the peaches quickly. *Not too much of a problem,* he thought.

He was on his third peach when he found – to his surprise – that he wasn't really enjoying it. In fact, he suddenly realised that he didn't want to eat another peach – ever. Something was wrong with them. They were not as sweet and juicy as they used to be. Probably due to the infernal pesticides. *Thank God, I've nearly finished with them. Although what it has to do with him, I don't know,* he thought, as his anger returned.

The third peach stone looked perfect and his mood lifted as he stared at it. 'You are it. Yes, you will do very nicely,' he raised his arms.

'I don't have to eat any more peaches,' he said loudly.

He carefully washed the stone and placed it next to the one already wrapped on the table. He picked the wrapped one up, carefully removed the covering and placed it next to the new peach stone.

'Just perfect … Just perfect …' he repeated with a quiet snigger.

He picked up the three uneaten peaches and walked to the bin in the corner of his spotless kitchen, pressed the pedal, opening up the lid, and smashed the peaches into the bottom of the empty container.

'Guess what? You won't have to worry about any more unsatisfactory peaches being thrown into you.' The lid closed.

'Neither will I, neither will I.'

CHAPTER TWENTY-NINE

Sam picked up the phone and dialled Jenny's number. 'Ma'am, I think we have the information that you wanted about the school.'

'Great, I'll be there within the next ten minutes.'

Jenny opened the door to data recovery. 'Morning, Jenny, take a seat,' he said. 'We were unable to get anything from the DBS, but I did some other searches and asked questions myself.' He spread some papers in front of her.

'Broomleigh House is still there and is still recognised as a good school for kids with rich parents, or for bright kids who've won a scholarship. I was unable to unearth anything else from the general information available. However, I thought I'd give the local police station a call and they were very helpful.' He picked up a couple of sheets and handed them to Jenny.

He pointed to the first page. 'That's a list of the current teachers. The information was available on their website. I can't find any records of previous teachers. That's not unusual, but they'll have more detailed records on-site in the school archives.'

'Most of the students achieve good academic grades and go on to university.' He pushed more paper around and picked up another sheet. 'I've made some notes for you,' he said, handing the page to Jenny. 'This is the information I got from the local police. As you read it, you'll see that in 1996 there was a scandal. A sports master had an affair with one of the students. She was underage and the girl's parents made a complaint to the police.'

'What happened?'

'Nothing. The girl eventually told the school that she'd lied, so the police took it no further.'

'What happened to the girl?'

'She left school rather suddenly. If you ask me, it looks like a case where the parents were paid off by the school, but there's no evidence to support that.'

'You're brilliant.' Jenny smiled at him. 'I intend to visit the local station before going to the school.'

'Broomleigh is expecting you,' said Mickey. 'Good luck.'

'Thanks, Mickey, you've been a great help.' She smiled at Sam. 'You too, Sam,' she said, as he turned back to his computer.

As she was walking up the stairs, Jenny's phone rang. She saw it was Peter.

'Hi, Jenny. Do you have some information?'

'Yes, Mickey and Sam have been very helpful. It's well worth us taking a visit to Broomleigh. Mickey told them to expect me, so I'll telephone to make an appointment now. I want us to visit the main police station in Bedford before we go to the school, though. I'll explain everything as soon as I see you.'

She walked towards her office. We're not there yet, but a few things seem to be slowly falling into place, she thought.

✳✳✳

On the short drive home, her thoughts drifted towards Andrew Baines and she smiled to herself. It was about time she started having a social life again.

Jenny opened the door to the house she had shared with Jonathan. It was warm and friendly, full of memories, both happy and sad. Just like any home, she had always thought.

Honey bounded happily towards her with a soft toy in her mouth. Their greeting usually lasted a few minutes and today was no different. She cuddled her dog's silky head.

'What would I do without you, Honeybun?' Tears were close as she recalled the injuries her beloved dog had suffered. Just one more trip to the vet for a final check, she reminded herself.

'Come on, girl, let's go for a walk. I've got a busy day tomorrow, and I need a good night's sleep.'

CHAPTER THIRTY

The drive to Bedford was uneventful. It was mid-morning when they arrived at the police station. Jenny introduced herself and Peter to the officer behind the desk.

'Good morning, Ma'am, I'll find out who's available to speak with you. Please take a seat.'

In a few minutes, a young police officer appeared and asked them to follow him. At the end of a long corridor, he stopped, knocked at a door, and introduced them to the officer inside.

'Come in,' said the man, with an outstretched hand. 'Good morning to you both, please take a seat. I'm Superintendent Lilley. I understand you're looking into an incident at Broomleigh House School in 1996?'

'Yes, Sir,' said Jenny. 'One of the sports masters was investigated for having an affair with an underage student.' Without waiting for a response she continued. 'You will, of course, know about the two murders in Sussex. There's a link with Broomleigh House School and we have an appointment with the headmaster later. I'd like to have as much information about the school as possible before we see him.'

'Nasty business down there, I must say.' He passed a folder across for Peter to pick up. 'It was before my time, but our records show there was a fourteen-year-old girl by the name of Julia Burrows who told her mother that she was in love with her sports teacher and was worried that she was pregnant. The mother, of course, was distraught, and only just managed to stop her husband from going to the school armed with a cricket bat.' He gave a faint grin as he looked up at Jenny. 'Anyway, the girl was not pregnant, but her parents came to us to report the sports master. The father wanted us to lock him up and throw away the key or, in his words, "hang him". Not an unreasonable request in the circumstances.'

'What was the name of the sports master?' said Jenny.

Lilley took back the file he had passed to Peter. He opened it and flicked through several pages. 'Paul Jeffery.' Closing the file, he pushed it back towards Peter. 'Our officers immediately went to the school, and Jeffery denied everything, smarmy bugger he was, apparently. Said all the young girls had a crush on him and Julia Burrows was one of them. Said he'd had to fight her off.' He looked at Jenny. 'His words. Anyway, our officers carried out a full investigation, and after talking to other girls and some of the staff they believed they had a case and we arrested him.

'The girl's mother came to see us while we were holding him in custody. She said that her daughter had told her she'd made the story up and that nothing had happened.'

'Was the girl interviewed by your officers again?' said Jenny.

'Yes, she was, and the mother and father, but the girl just kept saying it wasn't true and that she'd just been playing a game.'

'Some game,' Peter said wryly.

Lilley nodded. 'We didn't believe her, of course, but the girl and her parents were adamant that they didn't want any further action taken. The mother insisted that it would harm her daughter if we continued our investigations, so we dropped it. We asked Jeffery if he wanted to make a claim against the girl, but he declined.'

'What happened after that?' said Peter.

'The daughter left the school almost immediately.'

'What about Jeffery?' said Jenny?

'He left pretty soon after. The story went around that he was offered a post overseas somewhere. All the details are in the folder. Let me know how you get on, or if there's any further information you need,' he said, rising from his chair.

'Just one more thing, Superintendent,' said Jenny. 'What did the officers investigating the incident think about the case? They must have been pretty sure he was guilty?'

'That the family was paid off. Broomleigh has an extremely good reputation and a scandal like that would have been very damaging to them. Might even have finished them off.' He opened the door and smiled.

'Thank you, Sir,' said Jenny.

'Glad to be of help. Good luck with your investigations. If there's anything else we can help you with, you know where we are.'

***

The entrance to the Broomleigh House School was as Jenny remembered it from so many years before. The gardens were perfect, lawns freshly mowed, flowerbeds full of colourful roses, hedges and shrubs perfectly trimmed.

She felt a pang of nostalgia, the scene awakening memories of friends, and of hard work demanded by teachers committed to getting students to the high standards required for the best universities. As they drove to the area reserved for visitor parking at the side of the well-kept main building, Jenny wondered if she had ever shown her mum and dad her appreciation for their determination to give their only daughter the very best education and help that they could. Broomleigh's reputation was well-earned, students studied hard and academic standards were among the highest in the country. Jenny had been very happy there and felt a slight degree of remorse that she was investigating a murder in which the school was potentially implicated.

As they entered through large glass doors a young man rose from a desk at the side of the hall and, after introductions, disappeared off to find the headmaster.

Almost before they had taken their seats, a tall, impressive-looking middle-aged man walked towards them.

'Good afternoon to you both, I'm Dr David McAllister.' He turned his gaze to Jenny. 'I understand from the school records that you were a pupil here. Welcome back to Broomleigh House, Chief Inspector Trent, I do hope little has changed since you were here – in a good way, of course.'

'It looks remarkably the same,' said Jenny.

'Please, come with me. I warn you that once we're past the sanctum of reception the atmosphere changes to one of mild chaos.' He smiled at Jenny. 'Probably not much different to when you were here.'

Peter and Jenny followed the headmaster into a long, grand hall. The walls were covered with portraits of past masters, and of top students who had gone on to some of the best universities.

Many of them Jenny recognised, some were people she had never seen. The portraits and the lavish furnishings were designed to impress wealthy parents looking for the best education for their children. Large white double doors off either side of the hall led to grand dining and lounge areas. Places where introductions were made and gourmet meals set out for foreign visitors, politicians and important clients. Everywhere smelt of fresh flowers and polish. Jenny breathed in, remembering the same smell that she had loved years ago. She wanted to stop, to bring back time and memories, but instead quickened her step to keep up with Dr McAllister.

As they reached the end of the hall, they turned left. Dr McAllister led them through a door. 'Sorry for the long walk, but my office is just over there.'

Children were running and shouting at each other as they went on to whatever was the next part of their day.

Looking through a window, Jenny remembered the playground with the sports fields next to it. Older children were playing cricket, others were using the tennis courts adjacent to the sports field. To one side there was a large brick building with windows and an impressive double door. Jenny could not remember if the building had been there during her time. *Probably for parents and visitors to watch the children playing cricket,* she thought.

A boy of about fourteen pushed past Jenny and crossed in front of Dr McAllister.

'Wilkins! Come back here, immediately!'

Wilkins skidded to a shaky halt, turned quickly and walked slowly towards the headmaster. 'Sorry, Sir, I didn't see you there, honest!'

'And where do you think you're going, Wilkins?'

'To the refectory for a drink, Sir.' He looked down at his feet. 'I'm really thirsty, Sir, I've been playing cricket all morning.' He looked up appealingly. 'I got a sixer, Sir!'

'A sixer. Really.' McAllister lowered his head, his face almost touching the young boy. 'I suppose you think that entitles you to be careless and rude.'

'No, Sir,' the boy said defiantly as he backed away from the red face in front of him.

'Well, Wilkins, you can go to the refectory once you have washed your hands, and you can ask Mrs Jones for three coffees placed on a tray with milk, sugar, and biscuits. Bring the tray to my office without spilling a drop.' He rose to his full height again.

'Yes, Sir.' Wilkins looked at Jenny and Peter in turn. 'I'm sorry.' He turned and walked away. He looked back just once and, seeing Jenny's smile, he straightened his shoulders, raised his head, and smiled back.

'Please accept my apologies for the rudeness of young Wilkins. He is actually one of our most promising students. Loves cricket and is dammed good at it.' McAllister raised his hand and pointed. 'My office is just on the right.'

The office was small and beautifully furnished. A large highly polished desk took up most of the room. The walls were covered with bookshelves filled with leather-bound volumes of the nineteenth-century literary masters. Jenny had never been in the room before, but she felt comfortable as she sat down next to Peter.

McAllister looked enquiringly at Jenny. 'I understand that you are investigating the murders of two people who attended this school some time ago. Rather grisly matter by the sounds of it.'

Before he could say any more, Jenny leant forward and placed the folder that Superintendent Lilley had given to them on the desk.

'The names of the two people are James Williamson and Lynn Moore. They attended Broomleigh at the same time.'

McAllister tapped a white cardboard file on his desk. 'I've already pulled out the records of all the pupils and teachers that were here between 1981 and 1998 for you. Most of our students are with us from ages eleven to eighteen, at which time they go on to further education at universities, usually the top ones in the country.' He looked at Peter and Jenny. 'Some even go to Harvard in America.' He smiled. 'Those that don't make the grade leave at sixteen.' He pushed the file towards them.

'I understand from our records that you were one of our exceptional students, Chief Inspector,' he said to Jenny. Without waiting for a reply, he rose. 'Unless you need me to stay, I think you would do better to read the information on your own. Please use my office for as long as you like. Coffee and biscuits will be here very soon.' He turned towards the door. 'If there is anything else you need, or if you would like to ask me for any further information, press 1 on the telephone pad and ask for me.'

'Just one thing before you go, Dr McAllister.' Peter rose from his chair. 'Are any of the teachers that were here in 1998 still here?'

'I have had the ones that are still here marked in the folder.' He smiled and opened the door just as Wilkins arrived nervously with the tray of refreshments.

'Great timing, Wilkins. Well done, take the tray into my office for our guests.' He lifted a cup from the tray. 'I'll have mine later.'

As Wilkins placed the tray carefully on the polished desk, Dr McAllister left.

'Thank you.' Jenny's smile settled Wilkins down again and he gave a cheeky grin back.

'You're welcome,' he said politely as he left the room, closing the door behind him.

The file was thick with documents listing the names of pupils and teachers that were at Broomleigh House School during the years she had asked for. As McAllister had promised, the names of those teachers still teaching at Broomleigh House were highlighted.

Jenny recognised all of the names which had been marked, but one name was missing from the list.

'He's not there, is he, Jenny?' said Peter having also briefly gone through the names.

'Unless we've both missed it, Paul Jeffery isn't listed. Now, I wonder why?' she smiled at Peter. 'A question that no doubt Dr McAllister will be able to answer.'

James Williamson and Lynn Moore were listed within the same period, 1991–98. Both had achieved excellent academic grades and had gone on to university. Williamson had gone to Bristol to study commerce, and Lynn Moore to Cambridge to read law. Both had gained first-class degrees.

'Pretty impressive,' remarked Peter.

'We need to know why Paul Jeffery is not on the list.' Jenny closed the file. 'Before that, I need to talk with one of the teachers I remember. Joseph Green, he was one of the sports masters when I was here. Everyone liked him.'

Peter picked up the phone and pressed 1. 'Can you put me through to Dr McAllister, please?' he said, and waited.

'McAllister.' His voice was efficient and sharp.

'Dr McAllister, we would like to speak with Joseph Green please,' said Peter.

'I'll arrange that immediately, Inspector.' The line went dead.

Within minutes, there was a knock on the door.

'Come in,' Jenny called.

Jenny stood up as Joseph Green walked in. Even though almost twenty years had passed since Jenny had seen him, he was still a good-looking man and he looked fit and healthy – his career in sports had served him well.

'Good afternoon, Mr Green. I'm Jenny Trent, DCI with the Sussex Police, and this is my colleague DI Peter Branden.'

'Good afternoon, Chief Inspector.' He smiled as he looked at Jenny. 'I remember you as well as Jennifer Collier, and to be honest you haven't changed much.' He turned to Peter and shook his hand. 'Good afternoon, DI Branden.'

'Do you know why we've asked to see you?' Jenny said.

'Dr McAllister briefed us on the reason you're here. It sounds a nasty business, and both victims coming from this school ...' He shook his head.

'I know it's going back some time, Mr Green, but I wonder if you remember the two people who were murdered, and whether you can tell us anything about them that may help us with our enquires?' said Jenny.

'It was only when Dr McAllister told us that you were coming that some of us checked the details again. I can tell you it has been quite a shock, especially for the teachers who knew them.'

'What sort of students were they?' Jenny said.

Joseph Green shifted in his seat. 'I was the sports master for two of their years here, and neither of them excelled in any sports, but they tried hard. The girl, Lynn, was quite good at netball, but she wasn't really a team player.' He stopped looking down at his hands. 'Neither was that interested in sports.'

Sensing hesitation, Jenny reframed the question. 'Can you tell us what sort of *people* they were?'

Green met Jenny's eyes. 'Apart from sports, I didn't have much to do with them.'

'Well,' Jenny said abruptly. 'What were they like when you were with them and when they were with other people?'

'They seemed to be together most of the time and had a lot of friends as far as I could see.' He shifted uncomfortably.

'Mr Green, I really would like to know more about these two people. They have both been brutally murdered and there is a link with this school. I need to know what kind of people they were. Whether they were liked or disliked and, most importantly, if they made any enemies while they were here,' said Jenny.

'Chief Inspector, I can only tell you what I know from when they were with me in a sports capacity. There was nothing unusual about them except that they were always together. They had friends, and as far as I know, they worked hard at their studies.'

'Did they have any enemies?' Jenny looked directly at him.

'Everyone has some sort of enemies, Chief Inspector. I'm sure you know that's a fact of life.' He shrugged his shoulders, looking at Peter for acknowledgement. 'Perhaps one of our other teachers could tell you more? Mrs Davies, Head of Sixth Form – who was Miss Teal in your time – is still here. She will probably know more about them than me. I can get her for you. Dr McAllister said we should be as helpful as possible and I should get anyone you asked for.'

'Thank you, I'd like that, please,' Jenny said.

Green rose to leave.

'Before you go, Mr Green ...' Jenny held up her hand. 'Do you remember a Paul Jeffery? He was Sports Master.'

'No! I don't remember anyone of that name, I'm sorry.' He opened the door and walked quickly through. The door shut quietly behind him.

'He's defensive and lying,' said Peter, as he placed his notepad back on the desk.

Jenny sat back in her chair. 'You know what, Peter, I loved my time here. The teachers were so committed and ready to help you. I can't quite put my finger on why, but it just doesn't feel the same now.'

'I suppose we all change over the years, people, places, you, and me.'

'I wonder how long Mrs Davies will be. I remember her as Miss Teal, of course. All the boys had a crush on her.' Jenny smiled. 'She really was very beautiful and all the girls wanted to be like her, some even had a schoolgirl crush on her.' A loud knock at the door interrupted Jenny's reflections. 'Come in, please,' she said.

Mrs Davies walked in and greeted Jenny.

'How lovely to see you, Jenny, you look remarkably well.'

Jenny felt her old admiration for the woman in front of her return. As the years had passed, she had grown into a very attractive older woman. Tall, with her back held straight, her head high. Her hair was just showing shades of grey that only served to make her look more sophisticated and elegant. Her blue eyes shone as bright as they always had and her nails were manicured to perfection.

'It's a pleasure to see you again, Mrs Davies. Being here brings back so many memories. I'm just sorry that we meet again under such depressing circumstances.' Jenny smiled. 'Please, take a seat. Detective Inspector Branden and I are investigating the murders of two people who were students at Broomleigh House between 1991 and 1998. I understand that you knew them quite well. James Williamson and Lynn Moore.'

'Yes, I was their form teacher for two years when they first joined.' Mrs Davies took a file from the small leather case she had put on the desk. 'As you can imagine, Jenny ...' she looked up. 'I'm sorry, should I call you Chief Inspector?'

Jenny raised her hand and shook her head. 'Jenny is fine.'

'It was such a long time ago, so I looked up some records.' She took a piece of paper from the file and studied it for a few seconds. 'They were both good students, very bright and on the path to top universities. They boarded, seeing their parents during most of the holidays. James's parents worked in Nigeria and Lynn's lived in Sussex.'

'When you say "most of the holidays", what do you mean?' said Jenny.

'There were two occasions when James's parents couldn't get home, so he had to stay at Broomleigh during the Christmas break,' said Mrs Davies.

'How did he feel about that?'

'I was here during one of the breaks, and to be honest he didn't seem to mind at all.' She stopped, before adding, 'We try to make Christmas as good as possible for the children who for various reasons can't be with their parents. From their comments, I believe we achieve our aim.'

'I remember that all students had an assessment at the end of every term,' said Jenny. 'And that it not only assessed their academic progress but their behaviour and character too. Do you have a copy of any of the assessments regarding James and Lynn?'

Mrs Davies looked in the file and took out a sheet of paper, handing it to Jenny. 'I did the assessments on James myself.' The page was headed 'Student Assessment Report', the name of the child clearly marked together with the year and term of the assessment. She pointed to a box at the bottom of the page. 'That's where we made notes on their personal character traits and abilities.'

Jenny took the page from Mrs Davies. It was headed 'James Williamson 1996 Summer Term Assessment'. Her eyes drifted to the box at the bottom of the page.

James has many friends and takes the lead in and out of school activities. He must try to curb his enthusiasm for wanting to take charge and learn to be part of a team. He has the ability to help people and should do so, rather than ignoring those who do not have such a strong personality. He is a born leader, but he can be arrogant and uncaring. James has excellent academic abilities and providing he can control some of his less admirable characteristics he will probably excel in whatever career he chooses.

'Pretty strong assessment of him I must say. Did you like him?' Jenny handed the sheet back.

'I liked his enthusiasm for his studies,' said Mrs Davies. 'He was very clever and popular, but I found it hard to understand him sometimes.' She thought for a moment. 'I felt there was an underlying cruelty about him.' She smiled. 'But then most children can be like that, I think.'

'What about Lynn, have you an assessment of her character?'

'I never did any of her assessments, she wasn't in any of my teaching classes. I'm afraid I was unable to find any records of them. It's so long ago, I think some of the records have been lost.'

'But you knew her,' Jenny said.

'From what I remember, she was also bright. And Lynn and James spent a lot of their time together. She could be easily led and I think James had a lot of control over her.'

'Can you remember if anyone else spent a lot of time with them?'

'Not to any great extent, they had other friends that came and went.' Mrs Davies thought for a moment. 'I seem to remember that one boy spent some time with them for a short while. It was strange really, because he was nowhere up to their academic standard, and didn't really fit in with their friends, but he rather hung on to James for a while.'

'Can you remember his name?' said Jenny.

Mrs Davies thought for a moment. 'I believe you have a file with the names of students. If I look at the lists for the years that James and Lynn were here, I might recognise it.'

Jenny handed her the folder and watched as she turned several sheets before placing a finger firmly in the middle of a page.

'That's him, Jonnie French.'

'Can you tell us anything about him?' Jenny asked hopefully.

'Again, he wasn't in my classes, so I don't remember much about him.' She began searching through the papers in the file she had brought with her. She pulled out another sheet.

'Ah … believe it or not, I do have an assessment sheet on our Mr French.' She closed the file and placed it on the desk in front of her. 'No wonder the file is heavy, I seem to have everything in there.' She read the text from the box at the bottom of the page.

Very low academic ability but excels at sports, especially swimming. Jonnie will probably leave Broomleigh House at sixteen due to his lack of academic achievements. He should look for a career in sport. He is already an accomplished swimmer.

'That's all it says.' She passed the sheet to Jenny. 'I don't know if there's anything more I can help you with, Jenny, it's been a long time now but my memory usually serves me well.'

'Thank you. You've been very helpful, Mrs Davies.' Jenny rose from her chair at the same time as the older woman. 'It's been a pleasure seeing you again.'

'Congratulations on a successful career, Jenny. You always worked hard, I knew you would do well.' She shook Jenny's hand and turned to Peter. 'I hope you find the person you're looking for soon, it's very worrying for everyone.'

'Thank you, Mrs Davies, I hope so too,' said Peter. 'Just one more thing, Mrs Davies,' he said. 'Do you remember a sports master by the name of Paul Jeffery?'

Mrs Davies hesitated and looked back at Jenny. 'I'm sorry, Jenny, I don't remember anyone of that name.' She turned and left, closing the door behind her.

'They have been briefed very well.' Peter closed his notebook and, putting his hands to the back of his head, he yawned. 'Sorry, Jenny.' His hand moved swiftly to cover his mouth.

'I think I'd like to talk with Dr McAllister again,' said Jenny, as she lifted the handset.

McAllister arrived quickly. 'What more can I help you with?' He smiled as he sat down.

'Mr Green and Mrs Davies have been very helpful, thank you, Dr McAllister.' Jenny looked carefully at the man. 'But there's just one or two more things I would like to ask you.'

'Of course, if I can be of further help.'

Jenny took a short breath. 'We have information that there used to be a sports master by the name of Paul Jeffery at the school. I believe he was here in 1996.'

McAllister didn't move.

'When I asked Mrs Davies if she knew him she said she didn't remember anyone of that name,' Jenny paused briefly, 'and Mr Green said exactly the same thing.'

McAllister held up his hand to stop Jenny.

'I am afraid that is my fault, Chief Inspector. Your own police records will show that Paul Jeffery was investigated about an allegation of underage sexual activity with one of our students. It was totally without any foundation and the girl admitted that she had made the whole story up.'

'What were your feelings about the accusation?' Jenny said.

'Well,' McAllister gave Jenny a brief smile, 'Paul Jeffery decided to leave immediately after the incident, and it was decided the incident was never to be discussed again and that his name should be deleted from our records.'

'But if he was innocent of the allegations made, why was that necessary?'

'Allegations of that sort are serious and the reputation of Broomleigh could have been damaged if we had not closed them down quickly,' said McAllister.

'I understand the girl left Broomleigh House almost immediately. Why was that?'

'I think her parents were ashamed about the false allegations made by their daughter and they withdrew her. However, the school governors would have pressed for her to be expelled from the school if her parents had not taken the action to move her.' He brushed invisible dust from his trousers.

Jenny noticed, but her expression remained impassive.

'Have there been any other scandals?' Jenny said.

'None at all, Chief Inspector.' His voice rose defensively.

'Have there been any other incidents that might have caused Broomleigh House to worry about its reputation, such as bullying, for instance?'

'I am sure you will appreciate that every school has some bullying, Chief Inspector, and yes, there have been incidents of this at Broomleigh House. The housemaster and all my staff are well trained to look for any such signs, and it will have been dealt with immediately, I can assure you.'

'What about before you joined Broomleigh House, Dr McAllister? Do you know of any bullying that took place then?' said Jenny.

McAllister straightened his back. 'Broomleigh House School has one of the highest reputations in the country for academic excellence and sporting achievements, Chief Inspector.' He fixed his gaze steadily on Jenny. 'You were here for seven years, can you remember any bullying taking place?' He threw the question back at her.

'I saw very little bullying, Dr McAllister, but I do remember seeing a young boy being hit on the legs with a heavy stick by another boy. He stopped hitting when I ran up to him, and ran away.'

'Did you report it to anyone?' said Dr McAllister.

'Yes, I did, I reported it once, but I never heard what happened.'

There were a few moments of silence, and then McAllister rose from his chair.

'Chief Inspector, I hope we have been able to help you as much as possible. Now, I am a busy man. If you have finished with me I would like to carry on with my duties.'

'Thank you, Dr McAllister, you've been very helpful.' Jenny rose to shake his hand.

'Will the press have to know that the two victims were at this school?' he said.

'The press have a way of finding things out, Dr McAllister, and we mustn't forget that two people have been sadistically murdered. If it does get out, the publicity might help jog someone's memory.' She stopped for a moment. 'We want to catch the culprit before he strikes again.'

The door closed softly behind Dr McAllister.

Peter closed his notebook. 'I think he's a worried man.'

'He should be,' said Jenny.

'Come on, Peter, it's time to get back. We need to find out where Jonnie French is, he could be the next victim.'

Jenny looked back at the school where she had been so happy, something was wrong and she had a feeling that Broomleigh House was now tainted.

✳✳✳

Peter turned the car to take the short entrance road to the gate. As he did, someone came out of the side hedge and into the road, moving quickly towards the car, waving frantically.

Peter slammed his foot on the brakes and the car came to an uneasy stop just in front of an elderly man dressed in gardening overalls.

'Stop … stop! I need to talk to you.'

The man moved to Jenny's side of the car. 'I 'eard some of what was said in there, and I was 'ere when you were 'ere, Miss. I've been looking after the gardens here all my working life.'

'How did you hear?' Jenny asked.

He looked nervously around him. 'I'm not as daft as people think and I know a lot more of what goes on 'ere than anyone. When I saw you drive up I was weeding outside of his window.' He jerked his thumb in the direction of the school.

'Anyway, just thought you should know about that poor kid who was bullied 'ere years ago. Two of the kids that bullied him are the ones that have been killed.' He took a deep breath. 'They were merciless to him. Poor little sod.'

'What was his name?' asked Jenny.

'I only remember because it was a funny name and my granddad 'ad a big German shepherd with the same name.' He gave a slight laugh. 'Clever bugger he was too. Einstein. Einstein,' he repeated. 'That was his name. Why would anyone want to call a kid by that name? I wouldn't mind betting that was why he was bullied so much in the first place.'

'Do you know if any other children were involved in the bullying?' said Jenny.

'Not as much as those two.' He stopped as he thought for a moment. 'There was another boy joined in, a big one, but can't remember his name. Memory's not the same as it was,' he said, tapping the side of his head. He glanced towards the school. 'I've been too long talking to you. Have to go, just thought you should know.'

He disappeared quickly through a small gate at the side of the hedge.

'Should we go back to see McAllister with this information, Jenny?' Peter said as he started the engine.

Jenny thought for a moment. 'Not yet, Peter, I need time to think, and it would put the gardener in a very difficult position right now. If they frighten him off, he may not want to be so outspoken with us again.'

CHAPTER THIRTY-ONE

Jonnie French was sitting at a desk in the empty office. He had been told many times not to use the office. It was for senior members of staff and not for instructors. *Snotty cows,* he thought, as he reclined in the leather-backed chair, his hands cradling his head as he opened his mouth to yawn loudly. His boss was a woman and he didn't like it. In fact, he hated it. 'Only good for one thing!' he said loudly to the closed door. 'Probably no good at that either, and I certainly wouldn't like to find out.' *Thank God, she and her fat friend won't be here for three whole days. Three whole days without them,* he thought again, as if someone could hear him inside his head.

For the next three days, the spa was closed and his job was to empty the two swimming pools and ensure that the contractors brought in to clean them did their job properly. He was to supervise them. *Me! Supervise! I couldn't care less if they did the job properly, or not!* He had three whole days to himself. *Bliss. I might even bring that slut in for a shag in the pool after I've supervised the cleaning.* He laughed aloud at the thought.

His mood suddenly took a step into the dark as he remembered the attack a few days ago. 'I thought I'd had it and was a goner,' he muttered. 'Perhaps I should have told her about it,' he said, as he lifted his head from his hands and sat back up in the chair. 'Couldn't bloody sleep properly because of that.' His voice shaking. 'Ah, what the hell, I'm here and might as well get on with it. Three whole days to myself, no fucking woman telling me what to do.' He slammed his fist down on the desk, making it judder on the polished floor.

'I suppose I ought to think about getting ready for the cleaning guys before they get here,' he said to himself, as he rose from the chair and went to pick up the newspaper he'd placed on the desk in front of him to read later when he could have a rest and a drink. He misjudged the distance and his fingers pushed the paper, which slid from the desk and fell to the floor, spreading open. He bent to pick it up. The naked girl in the middle of the page caught his eye. *That's where women should be,* he thought, *not trying to play the boss!*

He turned the page and stared at the words in front of him.

TWO MURDER VICTIMS ATTENDED THE SAME SCHOOL

James Williamson and Lynn Moore, brutally murdered in West Sussex, both attended Broomleigh House School. The school is a private school in Bedfordshire and the police are asking anyone for information they may have regarding the two victims. A spokesperson for Sussex Police said that they are concerned there will be other attacks. Police officers are already in touch with the school and hope to gain information which will help the investigation into the murders.

Jonnie French slammed the paper down and took a deep heavy breath. 'I should call the police,' he said softly to himself. *Probably not a good idea though. They'd start asking me all sorts of questions, not what I bloody want at all!* He thought angrily.

He was muttering quiet words of hate about the police when he heard a sudden movement behind him. As he turned, an arm slipped around his neck, his legs were kicked forward and he crashed to the floor. He took a sharp breath in, but before he could let out a scream of anger and frustration a thick hard cloth was pulled across his open mouth and tied tightly around his neck, he couldn't make a sound.

As he tried to stop the onslaught with his arms, they were pulled above his head and bound at the wrists. He lifted his feet to kick out, but hey were held down. Another bandage was tied around his ankles. His hands were lifted, and he felt himself being dragged along the floor out of the office.

The slow drag along the polished floor of the hallway leading to the changing rooms and the swimming pools was agony. His fight to release himself only made the journey more painful. He stopped struggling, waiting for the journey to reach its end.

The end was the main swimming pool. The smell of chlorine and bleach filled his nose as his arms were released and he fell heavily to the floor.

The shiny black tiles on the floor reflected the tight white bandage, which was soaked with saliva from his half-open mouth.

He moved his head, trying to see his attacker.

A bright object lit up a reflection in the floor tiles. Before he could see what it was, it crashed down on his shoulder. Three times the object was raised and brought down, each time ripping through clothing, flesh, and bone. His arm fell away from his shoulder. The tiles lit up again as another crash split his other arm from his shoulder. His eyes watered at the excruciating pain.

He still couldn't scream, he couldn't do anything.

He felt his ankles being untied and he was pushed into the deep water of the swimming pool. Thrashing his legs, he pushed himself to the top of the water. Blood was flowing into the pool, surrounding his body. He felt sick as he began to sink beneath the surface, water filling his nostrils and running down his throat. The pain returned to his body, pain like nothing else he had ever felt in his entire life.

He heard a crash as his attacker joined him in the water, he felt arms holding him afloat.

'Come on, Jonnie French, use your arms, use your arms, you stupid boy, use your arms!' The voice screamed at him again, 'Oh dear, oh dear, you can't!' The bandage was ripped away from his mouth. As he tried to take a deep breath, something dropped into his mouth falling to the back of his throat.

He knew what it was. His tongue dug deep, winding around the peach stone. As he held the stone with his tongue, he coughed and it moved to the front of his mouth. He used all the strength he could get from his shoulders and neck and spat the stone from his mouth, watching as it floated away from him. He tried turning his head from side to side to see who was in the pool with him. He saw that the water was red with the blood from the wounds where his arms had been, and watched as the ruby liquid continued to spread. He felt numb as the pain suddenly stopped. *I must be dead*, he thought. Then the pain returned. His scream pierced the silence like a knife cutting through soft butter. His head was bursting. He felt hands holding it, the pressure squeezing all the breath from him.

'I'm so sorry you didn't like my peach this time, Jonnie French. You used to like them so much,' his attacker snarled, his eyes wide with hatred. 'Funny thing is, I don't like them anymore.' He coughed and a loud snigger burst from his throat. 'What's the matter, why can't you swim? You're a good swimmer, Jonnie French. Whoops! So sorry, you haven't got your arms with you.'

His attacker turned away. 'They're over here,' he said gleefully. 'Wait, I'll get them for you.' He climbed from the pool after fishing both arms out of the water. 'Here they are, Jonnie French, you can use them now.'

His attacker howled at him. 'Come on, Jonnie French, they're next to you so you can use them.'

The attacker ran up and down the side of the pool. 'Use your arms, stupid. Come on, use your arms. I've given them both to you!' He laughed cruelly as he picked up a training pole.

As Jonnie French kicked towards the side of the pool, he was pushed roughly back towards the centre with the pole. He screamed at his assailant. 'I'm sorry, I'm sorry, please help me, please! I can't swim ... I can't swim. I'm hurting so much ... help me, please ... I don't want to die ...please ...please!' He grew weak as he sank again under the water, his feet slipping on the bottom of the pool.

He choked as foul red water filled his lungs.

Jonnie French rose to the surface once more. 'Please help me! Please!' He used all the strength he had to plead with his attacker.

'Oh, by the way, before you go, you should know that I am not Einstein Luther Smith any more. I am not Einstein Luther Smith, any more,' he repeated more loudly. 'But you won't ever know who I am ... never!'

Jonnie French didn't hear him, his head was face down in the swimming pool.

CHAPTER THIRTY-TWO

Jenny and Peter arrived back late from Bedford and spent the evening at Jenny's house looking through the papers that McAllister had given them. The incident with the old gardener had made them look for more names.

Einstein Luther Smith was there.

'This case is about four people,' Jenny said, as she closed the file. 'James Williamson, Lynn Moore, Jonnie French, and Einstein Luther Smith. Apart from Jonnie French, all three were three years behind me. I didn't really know them and wouldn't have had much to do with them.'

'Do you remember any of the bullying the old man spoke about?'

Jenny thought deeply, her mind trying to bring forward long-forgotten memories.

'There was the incident when I saw a boy hitting another boy on the legs with a stick. I remember he was so adamant that I didn't report it or to get first Aid to see to his bleeding legs.'

Peter rose from his chair. 'I'm getting tired, Jenny, I'd better go. Should we have a briefing first thing in the morning?'

'Yes.' Jenny thought for a second. 'We must find Jonnie French, I think he's in danger. I'll contact the station when you've gone and get someone onto it.' She paused. 'And we need to know more about Einstein Luther Smith. I'll call the school again first thing in the morning. Come on, Peter, you get home. I'll see you out.'

***

Morgan-Jones met Jenny as she arrived at the station entrance the next morning.

'Come and see me with an update immediately, Jenny. I'm going to my office now.'

As she followed Morgan-Jones, she saw Peter already at his desk.

'Get as many of the team as possible in the incident room as soon as you can. I have a feeling we need to act quickly. As soon as I've updated the super I'll be with you,' she said.

'Was your visit to the school useful?' Morgan-Jones said as they went into his office.

'Yes, Sir. We were able to have it confirmed that Williamson and Moore attended the school at the same time. We also have information that during the time they were there, they carried out a campaign of bullying against one of the boys in their year. It also seems that another boy was involved. None of this was mentioned at all when we were talking with the teachers. They all made it quite clear that bullying was not tolerated under any circumstances. The school had already suppressed information on one scandal that happened a few years ago, and the people we spoke with certainly wanted us to know they knew nothing about it.'

'How did you find out about the bullying then?' said Morgan-Jones.

'As we were leaving, the gardener stopped us. He said he'd heard our conversation with McAllister and that he wanted to tell us about a boy who'd been bullied there.'

'Did he give you a name?'

'He could only remember the first name, which was Einstein. On further investigation of the information given to us by McAllister, we found the name of the boy the gardener mentioned.' She drew a sharp breath. 'Before the briefing this morning I want to speak to McAllister again to find out about a boy called Einstein Luther Smith. No one mentioned his name during our conversations. It's not a name that would be forgotten easily.'

'Do you think he might have anything to do with the killings?' Morgan-Jones leant forward, his eyes meeting Jenny's.

'I do, Sir. I also believe that the third person involved in the bullying, Jonnie French, may be in danger. We need to act quickly, and I've already alerted uniform and my team of the need to find him.'

Morgan-Jones walked her to the door. 'Well done, Jenny.' His hand rested on her shoulder. 'Take care, and don't forget you may be closer to these people than you think. You've already had a warning. Just be careful, please.'

∗∗∗

Walking to her office, Jenny pulled her phone from her pocket and dialled Broomleigh House School.

'Broomleigh House School, how can I help you?' The voice was now familiar to Jenny.

'I would like to speak with Dr McAllister please, DCI Jenny Trent here.'

'Just one moment, I'll put you through.'

'McAllister here, Chief Inspector.' The voice was friendly.

'Dr McAllister, do you have any information on a boy who attended Broomleigh between the years of 1991 and 1998? He had an unusual name – Einstein Luther Smith.'

The line was quiet for a few seconds.

McAllister coughed. 'The only information we have is in the file I gave you, Chief Inspector.'

'Yes, I've got that information, which was that he was very bright and gained a place at Aberdeen University to study for some sort of medical degree. Were there any incidents that may not have been recorded?' said Jenny.

'What sort of things do you have in mind, Chief Inspector?'

Jenny heard the caution in his voice. 'Was he bullied?'

'I thought we went through that yesterday.'

'We did, and you said that bullying was not tolerated and was dealt with very quickly. That indicates to me that there might have been some bullying, Dr McAllister.'

'I'm sorry, Chief Inspector, but as I said before all schools have some sort of bullying, and if we have any here at Broomleigh House they are dealt with immediately. No serious incidents come to mind. However, I'll certainly ask the teachers who were at the school during that time and come back to you later today.'

'I would be grateful, Dr McAllister, thank you.'

'Before you go, Chief Inspector, I should tell you that there was a rather sad incident to do with Einstein Luther Smith that was talked about a lot here, but is not recorded because it happened after he'd left Broomleigh House.' He hesitated, waiting for Jenny to respond.

'And what was that incident?'

'Luther Smith's mother died suddenly. According to reports, she died during a family picnic soon after the school had broken for the summer break, and before he went to university that autumn.'

'That's terrible, do you know how she died?' said Jenny.

'I'm sure you can get the full report, but it seems she choked on a peach stone.'

'What did you say, Dr McAllister?'

'She choked to death on a peach stone.'

'Thank you, Dr McAllister, you've been very helpful again.'

✳✳✳

Peter had written the details of their visit on the whiteboard and posted next to it a brochure of Broomleigh House School that had been given to them by McAllister. Jenny reached the incident room just as Peter had finished his account of the visit.

'Good morning, everyone.' Jenny waited for the noise to stop as she stood in front of the board. 'First of all, has anyone found the whereabouts of Jonnie French? It's likely that he could be the next victim and we need to get to him fast.'

DS Hughes raised his hand. 'We're on to it now, Ma'am.'

'Thank you, keep me informed. As you know, DI Branden and I visited Broomleigh House School yesterday.' She looked around the room, noticing Ben Seldon at the back. She acknowledged his slight hand raise with a smile. 'And I have spoken to Dr McAllister, the head of the school, again just now, and he has given me information that I would like followed up immediately.'

She looked at Peter. 'Have you told everyone about the meeting with the gardener, and his information about the boy called Einstein Luther Smith?'

'I've told them everything.'

'Good.' All eyes were on her. 'Einstein Luther Smith's mother died suddenly at a family picnic soon after the school had closed for the summer break in the year that he left Broomleigh House, and before he had taken up his place at Aberdeen University. She choked to death on a peach stone.'

Someone in the room groaned. 'Oh my God!' Others just let out whistles and grunts.

'Peter, organise someone to make enquires. Also, we need to know about what our Mr Einstein Luther Smith is doing now. I suggest we start at Aberdeen University. We need to move quickly. I'm off to see Mickey and Sam, I want them to find out more about the death of Einstein's mother.'

CHAPTER THIRTY-THREE

Jenny shook Honey's head. 'We're getting there, girl.'

Honey gave a squeaky grunt without moving. 'That man who hurt you will soon be caught.' She put her arms around her dog. 'I really have got to stop talking to you.' She laughed as she rose to her feet and walked towards the kitchen for a welcome cup of tea.

She stopped. *No, I deserve a drink!* She smiled. 'Come on, Hun, let's go into the lounge and see what's on.' Honey bounded excitedly after her.

After she'd poured herself a large vodka with lots of coke and ice, she picked up her phone and noticed that she had a missed call. She quickly pressed the button to find that the call had been from Andrew Baines.

'The evening could be getting better,' she said to Honey. 'I think I'll make him wait just a bit longer before I call him back.'

The *Six O'clock News* had just started as she sank weary but happy into a large chair, Honey at her feet.

'Police have released more information regarding their investigation of the so-called "Peach Stone Murderer".' *First time I've heard it called that,* thought Jenny. 'A police spokesperson revealed that the victims both attended Broomleigh House School in Bedford between 1991 and 1998. Police are continuing their investigations and have interviewed senior staff at the school. A representative on behalf of Broomleigh House School said they are cooperating fully with the police.'

'I'm not sure "cooperating fully" are the words I'd have used.' Jenny realised she was talking to herself again and put her drink down to call Andrew Baines.

'Hello, Jenny, at last, we speak. How are you?'

Jenny felt the warmth in his voice. 'I'm very well, thank you.'

'It sounds as though things are beginning to fall into place, you must be feeling a lot better about your chances of catching the murderer.'

'Yes, it looks as though we're getting somewhere at last, but we need to move faster before someone else is killed,' she said.

'What about talking it over?'

'I'd like that. When have you in mind?'

'What about later this evening? If you haven't eaten yet we could have a meal.'

'That sounds like a great idea.'

'There's a new Italian restaurant recently opened on the seafront. I hear it's pretty good.'

'Sounds good to me.' Jenny tried not to sound too excited.

'Seven-thirty at the Roma Italia then. Would you mind getting a taxi? It would save you worrying about having a drink, and I don't have my car at the moment,' he said.

'Of course. I'll be there.' She closed her phone and smiled. 'Honey, guess what? I've got a date! I need to get ready.'

Honey wagged her tail.

The taxi arrived at Roma Italia at exactly 7.30 pm, Andrew was outside waiting for her.

'You look lovely.' He walked towards her and put his arm gently around her shoulder. 'And you smell just as sweet.'

His protective arm made Jenny want to hug him, but she just leant towards him as they walked into the restaurant.

Dinner was smoothly chosen, each feeling relaxed in the other's company and savouring the quiet noise of other couples enjoying time together. The conversation was easy and Andrew was attentive, making sure they had the very best wine and food together with excellent service. Jenny discovered that he had moved to West Sussex three years earlier, having lived in the Midlands most of his working life.

'How do you get on with Ben?' Jenny said, as they waited for the dessert menu.

'Ben is brilliant at his job and he trusts me to give him the very best technical service I can. And I do,' he said. 'I know he can be difficult, but our job can be pretty testing.' He stopped, thoughtful for a few seconds. 'Especially when we're dealing with the death of a child.' He looked closely at Jenny. 'We get on very well, and,' he touched her arm softly 'he has a lot of good things to say about you.'

Jenny blushed.

The dessert menu arrived and Jenny passed it back. 'I really have eaten enough, it was lovely and I don't want to spoil it by having too much.'

'Let's just have coffee.' Andrew passed his menu back to the waiter too.

The evening was ending too quickly and Jenny sighed contentedly.

'We haven't talked much about the investigation,' said Andrew. 'But I would rather talk about you.' He took her hand as he spoke. 'First of all, though, how is Honey?'

'She's really well now, getting back to her old fussy self. She has to have a check-up and some stitches out in a couple of days. Other than that she's fine.'

'And you, Jenny. Now tell me about you.'

The coffee came just as he took her other hand.

Jenny felt at ease telling Andrew about her grief over her husband and the time it was taking for her to get on with her life. She told him about her pride at being promoted to Detective Chief Inspector, and her worries that Morgan-Jones didn't seem to have the same faith in her that everyone else appeared to have. She talked for a long time, her hands still enclosed in the warmth of his.

Andrew looked around the emptying restaurant and released her hands. 'It looks like we should be going.' He gestured to the waiter and paid the bill before Jenny had time to protest that she wanted to share the cost. 'I've already arranged a taxi and it should be here in ten minutes.'

Jenny rose from her seat. 'Good, I won't be long, just time to make sure I haven't got crumbs stuck to my face,' she said, giving Andrew a warm smile as she turned away from the table.

Her hand slipped into Andrew's welcome grasp on the way home, he put his arm around her shoulders, and she felt safer and happier than she had for a long time.

When they arrived at her house, Andrew led her to the door.

'Would you like another coffee?' She met his eyes. 'I'd love you to meet Honey, I know she'd be happy to meet you too.'

'I'd really love to, Jenny, but I have to stand in for Ben tomorrow and I desperately need to catch up on some paperwork. A child died after an operation yesterday and I have to ascertain the reason.'

He pulled her to him. Jenny felt the warmth of his closeness and lifted her face, looking into his strong blue eyes. His mouth found hers, the kiss rekindling emotions she had never thought she would feel again. She held him close, her arms around his neck, afraid that he would not come back if she let him go.

He turned and walked towards the waiting taxi, and was gone.

She turned to open her door and found Honey wagging her tail and holding a grubby toy in her mouth.

CHAPTER THIRTY-FOUR

Jenny was early getting to the station the next morning. She saw DS Hughes sitting at his desk. 'Anything happened overnight?'

'Not that I know of yet, Ma am' said Hughes swallowing the last mouthful of coffee. The phone on his desk rang as Jenny acknowledged his reply.

As usual, her office smelt of cleaning fluids and polish. She opened the windows to a cool, but sunny morning, and breathed in a welcome breath of fresh air just as Hughes knocked loudly at her door.

'Come in, sergeant.'

'Ma'am, one of the lads has just phoned. He's had a call from a woman who said she heard about the "Peach Stone Murderer" on the news, and wanted to tell us about someone who keeps coming to buy peaches in the shop where she works.'

'Is she still on the phone?'

'No, Ma'am. She said she didn't want to talk about it on the phone and that she has to get to work. She asked if someone could go there. She seemed a bit anxious.'

'Where does she work?'

'At the Welcome supermarket on the high street. She starts at eight-thirty when it opens.'

'As soon as DI Branden gets in I want you to go with him to talk to her. Did she leave her name?'

'No, Ma'am. Apparently, she said she'd rather not before she spoke to someone at work.'

'Just ask DI Branden to see me before you go,' said Jenny.

Could be a lead, or just someone trying to be helpful.'

Ten minutes later, Peter knocked at her door and poked his head around it. 'Hughes collared me on the way in. We're on our way.'

'You're good at getting the most out of people, Peter. Get Hughes to take the notes and you speak to her. It may be something or nothing. Hughes can let you know the details on the way.'

'I'll get all the information I can from her. Could be the break we need.'

Looking down, Jenny asked carefully, 'How are things with you and Maggie? I'm sorry, Peter, I've been thoughtless not asking before.' She looked up to face her friend, but he'd gone.

✱✱✱

As Peter and Hughes walked into the Welcome supermarket they saw two members of staff at the checkout in smart navy blue uniforms. One of them looked away from the customer she was serving and raised a hand.

As they walked towards her a tall young man approached them. 'Good morning, officers I'm Jim Gately, the store manager, how can I help you?'

'Good morning, Mr Gately,' said Peter, as he pulled his identification badge from his pocket. 'A young woman telephoned our station this morning and requested us to come and see her here, at her place of work. I'm sorry but she didn't leave a name.'

'Yes, that's Miss Matthews. She's already told me about the man who seems to buy rather a lot of peaches she seems to think it may have something to do with the recent murders. She's just finished with a customer. Ah … here she is.' He lifted his hand to encourage the young lady to come to him. 'Miss Matthews, these officers are here to speak with you. Take them to the office. Be as quick as you can, please, we're rather busy today.'

'I'm sorry, Mr Gately,' said Peter, 'but I'm afraid we won't necessarily be quick. We need all the information Miss Matthews has to tell us, no matter how long it takes.'

'Okay, officer,' Gately said a little grudgingly, and he turned and walked away.

Samantha Matthews was a young woman, dark hair tied back in a long plait with just enough make-up to enhance her pretty face. She was smartly dressed in the same style of navy blue uniform like the other two young workers in the store.

'This way,' she said. 'It's the door on the left.'

As they moved into the spartan room, furnished with just a desk and a few chairs, Peter held out his hand and put her at her ease with a friendly greeting.

She sat down on the nearest chair, her hands moving nervously in her lap. 'It was when I heard it on television last night.' She spoke well and her voice was clear. 'The "Peach Stone Murderer", I think they called him.' She hesitated nervously. 'There's a man who came in here a lot of times and just bought peaches, he was very fussy and took ages to choose the ones he wanted. I used to watch him at first because I thought he was trying to steal them. But he wasn't, he was just very fussy.'

'When you say "a lot of times", how often do you mean?' Peter asked.

'He would come in at least four times a week. I remember once he came in every day I was here. I worked six days in a row because we were short-staffed.'

'Did he buy anything else?' said Peter.

'No, that's what was so weird. Nothing else, just peaches.'

'What sort of person was he?'

'Well …' She hesitated for a moment. 'He was really very nice, always smart, and was tall, and good-looking I'd say.' She let out an embarrassed giggle. 'You know what I mean. He didn't speak very much, but always said good morning to me, which was nice because not many customers do that.' She paused, her eyebrows drawing together slightly. 'But I must say he was very fussy about the peaches. Some days he just looked at the peaches and left. Once, I asked him not to touch the peaches so much. At first, he looked a bit angry, but then he sort of smiled and said, *'I'm sorry, I won't do it again.'* She looked at Peter. 'He was just really nice, until …' she stopped and gave a nervous cough.

'Until what, Miss Matthews?' Peter gently pushed.

'It was the last time he came in. He spent even longer choosing his peaches this time. We'd had a fresh delivery so I thought he'd be a lot quicker.'

'What happened this time that was different? I know it can be difficult remembering everything,' Peter said and gave her an encouraging smile.

'When he came to the checkout, I said to him, *"They're lovely fresh peaches today, Sir, who's the lucky person you're buying them for?"* She looked down at her hands resting in her lap.

'Did he answer you?' Peter waited while she retrieved a handkerchief from the pocket of her uniform.

'Not really. He just stared at me, a horrible stare. Horrible, his whole face changed. It was far worse than before when I asked him not to touch the peaches. As he gave me the money he snatched the bag of peaches from me.' She shuddered. 'He snarled at me as he went out of the door.'

Peter tried to picture the man described by Miss Matthews. Snarling is harsh, and it's certainly made an impression on her, he thought. 'What do you mean when you say he snarled at you? Did he say anything?' he said.

'I think he said something like *"How dare you!"* His mouth was only just open and his teeth were clenched. And the look in his eyes, well … I've never seen such hatred, never. He was so angry and … and … well, as I said, *snarly*. He looked so different, didn't seem to be the same man. He was just … horrible.'

'You were obviously shocked by his actions. Did you feel anything else about him?' said Peter, raising his voice slightly.

'I was shocked, he'd always been so nice, and I thought I was only being friendly to him. He was just … so strange,' she said, and she shuddered again. 'I suppose I felt a bit frightened because of the way he was looking at me.'

'When was this? Asked Peter.

She hesitated. 'Not sure really, but I think about two weeks ago.'

'Has he been in here since?' said Peter.

'No, I haven't seen him at all since then.'

'Would you recognise him again?'

'I'm not sure.' She hesitated. 'But, yes, I think I would.'

'Is there anything else you can remember, Miss Matthews?'

'No, I'm sorry, that's all.'

'You told us that he came in a lot, I think you said sometimes four times a week. Yet you've only just rung the police to enquire about the Peach Stone Murderer. Did you not have any thoughts about that before?'

'Yes, I thought it was strange. I've never known anyone to buy so many peaches, be so fussy and not buy anything else.' She shifted in her chair nervously. 'But he was so nice I just couldn't see that he would be anyone like that. But then … he was so nasty when I asked who they were for and, well … his face was really ugly and he looked at me as though he hated me. It was horrible, he was like a different person. It was only then I thought I should call the police.' She shivered. 'Have I done something wrong?' she said, as she wiped her mouth with the back of her hand, looking Peter and Hughes each in turn.

'No, of course not,' said Peter. 'I'm very glad you called now. Can you remember what he was wearing, or if he wore the same clothes each time he came into the store?'

'We see so many people every day, hundreds, we don't notice what they wear. I'm sorry, I really don't know what he wore at any time. I just remember he always looked smart.'

'Don't worry, Miss Matthews, you're being very helpful. It would also be a great help if you could come to the station so that our police artist could make a sketch of the man from your description.'

She looked at Peter, her eyes wide. 'Do you think he's the Peach Stone Murderer?'

'We have lots of enquiries to make before we can make any assumptions, but your information is very helpful. Let's get you to the station. If our artist can make a good likeness from your description it could prove to be just what we're looking for.'

Gately arrived at the door. 'Excuse me, Sir. Are you likely to be much longer? We're getting busy now.'

'They want me to go to the police station so that I can give their police artist a description of the man I told you about,' said Samantha.

Gately turned to face Peter and Hughes. 'I would like to help you as much as I can, officers, but I'm sorry, I can't let Miss Matthews go now.' He turned to point through the opened door. 'As you can see, we're very busy. Two staff members haven't turned up.' He turned back. 'I'll be happy to bring her to you after we close at six o'clock this evening.' He turned to Miss Matthews. 'Please hurry, Samantha. We need you, now.'

Peter held up his hand. 'I'm also sorry, Mr Gately, but we have a serious murder enquiry going on, which is far more important than your shop being busy and the need for Miss Matthews to be here. Furthermore, there is someone brutally murdering people in this area. I do hope you understand that it is our responsibility to keep people safe, which of course includes your customers.'

'I understand, Inspector, and I can assure you that Miss Matthews and I will be only too pleased to help as much as possible. But, as you can see,' he repeated abruptly, 'we are extremely busy. Miss Matthews is employed by me, not you or the police, and she is needed here, right now.' He pushed the young woman lightly on the shoulder. 'Please go, Miss Matthews. Aisle six is not manned and customers are getting annoyed because of the queues.' He turned to see Peter raising his hand again, but ignored him. 'As I said earlier, Inspector, I will bring the young lady to the police station myself after the evening staff arrive at 6.00 pm. I assume you will be there to speak to her?' He turned to walk away.

'Whoa ... Mr Gately. I sorry, it doesn't work like that. Miss Matthews may have seen the killer. Her description may well be the vital link we need to catch what is probably one of the most brutal murderers we have encountered for a long time. You have no jurisdiction over whether she can stay here or not. I have no option but to insist that the young lady come with us. *Now.*'

Gately turned quickly to face Peter, his hands curled into a fist but held tight to his sides. 'You may have missed what I said.' He glared at Peter. 'Miss Matthews is employed by me.' He brought a closed right hand to his chest. 'Me ... for this company. I say what she does, not you, or the police. He made to touch the woman's shoulder again.

Peter nodded to Hughes, who moved swiftly in front of Gately.

'Sorry, sir,' said Peter. 'I appreciate your need to keep the young lady, but our need overshadows yours. I am afraid you have no right whatsoever to keep her here when such a high profile case needs her input immediately. We will take her to the station now. I assure you that she will be returned to her work as soon as possible. It may be too late for today, in which case we will escort the young lady home.' He looked at Hughes. 'Officer, please take Miss Matthews to the car now.'

Gately looked at Peter. 'How dare you give me orders? This is not the last you'll hear from me. Give me your card. I will certainly telephone your superior about your behaviour.' He continued to glare at Peter, before taking his card and stalking out of the office.

Hughes was standing on his own. 'Miss Matthews has just gone to get her coat, she'll be here in a moment. Do you think the peach-buyer is our killer?'

'If we're still allowed to have a hunch, then I think he could be. Let's go through your notes when we get back and report to Chief Inspector Trent, and arrange for our talented artist to listen to what this young lady has to say when she describes him.'

Samantha Matthews arrived at the office door. 'I'm ready,' she said, 'but I'm a bit nervous.'

'Totally understandable,' said Peter.

✳✳✳

'Miss Matthews, please take a seat.' Peter smiled at the nervous young woman in front of him as she sat swiftly on the chair facing him. 'You'll like our artist. He's very good at what he does and will put your mind at rest very quickly.'

She smiled as she looked down at her hands.

There was a sharp knock at the door, and a young, rather untidy young man opened it halfway.

'Right, I'm ready, Sir. Can I take this lovely young lady with me now? I'm all set up and raring to go.' He held out his hand to her. She rose slowly and he guided her through the door.

CHAPTER THIRTY-FIVE

He was angry. Very angry.

How dare that stupid bitch ask why I bought so many peaches? How dare she ask who I was buying them for? What the hell was it to do with her? I shouldn't have been friendly to that stupid woman. It was a mistake.

He didn't like mistakes.

The key turned in the lock easily and he felt the warmth of his home easing his temper slightly. Walking to the kitchen, he threw the bag of twelve fresh peaches into the waste bin. Tears of anger rolled down his cheeks, his longing for the taste of the fruit gone, but his search for the last two perfect stones not yet complete. *Thanks to that stupid vile woman.* Although he felt uneasy in his anger he knew he could buy more peaches from somewhere else soon, and that he would never have the same question asked again.

He woke refreshed from a short, deep sleep and went to the large black leather box in the corner of the room. He glanced up at the photos on the wall, all pinned at the top in the middle, allowing the edges to curl slightly. He touched the photo of James Williamson taken almost two years earlier, now with a thick red cross crudely covering most of his face. He drew his fingers across the face and sniggered.

Next to the photo of Williamson was one of Lynn Moore, her smile happy and relaxed, but distorted by an even thicker red cross. He touched the picture carefully, pressing his thumb hard on the side of her face, laughing as he brought his fingers to his mouth, carefully licking off the slimy dust from the picture. He had never found a picture of Jonnie French. He told himself he didn't need one. After all the man was so filthy and ugly, he wouldn't have a place for it. His laugh faded as he made himself glance at a third picture. *I will have to wait a bit longer now,* he thought.

His anger returned as he thought again of his mistake. He hit the wall with his fist and closed his eyes as the pain in his hand registered. Turning, he opened the box and took out the largest of the long-bladed knives, carefully and slowly removing its soft leather cover. The blade was as long as a machete, and as sharp as a surgeon's scalpel. He caressed it, putting the blade close to his lips, feeling his blood warming as the thinnest sharp edge caressed his lip. *Perfect, just perfect,* he thought as he stroked the handle of the knife, replaced the leather sheath and threw it back into the box, slamming the lid shut.

'Unfortunately, thanks to that bitch,' he snarled, 'I don't have your partner in murder.'

His search for peaches lasted two more days and took him to several shops, his quest ending with peaches from three shops, all bought, as usual, with care and attention to size, colour, and feel. He had eighteen, he only needed two to be perfect.

It took six days to eat the peaches. Although every bite was hateful, he just had to eat them. After he'd tasted the flesh and swallowed the juice of each one, he carefully washed and placed the stones exactly one inch apart on the shelf.

He studied each one, touching and turning them until he found the one he was looking for. He held it against the perfect stone he already had. It matched it in every detail. He was exhilarated, and happy again.

Gathering the redundant stones, he swept them into a plastic bag, ready for disposal the next day.

He slept deeply that night, but woke twice, crying for his mother.

CHAPTER THIRTY-SIX

Two women in their early thirties hurried towards the doors of the spa, their high-heels clicking sharply on the smooth tiled path to the steps.

'First, break for months, and it's spoilt by this,' muttered the first woman. 'He's had it this time.' Her voice was loud and angry. 'I'm fed up with his moaning, his bad moods, not to mention his rude and arrogant manner with our clients.'

A young man came up to them wearing blue overalls with a bright yellow 'HSP' across the front, and 'Hygiene for Swimming Pools' written underneath the bold initials. 'Good afternoon. I'm so sorry to have called, Miss Nicholls, but your man has not answered the door all morning.

Taking keys out of her handbag, Amanda Nicholls opened the door leading into the reception area. 'Sorry, I didn't catch your name?' she said.

'Jason Caruthers, Miss Nicholls.'

'Come with me, Caruthers. I'll take you to the pool. I would hope there's more than just you, to get the job done properly?' She turned to the woman with her. 'Please stay here, Kathy. Let's hope more people come soon.'

'A team will be here as soon as we're ready to start,' said Caruthers.

They walked along the corridor leading to the first swimming pool.

'This place is still filthy. French has not been doing his job at all.' She felt satisfied that she now had the justification needed to get rid of the horrible man. 'Leaving my spa in this dreadful state is surely gross misconduct, not to mention the ghastly smell.'

She opened the door to the main swimming pool. 'This door is not just dirty, it looks disgusting.' She peered at the door, her face almost touching it. 'Look, I think that's blood on it.' She stepped back. 'What on earth was that man doing? Nothing seems to have been cleaned at all, nothing ... it should be spotless!'

The pool was dark, with a smell of wet flesh and body odour. Nicholls took a towel from a hanger and held it to her face, then took a small step forward and raised her hand to put the light on.

Caruthers put up his hand to stop her. 'Wait ... wait, Miss Nicholls, let me do it. Something's very wrong in here, I've never known a swimming pool to smell like this.'

She lowered her hand and he ushered her behind him.

At a flick of a switch, the lights came on.

She pushed past him and stopped, her mouth open wide. 'What the hell?' Her legs wobbled and she sank to her knees on the wet black tiles. She tried to scream, but nothing came out. She looked up at Caruthers, who was standing still taking in the scene them. 'What's happened here? What's going on?' Her voice was a shaky whisper.

Caruthers made no move, nor attempt to answer her questions.

She tried to move her legs so she could stand, but the effort was too much.

A large area of tiles was covered in watery blood. The body of a man was floating face down at one end of the pool. Blood had clearly washed from his clothes, leaving wet pink cloth sticking to his torso. Further along in the water, there was an arm, floating and bobbing gently up and down on the soft moving water. Further on, another arm was close to the edge of the shallow end of the pool, banging gently against the side.

'What on earth is going on? The smell, it's just disgusting,' she said. She retched, but only pain filled her throat. 'I can't bear it. What's happened here?' She stared, open-mouthed at the scene. 'It is ... it is.' Her voice a whisper. 'It's him, it's Jonnie French, and someone's killed him.' Hysterical sobs wracked her body.

Caruthers pulled out his mobile and dialled 999.

CHAPTER THIRTY-SEVEN

The team listened to Peter's account of the interview with Samantha Matthews at the supermarket. There was a sense of anticipation in the air, things were starting to come together and the buzz made Jenny raise her hand.

'Before we get too excited, let's remember we're not there yet.'

A groan from Eddie Callam sounded as the room became quiet again.

'Eddie.' Jenny looked at him. The young officer blushed and stood up. 'Eddie, you seem disappointed.'

'Well, Ma'am, over the last few days we've ascertained that both the victims went to the same school, even though it was a long time ago.' He looked apologetically at Jenny. 'We also know that you went to the same school, and that's why you were warned when your dog was attacked. In spite of what they said at the school, we know that there was bullying going on.' He took a deep breath. 'And now we can assume that the murderer is local because he shops in a local store to buy peaches. I just think we're doing better now, that's all.' After a short pause, he sat down to a smattering of applause that made him blush even more than usual.

'Eddie. You are quite right, and yes, we're doing much better. It's good to be reminded now and again, thank you,' said Jenny. She liked the young officer, with a bit of encouragement and a lot more training he could become another valuable member of her team.

She tried to smile as she spoke. She remembered how Jonathan had been in these situations. He had been so good at spotting promising young officers, and had made it a priority to mentor and encourage their talents. He'd have instantly spotted Eddie's potential. Maybe she could continue her husband's legacy by continuing to help this young officer. Yes, he's like that. She quickly turned her attention back to the faces in front of her.

'Right then, a few more questions and answers, please.' She waited again for the room to quieten.

'Has anyone found Jonnie French yet?'

A hand went up.

'Nothing yet, Ma'am, but the data boys are still looking. There's no one of that name with a criminal record, anyway.'

'Fine, keep pestering. What about Einstein Luther Smith, who was looking into his whereabouts?'

Another hand shot up.

'We know that he went to Aberdeen University and gained a first in medicine. At the moment that's it, apart from one thing.'

'What do you mean?' Jenny said.

'Well, it could be that he's changed his name since then. We're searching electoral rolls across the country, and the records of the UK Deed Poll Service to see if anything crops up. With a name like Einstein Luther Smith, it shouldn't take that long.'

'Good work. As soon as you have anything, speak to me immediately.'

Just as she was about to close the meeting, PC Spencer came in with a note in her hand. 'Ma'am, Bedfordshire Police want to talk to you immediately. They said it was urgent, but wouldn't tell me what it was about, except to say that they've found Jonnie French. The call is being put through to your office now.'

A murmur went round the room.

'I'd like everyone to stay until I come back.' Jenny walked quickly to her office. 'Good afternoon, Chief Inspector Trent here. I understand you want to talk to me about Jonnie French.'

'DCI Bellingham here, Chief Inspector. We've found him.' The line went quiet for a moment. 'I am afraid he's been found murdered.'

Jenny felt her blood go cold. 'How was he killed?'

'He worked at one of those posh spa places. I think he was a swimming coach. The owners were called because a pool-hygiene company couldn't get in. It sounds pretty gruesome.' He took a quick breath. 'He was found in the swimming pool, both his arms had been cut off and were floating in the pool with him.'

'It sounds like our killer has found his third victim.' Jenny sighed. 'What's the situation now?'

'Our forensics team and SOCO are at the pool, but because of the similarities between this and the scenes with your victims in Sussex, we'd like your senior forensic chap to come and assist us. Would that be possible?'

'I'm sure it would be. I'll contact him. It will be Dr Ben Seldon or, if he's not available, his assistant Dr Andrew Baines.'

'Thank you, I look forward to hearing from you,' said Bellingham.

The line went dead. Jenny sat down heavily in her chair.

After a knock on the door, Peter walked in. 'Is it bad news, Jenny?'

'Bedfordshire Police have found Jonnie French's body in a swimming pool.' She sighed. 'Both his arms have been chopped off.'

'That's his third tormentor killed, what next?'

'We have to update the team. And they want Ben to go there to assist in the forensics investigation.'

As Jenny returned the incident room she felt all eyes on her. She told her team the news she had just received.

'Was there a peach stone in his throat?' someone said.

'Forensics are there now. We don't know the full details yet, but we can be pretty sure it's our murderer. They've asked Dr Seldon to assist them.'

She turned to Peter. 'Can you please find Ben? And obviously, we need to know who or where Mr Einstein Luther Smith is, and we need to find out quickly. Keep me informed with any updates immediately. No matter what time of day it is.'

Jenny walked abruptly from the incident room towards Morgan-Jones's office. She knocked loudly at the door and waited for the instruction to enter. There was no reply, so she pulled her phone from her pocket. He answered immediately.

'Good afternoon, Jenny, you must have some news for me.'

She told him the details.

'Get Ben there fast,' he said.

'We are already arranging that, Sir.'

'Good.' The line went quiet for a short time. 'Jenny, I want you in my office first thing in the morning. I would come over now, but I am heavily tied up.'

'I was just about to go down to speak to Mickey and Sam, I want to find out where Einstein Luther Smith is. I'm certain he's our killer.'

'I doubt if Mickey or Sam will be there now. See me in my office first thing tomorrow.' The line went dead before she could respond.

At the reception desk, the duty officer was discussing the case with the officers getting ready for the night shift.

She stopped to remind them to call her if there was any new information at all. 'Even if it's the middle of the night, call me.'

'Of course, Ma'am.'

As she reached the doors, Peter met her. 'Ben is away at a conference, so Andrew Baines has left to go to Bedford.'

'Do you know if Mickey and Sam are still in data recovery?' Jenny said.

'No, I saw them leaving about thirty minutes ago.'

'Never mind, I'll see them as soon as I can in the morning. Peter, do you fancy a drink?' She suddenly realised how badly she needed to relax, a large vodka and coke with lots of ice seemed remarkably inviting.

'A quick one would be nice.'

The Red Bull was unusually quiet. 'It's my shout this time, Peter. Find a table and I'll be with you.' She arrived with two drinks in hand and sat down opposite him. 'You look either tired or thoughtful, which is it?' Jenny tried to be light-hearted. She took a sip of her drink.

'A bit of both, I'm afraid. I'm tired of wondering how my marriage is going to carry on,' he looked past Jenny. 'Or not ... Maggie is still with her parents and her mother has told me she's not happy.' He looked hopelessly at Jenny. 'But she just won't talk to me, except to say I should know what I have to do. She has raised the stakes and time doesn't seem to be on my side.'

'And do you know what you have to do?'

'Yes, I think I do.' He stared into his glass. 'But I not sure that I can do what I think she wants me to do.'

'Peter,' Jenny's voice rose and Peter looked directly at her. 'This job can be one of the hardest, loneliest and most gruesome jobs in the world. It's difficult for families, especially for families with children. Sometimes it's too much, and you have to stand back and decide what to do. You put everything into your work, Peter, perhaps everything is too much.'

'Once we've cracked this one, Jenny, I'll step back and look at what I need to do.' He took a deep breath. 'I just hope Maggie can wait a bit longer.' He gave Jenny a brief smile. 'Whatever I do, Jenny, I do hope we can still be friends.'

Jenny smiled back as she put a hand over his and pressed gently. 'No need to ask, Peter.'

CHAPTER THIRTY-EIGHT

As Jenny arrived at the station she was met by the duty sergeant.

'Good morning, Ma'am. Dr Baines telephoned and asked you to contact him as soon as you came in. It seemed urgent.' He handed her a note with a telephone number on it. 'He said he's not on his normal number and to use this one.'

'Thank you, Sergeant, I'll call him immediately.'

As she reached her office, the phone was already ringing.

'I have Dr Baines on the line, Ma'am, I told him you were in.'

'Put him through, please.'

'Good morning, Jenny.' His voice was light and cheerful. 'Hope I haven't got you too early. I thought you'd like to know that the autopsy has already started and the similarities to the attacks on the other two victims are evident.'

'Was there a peach stone in his throat?' said Jenny.

'No, but there were some pretty deep scratches on the inside of his mouth leading to the throat, so it looks as though something had been pushed into his mouth at some point.'

'What's happening now, then? I have to make a report to Morgan-Jones very shortly and I need as much information as possible.'

'The spa is closed off and the pool where the attack took place is still being searched. They haven't emptied it yet because they're still hopeful of finding evidence in the water. Trouble is, water and chlorine are great cleansers, and a lot of the evidence has probably disappeared already.'

'Thanks, Andrew.' As Jenny put down the phone it rang again almost immediately, she recognised Morgan-Jones's number and gave a brief sigh.

'Glad you're in early Jenny. Can you come and see me right away.' Without waiting for a response, he hung up.

At least I've got something to tell him, she thought, in spite of his abrupt, rude manner.

As she entered Morgan-Jones's office, he was already pulling a chair out from the desk, and he gestured for her to sit down. 'I understand you've had a call from Baines this morning, what did he have to say?'

She carefully repeated the conversation she had had with Andrew.

'I have a meeting with the Chief Constable of West Sussex in about an hour, Jenny. Can you please give me a verbal report on where we are with the investigation at this precise moment? I'll have to tell him we have yet another body, therefore it's vital I can give him information that you and your team are at least getting nearer to understanding the why, how and whom of these murders. I'm assuming we know the how. The autopsy report is pretty graphic.' His tone was not missed by Jenny. He was under pressure and making sure she knew it.

'It's obvious that all three murders are connected,' said Jenny. 'All the victims went to the same school. From the interviews we've carried out so far, it seems that the three victims consistently bullied a boy attending the same school. The school did nothing to stop the bullying and in fact, tried to deny that any such activity took place. There was also a sex scandal which was hushed up, so the school doesn't come out of this very well.'

Morgan-Jones raised his hand to stop her. 'We've already had a call from the headmaster, a Dr McAllister, I believe? The press has been hard on him and it seems that parents are questioning the integrity of the school and are already talking about removing their children. He's not very pleased about your visit, Jenny, and is threatening some sort of investigation into your approach. Anyway, I am not concerned about that, but thought you should know about it.'

'I'm not surprised he's upset,' Jenny replied. 'If the school had taken action when the bullying started, these murders might not have been committed.'

'You were at the school, Jenny, and the attack on your dog indicated that you might have been involved. Can you remember anything about bullying?' said Morgan-Jones.

'I was definitely not involved in any bullying. However, I do remember coming across the same boy in trouble. Once he was locked in a cupboard. I heard him shouting and screaming, I unlocked the door and let him out. He was in a terrible state, shaking and crying. I wanted to report it, but he wouldn't let or take any action at all. In fact, he pleaded with me. In another incident I found the same boy running on the playing field and another boy was hitting him on the legs with what looked like a very heavy stick. When I shouted and ran towards them he ran off. The boy's legs were bleeding badly, he was shaking with fear, scared and frightened, but again he wouldn't let me do anything about it. And there was the time was in the swimming pool when he was being made fun of because he couldn't swim. A tall strong-looking boy was shouting at him repeatedly. It really was awful, many of the students were joining in. The sports master wasn't stopping them, in fact, I was shocked to hear him joining in with them. I got very angry with him and told him to get the boy out of the water, which he did.'

'Was anything done about it?'

'Not that I know of,' said Jenny.

'Did you report it further?'

'No, I didn't.'

'What was the boy's name?'

He had a strange name, Einstein Luther Smith. After the meeting with the headmaster, as driving out, we were stopped by the gardener jumping out in front of us. We managed to stop and he said he'd been keeping an eye on the boy and his name was Einstein Luther Smith. He told us that he's been bullied a lot and that no one had stopped it. It seemed that he felt very sorry for the boy.

Morgan-Jones swung round in his chair, rose and walked slowly to the window. 'I want you off the case, Jenny. I told you I would take you off it if there was any danger to you.' He turned to face her. 'I now think there is, and I don't want to take the chance of anything happening to you. Can you imagine what a field day the press would have if a Detective Chief Inspector got attacked, or even worse?' He stopped Jenny from answering. 'It seems to me that he is killing off his tormentors, and he's doing so in a way that relates to the bullying he received from them. He could be targeting you next because he believes you did nothing to help.' He paused for a second. 'The note he put inside your dog's collar said you weren't trying hard enough. I think you're the next one on his list, Jenny, and I can't afford to take that risk.'

Jenny met his eyes and blinked back an angry response. 'Sir, I just can't come off it now. It would upset the flow of our investigation, which is just starting to come together. We'll lose a lot of time, and time will give him just what he wants.'

Morgan-Jones sank heavily into his chair.

Jenny continued. 'We haven't been able to trace Einstein Luther Smith yet. We suspect he changed his name and we have Mickey and Sam looking into that. I would like another week, Sir.' Her eyes met his. 'Please.'

The silence lasted for a full minute. 'You have one week, Jenny.'

'Thank you, Sir, I won't let you down.' She rose from her chair with a determined shake of her head and walked towards the door.

'I know you won't, Jenny,' said Morgan-Jones, and he gave a brief smile.

Peter met Jenny as she walked towards her office. 'Mickey and Sam called. They want to see you as soon as you're free, shall we go now?'

'Yes, we need to get a move on. Morgan-Jones wants me off the case. Thinks I'm in danger. We have one more week.'

Peter stopped, ready to say something, but didn't.

They headed quickly along the corridor towards the stairs leading to the data recovery unit.

'He could be right, Jenny. I'm sure that's crossed your mind.'

'Yes, it has, but only briefly. She stopped on the stairs and turned to look at Peter who was a few steps behind her. 'If we don't clear this up, I'm off the case. Morgan-Jones is getting pissed off, to say the least. Not sure if he's really worried about my safety, or his reputation if anything happens to me. Probably both.'

They reached 'data recovery' and Mickey raised a hand in welcome.

'Hi, you two. Before we start on our Einstein, we did a bit of digging and have some information about the death of his mother. The autopsy revealed that there was bruising around her mouth, but reported that it was likely to have been caused by the husband trying to get the peach stone out of her throat. Strange coincidence though, don't you think?'

'I don't think it's quite so strange now,' said Peter. 'Looks like his revenge issues could go back a long way. Quite possible to his mother, after all giving a child such a ridiculous name was surely asking for trouble for a young lad at school.

'Thanks for that, Mickey,' said Jenny. 'Every bit of information is very welcome at this stage. What have you got for us on the name situation so far?'

'Sorry it took a bit longer than you wanted, but we had to send off a declaration form for data use and only received the authorisation today. Even the police don't have authority over the Data Protection Act.' He opened a plastic folder on the desk in front of Jenny and took out several sheets of printed paper.

'Do you want the good news or the bad news first, Chief Inspector?'

'At the moment any news is good news, Mickey.'

'Your Einstein Luther Smith changed his name by deed poll in September 1998.'

Peter looked at Jenny. 'We could be getting somewhere,' he said.

Mickey raised his hand. 'Now, the bad news. He changed his name to John Smith. And yes, it's still one of the most common names in the country. And, believe it or not, a lot of people change their names to John Smith.' He stared at Jenny over the top of the sheet he was reading from. 'A lot of digging still to do, Chief Inspector.'

Jenny sat back in her chair as Peter put his hands to his head and groaned.

'We're still making enquires,' said Mickey, but anyone can change their name as long as it's not for a criminal reason and, not only once, but as many times as they like. They don't even have to do it legally, they just have to be known by whatever name they choose, and so, although he was a John Smith at some point, he could be anyone now. I've spoken with someone at the Deed Poll Service and they're making their own enquires for us.'

'Don't people change their names *from* John Smith rather than *to* John Smith?' said Peter.

'You would have thought so,' Mickey replied helpfully. 'But it doesn't seem to have worked that way in the case of our Mr Einstein Luther Smith. Although, he may have wanted a very ordinary, if not common, name after the one his parents gave him.'

'What's the next step then?' Jenny couldn't hide her disappointment as she asked the question.

'We just keep digging. It's what we do. Sorry, we can't be more helpful at this stage.'

'Why didn't the police look more into his mother's death?' said Jenny.

'Because they believed she swallowed the peach stone accidentally and there was no evidence to suggest otherwise. Her husband and son were unable to release it in time.'

'Thanks, Mickey. We don't have a lot of time, keep looking and let me know immediately if you come up with anything.'

Mickey touched his head in a loose salute. 'Will do, Chief Inspector, but we need a bit of luck on this one, I think.'

✳✳✳

Just as they reached the main office, Jenny's telephone was already ringing. It was Andrew.

'Hello, Jenny. I've just heard from the chaps at the spa. They've found a peach stone and are bringing it to me now, but I doubt there will be any evidence on it. Too much water and chlorine.'

'Not really much help, then,' said Jenny.

'Only that we can be reasonably certain it's the same person who killed him. It's just that the peach stone didn't cause the death this time, but it played a part in it.'

'What do you mean by that?'

'The first two victims had a peach stone pushed into their throat so far that it choked them to death. From what you've uncovered elsewhere, it seems likely that their other injuries were significantly related to instances of bullying that the suspect experienced at school.' He waited for a response from Jenny, but she was quiet. 'The brutality is a common factor in each case, as is the peach stone, but in this case, the victim obviously managed to spit it out, there are scratches in his mouth,' said Andrew.

'Thank you. How long will you be there now?'

'I'm nearly done. Mr French was in good health up to the point of his death. Doesn't seem to have any family. Apart from the people at the spa who have already identified him, there doesn't seem to be anyone else we should be contacting.'

'We'll look forward to seeing you again, Andrew, take care.'

'Thank you, Jenny. Perhaps we can have another meal soon.'

'That would be very nice. I'll look forward to it, call me as soon as you're back.'

She replaced the phone into her pocket.

'Peter, we need to make a visit to Broomleigh to talk to the gardener again,' she said. 'Can you arrange it, please? This time I want Dr McAllister to know that we want to talk to him and to the gardener. If we can go immediately we can see them both as soon as possible today.'

'I'll get on to it immediately.'

Ten minutes later Peter returned to Jenny's office.

'He said if we can get there by four o'clock he can see us then. He's not very happy though and wants to have his solicitor with him. He also wants him to be there when you interview his gardener.'

'I'm sure he's not happy. His school is falling to pieces around him. Fortunately for him, it's not his fault. When you get back to him, can you ask him if he has the telephone number of Dr Brian Cook, he was the headmaster when I was there. It might be useful to talk to him if we can. Did McAllister give you the name of the gardener?'

'No, but I'll get it from him when I call back.' Peter walked towards the door. Holding on to the door handle, he turned to face Jenny. 'Something's bugging you, Jenny, I know the signs.'

'You know me well, Peter.' She smiled as he closed the door behind him.

CHAPTER THIRTY-NINE

The drive to Broomleigh School was warm and sticky. The usual mayhem on the M25 was made worse by the inevitable roadworks, and an overturned lorry. They were relieved to arrive in Bedford in time to get a coffee and a break to freshen up.

'I'll let you do the talking this time, Peter. McAllister might be a bit more open with someone different asking the questions,' Jenny said. 'And let's try the gardener together.'

'That's fine,' said Peter.

When they finally arrived at the school, Dr McAllister was standing on the steps waiting for them.

'Good afternoon, Chief Inspector.' He turned and nodded to Peter. 'Please come through.' He didn't offer his hand in greeting.

'This is a very nasty business, I can tell you.' The friendly voice from their previous visit was absent. 'As I have already told you, I have asked my solicitor to attend both meetings. The press have been very aggressive in their accusations about the school so, if you don't mind, I want everything said in my office recorded properly.'

'We have no objection to your solicitor being present, headmaster,' said Jenny, recognising the hostility in his tone. *There's no doubt he would rather we weren't making more enquires,* she thought.

Dr McAllister opened the door of his office and a tall man with thinning hair and thick glasses turned from the window to greet them.

'This is Mr Clive Robertson from Robertson and Brown, the school's Solicitors,' McAllister said. He introduced Jenny and Peter and gestured for them to take the two seats facing him and the solicitor.

'When we met last time, I thought I told you everything. However, the press seems to have speculated widely about our involvement in this ghastly situation.' McAllister looked at Jenny and Peter. 'I don't know how I can help you any further. Perhaps one of you can tell me what's going on.'

'Before I answer that, headmaster, did you manage to find Dr Brian Cook's telephone number?' said Peter as they sat down.

'I'm afraid not. It has been some years now and no one seems to have kept in touch with him. One of my staff mentioned that she thought he had gone to Canada.'

'Thank you.' Peter placed a thick folder on the desk in front of him. 'I'm not sure what you've read in the newspapers, but there was a lot you didn't tell us the last time we spoke. Information which has a huge bearing on the case we're investigating.'

McAllister shifted in his chair. 'If you're talking about something the gardener said, he was quite out of order. It had nothing to do with him.' He glanced at Robertson for support.

'You know how things can get blown out of all proportion, Inspector,' said Robertson. 'The gardener can hardly be called a reliable source. He finds it hard to put two words together, let alone make any sort of judgement.'

'He has already put quite a few words together, Mr Robertson. I can assure you that what the gardener told us was a great help in furthering our enquiries.'

'I see,' said Robertson.

'Headmaster.' Peter looked directly at McAllister. 'We don't think you are aware that another person has been murdered, also a past pupil at this school. We, therefore believe that the three people who have been murdered were killed by the same person and that that person was also a student at this school.' He paused.

McAllister took a white handkerchief from his pocket and blew his nose noisily. Wiping his handkerchief across his face, he shifted uncomfortably in his chair. 'That's all been well published in the newspapers. It was a shock to me, I can tell you. And I knew nothing about any bullying.'

His solicitor touched his arm and he shut up immediately.

'Well, then, it's clear that your gardener knows a lot more than you do, Dr McAllister.' said Peter, He could feel his frustration creeping up.

Robertson held up his hand. 'Exactly where are we going with this, Inspector? Gardeners, cleaners and the like always gossip about what's going on, and you know that most of it is a load of hogwash, not to be taken at all seriously.'

'James Williamson, Lynn Moore, and Jonnie French were all brutally murdered, Mr Robertson,' said Peter, calmly. 'While you may not have any particular feeling about that, the families of these three people will have deep and very upsetting feelings.' Robertson didn't move. 'There was a reason for the murders, and the reason that seems obvious to us is revenge for bullying that took place at this school. Mostly in front of people that should have stopped it, but didn't. It wasn't playful, it was sadistic and cruel, and very serious. Even you must agree with that.'

McAllister rose abruptly from his chair. 'It all happened before my time, Inspector. I didn't come to the school until 2000 and I didn't meet Dr Cook. He left before I arrived at the school.' He glanced at his solicitor, who said nothing. 'I don't see how you can blame me for what happened before I arrived.' He sat down again.

'Did you have any reports of *any* bullying?' said Peter.

McAllister shook his head.

'Did any of the teachers who had been at the school at the time talk to you about anyone being bullied?'

'No.'

'But your gardener knew.'

'How would I know what the gardener knew? Isn't this questioning becoming a bit ridiculous? You'll be asking me what the butler saw soon!' He smirked, his solicitor glared at him.

'Do you even remember the name of Einstein Luther Smith?'

'It's not a name you would forget, but again, he left before I arrived at Broomleigh.'

'But you do recall his name being mentioned,' Peter pressed.

'Of course, not a name that's easily forgotten, nor was the unfortunate incident that I told you about with his mother. And when I was researching past student grades and university entrants I noticed that he was a clever student and went to the University of Aberdeen. But I've told you all of this.'

'He was the one that was bullied, headmaster.'

'Well, I'm glad he got over it and did well for himself.'

'That's the problem, he didn't. Everything points to the fact that he is the killer. It's also a fact that if Broomleigh House school had taken action to stop the bullying all those years ago we might not be sitting here asking you questions that you are reluctant to answer.'

Peter stood and moved closer to McAllister. 'And, three people would not have been brutally murdered.'

I don't think he cares a jot, Jenny thought.

McAllister stood up, his face was red with anger, his eyes wide.

'What are you insinuating, Inspector? Remember my solicitor is here and you will not be exempt from any legal action if the school suffers from any spurious allegations.'

Clive Robertson pulled at his client's arm and looked at Jenny. 'If you know who it is, why haven't you arrested him?'

'Because we can't find him. We believe he's changed his name,' she said.

'Before we talk to the gardener,' said Peter, 'is there anything else that you can tell us that might help us. Any small thing that might have come to your mind?'

McAllister glared at him. 'No! None at all. If you've finished with me, I have work to do.'

'One thing before you go, headmaster. What's the gardener's name? He left in rather a hurry after he'd spoken to us as we were leaving the school, and we didn't have a chance to ask his name. I think he was frightened of being caught talking to us.'

'Fred. Fred Elliott, he's waiting outside for you.' McAllister walked through the door and closed it quietly.

Peter rose from his chair and walked to the door. 'Are you ready for him, Ma'am?'

'Yes, unless Mr Robertson wants to ask us any questions before we speak to him.' She glanced enquiringly at the solicitor.

'Not at the moment,' he said, waving his hand impatiently.

Peter opened the door to Fred Elliott. Instead of the dirty overalls, he had worn when they last met, he was dressed in a smart, well-pressed suit.

He held out his hand as he saw Jenny and shook hers firmly.

'Nice to see you again, Miss.' He turned to Peter, taking his hand just as firmly. 'You too, Sir.'

He looked at Robertson. 'I already met 'im earlier.'

'Take a seat, Mr Elliott.' Peter pointed to the seat vacated by McAllister.

'Oh, please call me Fred. Everyone 'ere knows me as Fred.'

'Thank you, Fred. You remember when you spoke with us last time as we were leaving Broomleigh?' said Peter.

'Remember it well, Sir. Got into trouble for talking to you, too. Somebody saw me and told Dr McAllister. Thought I was gonna lose me job at first.'

Robertson coughed as he glared at Fred Elliott. 'Just answer the questions please, Mr Elliott.'

'Fred, can you tell us again about the boy that was bullied here some years ago? Anything that you can remember, no matter how trivial,' said Peter.

'There was nothing trivial about it, I can tell you. Poor little sod's life was made a misery by some of the other kids.'

'What happened to him?' asked Peter.

'Like I told you before, two boys and a girl took it upon 'emselves to bully him. I remember the girl screamed at him a lot. Really loud, screeching, seemed to hurt his ears, 'cause he was always 'olding them and looking as though he were crying.' He coughed noisily, before putting a hand over his mouth.

'One of the two boys used to yell at him to run, and once I saw him hitting him with a big stick on the legs. The other boy, the bigger one, made fun of him all the time, but mostly when he was in the swimming pool. I was cleaning one of the rooms once and I saw him yelling at him in front of everyone. He kept yelling at him, *"Use your arms, stupid,"* and called him stupid all the time. 'e had a birthmark on one of 'is arms. He got yelled at about that as well, poor bugger. No-one stopped it. Someone tried at the swimming pool once, but nuffin was done about it. I fink I told you that before.'

'Doesn't matter, Fred, sometimes just a little thing that was forgotten might come out when it's told again. Do you know why they were bullying him so much?' said, Peter.

'Not really, but could 'ave been because of his name, I wouldn't wonder. Why a mother gives a boy such a name. I dunno. Just asking for other kids to make fun of him, if you ask me.'

'Remind us of his name?' Peter prompted.

'Einstein … Einstein Lufer Smith. I ask you, what kinda name is that for a lad?' He thought for a second. 'Like I told you last time, me granddad 'ad a German shepherd dog called Einstein, booiful dog he were too, but a kid? Well, that's a lot different … giving a kid that name … just asking for trouble, if you ask me.'

'How did you know about all the bullying when no one else seemed to?'

'I suppose I just wanted to keep an eye on him, Sir. Felt sorry for him, so tried to be where he was if yer knows what I mean.' He stopped, and he tapped his head. 'I wasn't the only one who knew about it though. Lots did, but nuffin was done about it. You see, he wasn't really a very nice lad. Bit shifty, if you ask me.' He looked for a reaction from Peter. 'Didn't deserve the things that 'appened to him though.' He stopped.

'Did you report what you saw, Fred?' Peter said.

'Me … report it? Didn't 'ave to really. Lots of 'em knew about it. Anyway, I tried once and was told to get on wiv me gardening, so I did.'

'Who did you try to tell?' Peter said.

Fred thought for a few moments. 'Can't remember his name. Too long ago now, but he was the 'ousemaster.' He stopped to think again. 'Nope, can't remember his name,' he repeated.

'Is there anything else you remember?' Jenny pushed gently for more information. 'You told us some of this in the garden. I just want to make sure that you haven't forgotten anything.' *There's got to be more. We need more, much more, to give us the clues we're looking for.* She looked at Fred, and could almost feel the effort he was making to remember.

His fingers clicked as he lifted his hand to tap his nose with his finger. 'Got it! There was one thing … silly really. This Einstein kid, he used to bring a peach to school every day, every day I tell you. And every day these three kids used to pinch it from him. Yeah, every day. You 'ave to wonder why kept bringing 'em in, don't you.' He snorted as he looked down at his hands. 'The worst was when they threw the peach at the wall and made him lick it off. He had blood running down him. It was 'orrible, poor bugger. Couldn't tell anyone about it 'cause, as I said. I was frightened of losing 'me job. It was just by the fence near the sports ground. I was there, I knew that's where he was at lunchtimes, and most days when he came to school and the bell adn't gone off.'

'What about friends, did he have any?' said Jenny.

'Wouldn't know that, see it wasn't my place to mix with the kids. Got into trouble if I was found talking to 'em. Didn't stop me knowing what was going on though!' He touched his nose with his forefinger again.

'Did you ever see his parents, Fred?'

'Never saw 'em at all, but 'eard his mother died soon after he left the school. Somebody said she died 'cause a peach stone got stuck in her mouth.' He thought for a few seconds. 'Funny that, eh?' He sat back in his chair and sighed. 'I think 'e was a clever lad though. We did have a chat once when he was on his way home and I was working by the gate. Told me he was going to University. Aberdeen, I think. Couldn't wait to get away from 'ere.'

'Do you know if anyone heard from him again, Fred?'

'No, once they're gone they're gone if you know what I mean.'

Jenny looked towards Robertson. 'Do you have any questions for Mr Elliott, Mr Robertson?'

'I haven't come here to ask questions, Chief Inspector.'

'Thank you, Fred. You've been very helpful, you may go now.'

Fred rose from his chair. As he opened the door to go through he turned back to face Jenny.

'He really was a strange lad, you know. Not many people liked him. Good-looking though, and tall for his age. Shame really.' He passed through the door shaking his head. 'Poor sod!'

Jenny stood and held her hand out to Robertson. 'We've finished here for now. If we need to speak with Dr McAllister again, we'll contact him.'

'Have you found out anything more from this visit, or was it a waste of everyone's time, Chief Inspector?'

Jenny lowered her outstretched hand. 'We've learnt a lot from this visit, Mr Robertson. Most importantly, that Dr McAllister went to great lengths to hide the true nature of events that had taken place at this school, and that had he been more forthcoming at our previous meeting, the last murder may not have happened.'

Jenny and Peter moved towards the closed door. Jenny turned to face Robertson, who was collecting papers and files from the desk.

'I know that some of the younger members of staff who were at the school at the time of the bullying are still here,' she said. 'Because the reputation of the school was more important than the wellbeing of the children, they were probably told to ignore it. If the bullying had been stopped, three people wouldn't have been killed, Mr Robertson and a young boy's life wouldn't have been ruined by the need for an act of violent revenge. You will, I am sure, be aware of the term "suppression of evidence", Mr Robertson. It might be an idea to make Dr McAllister aware of it.'

Robertson pushed past Jenny and out of the office without replying.

***

When they got to the car, Peter clenched his fists as he raised them. 'Thank God the gardener remembered the peaches. I'd say we can be absolutely sure now that this Einstein bloke is definitely the killer. All we have to do is to find him.' He got into the car and looked across at Jenny, clicking his seat belt in place. 'Is there anything else that you remember? It was at the time you were here wasn't it?' He started the engine and slowly moved the car away from the school premises.

Jenny studied the countryside as she thought about her answer. 'That's why he's targeting me, Peter. I did know. I saw it happening, only twice, and although I tried to help, I didn't try hard enough to follow it through. What Fred has told us just cements what I saw. The note in Honey's collar said I wasn't trying hard enough. At least we know what all that means now.'

She looked out of the window again, her mind reliving the incidents from so long ago. 'I don't think he wants to kill me, but I think he wants to hurt me in some way.'

'If that's the case, then he's met his objectives apart from one, and that one is you. Morgan-Jones was quite right to want you off the case. You must step down, for your own safety.' Peter's voice was heavy with anxiety. 'Perhaps you should go away for a short time until this is over.'

'I'm not going anywhere. If I did, he'd find me. Whoever Einstein Luther Smith is now, I'm pretty sure he's close by. He knows every step we take and is waiting for the right time. If it takes me to draw him out, then so be it, we'll be ready for him. I need to talk to Mickey to see if he's found any hint of who our man is now.'

She leant back in her seat as she thought about the school she had enjoyed so much. How could a boy become so traumatised without someone doing something about it? They must have known about the bullying. There's more work to do, but things are definitely starting to fit together. No time to waste.

CHAPTER FORTY

Jenny arrived home still tired, even though she'd rested on the way back from Bedford. In order to avoid more questions from Peter, she had pretended to sleep most of the way, but her mind had been working, trying to remember every little detail of the times she had tried to help Einstein Luther Smith at Broomleigh. There was still a lot to do, and she needed to get to work early in the morning.

Honey bounded excitedly down the stairs to greet her. Finding a toy on the way, she followed Jenny into the lounge, her tail wagging and batting noisily against the chair.

'Come on, girl, let's get dinner. I just might give Andrew a ring tonight. Perhaps we can go out tomorrow evening, while you're having a sleepover at the vets. Or,' she said mischievously, 'I might invite him here this evening. It's about time he met you. He's bound to love you as much as I do,' she said, as she ruffled a furry ear.

Honey grunted and followed her mistress into the kitchen.

When Jonathan had been alive, their evening meal together was one of the most enjoyable times of the day. They had chatted about work, laughed and enjoyed each other's company. They'd taken it in turns to prepare and make the meal, and Jonathan was by far the better cook. He delighted in teasing her about her lack of culinary skills and felt no shame in telling their friends that his wife could only manage egg and chips and that the only reason they had a kitchen was that it came with the house. She cooked even less now. Perhaps the time had come to make some changes.

Ready-made lasagne warmed, Honey fed, and her usual early evening drink poured, she sat pondering on a call to Andrew. She was not used to asking men out. She moved towards the telephone on the hall table. Just as she was about to pick it up, it burst into life. Reluctantly, she answered. 'Hello, Jenny Trent.'

'Hello, Jenny, nice to hear your voice again. It's Andrew Baines. I'm back from Bedford and I was thinking we might meet again and have a coffee or a meal together. I can tell you all about my visit. We can talk shop for a short time.' He hesitated. 'Of course, that's if you'd like to.'

'Andrew, it's nice to hear from you. I'd love to meet again.'

'That sounds great.'

'What about dinner here, this evening? You'll have to risk my cooking though, and know Honey would love to meet you.'

'I'd love that, Jenny, but to save you cooking, what about I take you out to dinner? There's a new Italian restaurant opened in the High Street, I hear it's very good,'

'Well, that would be nice, but Honey will be at the vets for a thorough check tomorrow, which means she'll be there all night as she has to be anaesthetized. It would be nice just to relax in front of the television or listen to some music, without her grunting in the background.'

'In that case, I would love to. What time would you like me?'

'Around seven would be great,' said Jenny.

'I'm already looking forward to it. See you tomorrow.'

'Just one thing before you go,' said Jenny. 'I'm under pressure from Morgan-Jones to solve this investigation and would like to have any information you have as soon as possible. I was wondering if I could call in tomorrow morning so that we can talk about it. I could have mentioned it tomorrow evening, but you did say no shop talk.' She gave a soft laugh.

'Of course, I'll mention to Ben that you'll be coming in. I am sure he'll be pleased to see you.'

'Thanks, Andrew. She closed the phone and turned excitedly to Honey. 'I've done it, Hun, I've got a date with Andrew tomorrow, and he's having dinner here. You will have to meeting him another time.' She ruffled a shaggy neck and Honey rolled over with a bored, but happy snort.

Jenny rarely slept soundly, and the thoughts of her visit to her old school kept her mind working throughout the night, trying to remember long-forgotten details.

When the alarm woke her earlier than usual she didn't feel at all refreshed, but she was anxious to get on with the day.

***

Jenny arrived at the station to find Alan Hughes and Eddie Callam already there.

'Morning, Ma am.' Eddie greeted her. 'There was a call last night from Samantha Matthews. You know, the young woman who served the peaches to our man? She said she thought she saw him again last night.'

'Did she say where?'

'No, Ma'am, she just wanted to talk to you. I've got her telephone number.' He passed Jenny a small yellow Post-it note with the number written on it.

Jenny looked at her watch, it showed 7.30 am. *Probably a little early to call.* She decided to get herself a coffee.

'Eddie, what time did Samantha Matthews call last night?'

Eddie Callam looked at his notes. 'Eleven fifteen, Ma'am. She sounded anxious, but wouldn't say anything else.'

Jenny collected a coffee and went to her office, closing the door as she went in. She placed the note by the phone and rang the number. 'Hello,' said a sleepy voice.

'Is that Samantha Matthews?'

'Yes, who's this?'

'Hello, Samantha, its DCI Trent here. I hope I haven't called too early, but I understand that you called the station last evening to say that you might have seen the man who bought the peaches from you.'

'Well, I'm not sure now, but I think I did. There was something about him that made me think so.'

'What was that? Any small thing that made you think it was him will help us in finding him.'

There was silence for a few seconds. 'I forgot when we spoke before, but the man who bought the peaches had a scar on his arm.' She hesitated again. 'Well, I think it was a scar, it could have been a birthmark. You see, he only wore short sleeves once when he came into the store, that's when I noticed it. It wasn't very big so I could have been wrong.'

'And the person you saw last night, what made you think it was him?' said Jenny.

'When I walked home yesterday evening it was quite cold, so I was surprised to see this man without a coat and in short sleeves walking towards me. He stopped to cross the road, just ahead of me. Then as I reached him the lights changed to green, so we walked across the road almost together. The streetlights are quite bright by the crossing. As he turned to walk along the pavement, I saw his arm had the scar on it. 'I didn't think much about it until I got home, and then I realised who it might have been, so I rang you.'

'Thank you for doing that, Samantha. We may want to speak to you again. Will you be working today?'

'Yes, I start at ten.'

Thank you again, you've been very helpful. Just one more thing before you go. Do you know what arm the birthmark was on?

'Yes, it was on his left arm,' said Samantha.

Thank you again, said Jenny as she put down the phone and spun her chair to face the window. 'That's it,' she said loudly. 'A scar on his arm.' That's what she'd seen on Einstein Luther Smith when she tried to help him at the swimming pool.

She rang Peter. 'Peter, our man has a distinctive scar or birthmark on one of his arms. Samantha Matthews saw him last night and remembered that she'd seen it on the arm of the man who bought the peaches.'

'Is she sure, Jenny?'

'Well, she wasn't at first, but sure enough to call us. But that's not all. It's what I was trying to remember. Einstein Luther Smith had a mark on his arm. I remember seeing it once when he was swimming. I'm sure he's our man now and that he's somewhere close to us. Get everyone in this afternoon, Peter. I need to go to the pathology lab first to speak to Andrew. About two o'clock should be fine.'

'I'll arrange it.'

✳✳✳

Although Jenny had visited the pathology lab many times she could never quite rid herself of her nervousness at the surroundings, the smell of dead bodies and blood in a cold room that always felt warm and airless gave her the chills. It never ceased to amaze her that people actually studied hard to work in a place like this. *Thank goodness they do,* she thought with a shiver.

As Jenny cautiously opened the door, she saw the two men bent over the prostrate body of a young child. She wanted to leave but made herself walk into the room.

Ben looked up as he heard a movement. 'Come in, Jenny.' He waved his hand, signalling for her to move closer to them. 'It's always nice to see you.'

Andrew turned to face her, his smile warm. 'How can we help?'

'Hello, Ben nice to see you too.' She acknowledged Andrew's smile.

'I have a briefing with the team this afternoon and want to get every bit of information together. I'd be grateful for a report on the autopsy of Jonnie French.'

Andrew stopped his investigation of the dead child in front of him and placed his scalpel in the tray beside the table.

'You talk to Jenny, Andrew,' said Ben. 'I'll carry on here. I've left the report on the desk.'

Jenny followed Andrew to his desk and pulled up a chair.

'It really is nice to see you again, Jenny, I'm looking forward to this evening.'

'So am I,' said Jenny. 'If you'll risk my cooking? I'm brilliant at lasagne, or steak and kidney pie, you can choose.'

'Anything would be wonderful.' He gave a light-hearted laugh, before picking the folder up from his desk. 'Jonnie French was in pretty good health before he was murdered, although his liver and kidneys were beginning to shows signs of alcohol abuse. His death was caused by massive blood loss and drowning.' He stopped for a few seconds. 'Nasty way for a swimming coach to die, I'd say.'

'You said his throat was damaged, do you think it was by a peach stone?'

'The damage to his throat was very similar to that seen in the other two victims. I was told about an hour ago that a peach stone was found in the pool.' He gave a small sigh. 'But, it hasn't reached us yet, and it is extremely unlikely to give up any information due to the length of time it was in the water.'

'Even so, can we assume a peach stone played an important part in the murder, as with the other victims?' said Jenny.

'It might have done, but Jonnie French drowned because he couldn't swim due to his arms being cut off.' He looked at Jenny, his expression soft. 'Drowning is a silent killer, Jenny. He couldn't call for help because he would have used all his energy trying to breathe and keep his head above water. Once he swallowed water, his voice box could have gone into spasm.' He sat back in his chair. 'Sorry for getting technical, but it takes a few minutes for the brain to stop working, and those minutes must have been the most terrifying of this man's life. He was a swimming coach, yet he was drowning in his own bloody water! He would've been in excruciating pain. The shocks and traumas caused by his killer were pretty horrifying to him.

'Can we be absolutely sure that the murder was committed by the same person who committed the first two?'

'That's for you lot to decide, but the results of all three autopsies would indicate that,' Andrew said.

'Thank you, that's very helpful.'

'How are you getting on with the investigation? Are you any nearer to solving it?'

'Well, time is running out. Morgan-Jones is threatening to take me off the case. I've only a few days left, but we've received some encouraging information recently.

We have a briefing this afternoon so that the team can have all the up-to-date information and we can exchange ideas. I think we're very close now.' She smiled at Andrew, and her face flushed as she suddenly became aware of how close their chairs were. 'Depending on what happens today, I may have to cancel our evening if so I'll call you.'

'I hope not,' said Andrew as he took her hand. 'I'm so looking forward to it.'

***

Back at the station, Peter had prepared the incident room.

'Eddie Callam will be late,' said Peter. 'He's gone to talk to Samantha Matthews. We may have some more news before the meeting is over.'

'Great, just time to get a sandwich. Would you like to join me in my office?' Jenny said.

'Sounds good to me.'

Jenny picked up two sandwiches from the cafeteria and took them into her office, where Peter was already waiting for her. 'Sit down, Peter. Just a little time to ask you about Maggie, while we're eating. Are things working out?'

'She wants me to give up my police work, says it's ruining our marriage. She told me that she loves me too much to spend so much time on her own and that it's affecting Josh. He keeps waking up in the night and asking if the nasty man has killed daddy.'

'That's serious. Do you know yet what you're going to do?'

'My family means the world to me, Jenny. Life would be unbearable without them.' He looked at his uneaten sandwich. 'I told Maggie that I wanted to see this case through. Then I would seriously consider what she wants. My only worry is what I'll do.' He took a small bite from his sandwich followed by a swig of coffee. 'Her father owns Charlton's Furniture Stores and he's told us many times that he'd welcome me into the business. He's a good man, Jenny, and I like him a lot, but …' His voice trailed off as he finished his sandwich.

'You're a good detective, Peter, but you know no other way than giving more than you should. You work far too many hours and I can understand Maggie's feelings,' said Jenny. 'There are worse things than being in a family business, especially one that's as successful as your father-in-law's.'

'There's another thing,' said Peter. 'Maggie wants more children. We always said we wanted two or three, but she won't consider it while I'm still in the force.'

'Only you can make the decision. And, only you can decide which is most precious to you,' said Jenny.

'I know, I know, and I don't have to tell you which it is.' He picked up the two empty cups from the table. 'Come on, it's time for the briefing.'

✲✲✲

The buzz quietened as they walked in. Jenny made her way to the front of the incident room. 'Good afternoon. Thank you for coming in at such short notice.'

As everyone was sitting down, Eddie Callam walked in. 'Sorry I'm late, Ma'am. Just finished speaking to Samantha Matthews.'

'Perhaps you could update us then, Eddie.'

'Miss Matthews is now absolutely sure it was the same peach buyer that she saw again last night. She said she'd recognise the mark on his arm anywhere.'

'Did she say what sort of mark it was?'

'She said it was on the top of his left arm and thought it was probably not a scar, but a birthmark.'

'Did she say what it looked like or what shape it was?'

'She gave me a rough drawing.' He held up a piece of paper and handed it to Jenny.

Although the drawing was sketchy, the outline looked like a bunch of grapes. Jenny immediately remembered the incident at the swimming pool of Broomleigh House School. 'That's it!' She held the drawing up and then pinned it onto the board. 'I would like everyone to take a good look before we finish here.'

Alan Hughes held up his hand to speak. 'Can we be absolutely sure that our killer is, or was, Einstein Luther Smith?'

'Absolutely sure. As you all know I attended the same school, three years ahead of him. I can remember seeing this birthmark on him at the swimming pool.' She turned to Peter, who was standing close to her. 'Peter, I'd like you to outline the events of our meeting with Dr McAllister at Broomleigh House School yesterday, including Fred Elliott's accounts of the bullying that went on there. There's another link, which must have a clear line to our Mr Smith. Einstein's mother was killed by a peach stone getting lodged in her throat. That's not just a coincidence. Apparently, there were no suspicious circumstances noted in the police report at the time, but they're now looking into it again.'

Peter took out his notebook and relayed the conversations from the school meetings. 'Any questions?' he said as he closed the notebook.

'Do you think you're in any danger, Ma'am?' said Eddie Callam.

'I can't answer that with a definite yes or no,' said Jenny. 'What I do know is that we are getting nearer to finding our murderer. In the meantime, I want all of you to revisit all your recent investigations and talk to everyone again. There must be people who recall seeing someone with a birthmark like this one.' She pointed at the drawing on the whiteboard. 'We don't have long to find this person, or you'll have a new boss. If you don't have any more questions from us we should just get on with it.'

The team dispersed, but Peter remained next to her. He gave her a quizzical look. 'Something's puzzling you, Jenny. I can read you like a book. What's wrong?'

Jenny stood still. Her eyes closed tight.

I invited Andrew to dinner. It's been such a long time since I felt I could get close to someone, Peter, I'm worried I am being a bit pushy

'You, pushy? Everyone knows you're pushy, Jenny, but only when you want something done at work.' He smiled. 'Anyway, you like Andrew and it's about time you had someone close to care about you. It's almost as if you're looking for reasons not to get too close.'

'Yes, Peter, I like him, a lot, and we seem to be getting on very well. I'm looking forward to spending the evening with him. Please don't hesitate to contact me if you need to, though. It's one of the perks of dating someone from work – they understand the score. So I can easily cancel my evening if I need to.'

As Peter got to the door, he turned and smiled at Jenny. 'I hope you have a great time. You deserve to relax. There's nothing more you can do while sitting at your desk waiting for Sam, Mickey, and Ben to do everything you asked them to.'

'If Sam or Mickey can't get me, I know they'll call you if it's urgent or something I need to know, please ring me immediately. I know Andrew won't mind if I'm needed.'

'You can be sure of that Jenny, just keep your phone near to you.'

'Of course, I will.' Said Jenny, as she said 'goodbye.'

CHAPTER FORTY-ONE

'You look fine to me, young lady,' said Stephen Wade to his four-legged patient, as he came into the waiting room. 'Hello, Jenny, how's she been?'

'She seems to have recovered remarkably well, thank you. I'm rather hoping that when I pick her up tomorrow you'll be able to give her the all-clear.'

'I'm sure I will.' Stephen took the lead from Jenny and led Honey through to the back of the surgery. Honey wagged her tail and followed him, looking back at Jenny just once.

Shopping for dinner was easy. She had decided on lasagne, a dish she enjoyed cooking and probably the only one that Jonathan hadn't teased her about. She bought garlic bread and settled on fresh fruit and cream for a dessert.

Jenny placed the bags full of shopping on the kitchen table and realised that she hadn't thought about Einstein Luther Smith since she had spoken to Peter. She checked that her mobile was easily available and ready if Peter or Ben called her.

Her bath was extra special, the warm, perfumed water relaxed her, she felt the muscles in her body soften and tingle. The smell of the lasagne in the oven revived memories which at first disturbed her, but she quickly reminded herself why she was cooking and allowed herself to smile. *Things are definitely getting better.*

She dressed carefully in a new light-green sweater, with black trousers, and black shoes with a small, slim heel. She applied her usual modest amount of make-up and brushed her newly-washed hair. Looking in her long mirror, she felt pleased with what she saw. 'You scrub up pretty well, girl,' she told herself.

The table looked good and Jenny felt a stab of satisfaction at seeing her best cutlery and crockery on display. 'You lot haven't been used for over three years.' She laughed, as she realised she was talking to knives, forks, and plates. By seven o'clock, everything was ready, she poured herself a glass of cooled wine.

Andrew walked up the path and Jenny opened the door before he had a chance to ring the bell.

'Please, come in.' She smiled.

He placed a large bunch of white and red roses carefully in Jenny's hands.

'For you. You look as beautiful as the flowers.' He kissed her gently on the cheek. 'This is for both of us.' He had a bottle of champagne in his other hand. 'It's already cold.'

Jenny put the roses in the sink. 'I'll put them in my best vase later. They're beautiful, thank you so much.' She turned and placed her arms around his neck, kissing him on the cheek. He moved slightly, his mouth finding her lips for a welcoming kiss. Jenny stepped back nervously.

'Jenny ... don't worry, I'm not going to rush anything. I just needed to do that.'

She smiled, relieved at his reassurance that he would take things at her pace, and went to a cupboard to get two glasses. 'I'm afraid I don't have champagne glasses.'

'We will never have champagne glasses then.' He smiled as the cork flew with a loud 'pop' out of the bottle. Champagne was carefully poured into the glasses and he handed Jenny the nearest one. 'Now, you make a wish.' He lifted his glass. 'But, don't tell me.'

She made a silent wish as she took a sip of the bubbling wine. 'Dinner's ready.'

'Good, I'm starving.'

As they sat down, Andrew said, 'I'm glad we could do this. I wanted to know more about you. About what made you the person you are.'

She smiled, almost blushing. 'I don't know,' she said.

'You do,' he replied with a smile. 'You're just being modest.'

Jenny looked down, her mind recalling precious memories. 'My husband,' she said. 'I mean...'

Andrew took her hand gently. 'No, he was important to you. We all have people in our lives who influence us, don't we? But I want to know about you, what you like? What you don't like? How do you feel your career will go? Apart from Jonathon what has been the most important person and time in your life? What school you went to and if the school guided you to the career that you seem to love? It's all about you. Your ambitions and your fears, Jenny. Is there anything you believe you should have done but didn't? His voice was gentle. Tell me about your school first.' He squeezed her hand softly.

'I think everyone will have thoughts about things they should have done but didn't Andrew. The school I went to was really a great school, but like everything you go back and think about there are things that could be done better.' She cast her mind back to her school years. 'I think they could have looked after some of the more vulnerable children more. There was some bullying that took place in a class a few years below me. I remember trying to help a young boy who was being bullied. He had a strange name. Einstein Luther Smith,' she wiped her mouth with a clean napkin. '

'Who would give a boy a name like that? She said. I think that was what the bullying was about. He used to bring a peach to school every day and from what I can remember, I think it was the same bullies' every time. They seemed to have it in for him. There was also a girl with them. I did mention it the House Master, but nothing was done about it. But generally, I think it was a good school, Andrew. But,' she glanced away. 'But then maybe I should have reported it properly.' She went quiet, thinking hard. 'Yes, I believe I joined the police force because I wanted to do more for people who were being hurt by others. I wanted to do more than the school did.' She looked at Andrew. 'Does that make sense?'

'Of course, it does Jenny,' said Andrew releasing her hand. 'Everyone, I am sure has feelings about what they should have done but didn't.' He gave her a broad smile as he took her hand again.

'You don't have to answer this Jenny. How are you coping with the loss of Jonathan now? You work so hard, does that help?

'Yes it has, and everyone at the station has been so understanding and supportive. Without their help I would not have been sitting here with you Andrew, I never thought I would ever ask anyone to have dinner with me again. And here we are.'

'Well, I am not going to tell you about me.' He raised her hand to his mouth and kissed it gently, before placing it carefully back on the table.

'I didn't think you would,' said Jenny, smiling as she rose.

'I'll clear up tomorrow,' she said. 'Shall we have coffee in the lounge? If I don't bore you I can tell you more of my life story, but then,' she said. 'It will be your turn.'

As they reached the lounge, she heard her phone's urgent tones. 'Sorry, Andrew, I left my phone in the kitchen. I have to get that. Please go through.'

'Please don't,' said Andrew. 'I just want you to relax with me for a while.' He took her hand protectively. 'Please.'

'I'm really sorry, I have to, Andrew – you know that. It may be Peter or Ben. I left a few things for them to check, with instructions to contact me if it was important.' She moved past Andrew to the kitchen.

It was from Peter. 'GET OUT NOW!' The line went dead.

She felt a sudden movement behind her. The phone was ripped from her hand. 'Didn't you hear me? I said don't answer it.' His eyes were dark with anger as she spun round to face him. 'Why don't you do as you're told? You've gone and spoilt everything – so typical. And it won't be Ben.'

Her voice was shaking, and she tried to move away, tried not to think the unthinkable

He threw the phone across the room and grabbed her arms, pushing them hard behind her back. Kicking a chair towards her he pushed her roughly until she was sitting down.

'Just sit down and shut up or I'll make sure you do DCI Trent,' he snarled. 'Oh yes, and before you ask why it won't be Ben, it's because he's probably dead by now. Once he heard about the birthmark he would have found it easy to put two and two together and realise it was me. He's probably seen the birthmark on my arm. You see, Jenny, I might just have been careless enough to roll up my sleeves.' He raised his hands in the air. 'Everyone can be a bit careless sometimes. Even you. He's probably dead,' he repeated, 'because I fixed that stupid car of his. I'm not a car mechanic, but I know how to fix one. Steering would have been all over the place, and the accelerator would have been uncontrollable. Oh yes! He really is quite possibly dead by now.'

He stared at Jenny, moving his face close to hers.

She felt his hot sticky breath on her cheek and stared back, horrified at the change in him. How had she ever found that smile of his attractive?

'It's a shame because I liked him. But I had to get to him before he told you about the mark on my arm.' He rose, shaking his head. 'But he was a bit of a bully. Don't like bullies much, they deserve to die.' He stared at Jenny. '*Don't they?*' he shouted. 'You're not a bully, Jenny, but ...' He turned away from her. '*But ...*' his voice even louder now. 'In some ways, you were worse, DCI Trent. *You did nothing ... nothing ... nothing at all!*' He turned back to face her, his face a deep red, screwed up, tears brimming in his eyes. 'Because you did *nothing ... Bitch!*' he screamed.

Jenny flinched.

'*I have suffered!*' He stood up straight and raised his eyes to the ceiling. '*Suffered!*'

Fear running through her body, Jenny tried to get up, but she was immediately pushed back into the chair. *He's right. If I had done something all this wouldn't have happened.* She was shaking as she straightened in the chair, unable to move further.

'Look at me, Bitch, look at me,' he demanded. 'See what you've done to my life ... ruined it. *Ruined it,*' he repeated as he slammed his fist on the table. 'DCI, no less.' His voice became soft and snarling. 'I bet you've done a lot to help people on the way up. After all, that's what DCIs do, don't they? Help everyone that needs it.' He thumped the table again as he leant closer to her. 'But not me ... not me. *Not me!*'

Jenny looked up at his bloated red face, wondering if he was too far gone. Could she reason with him? 'I wanted to help you, but you wouldn't let me. Every time, I wanted to get help for you and report it. Every time, you told me not to.'

'You could and should have reported it, but you didn't. *Did you?*' he roared, before abruptly looking away and muttering, 'Never mind, never mind. I enjoyed making them suffer. They deserved what they got. After all, I had planned it carefully over the years. Every one of my academic successes brought me closer to achieving my goal. University was good for me. I had no bullying about my name. Well ... very little.' He moved away from her, speaking almost normally. 'In fact, I made a few friends. One actually said my name was cool. But then university students are so much more open-minded than those ignorant buffoons at Broomleigh House.'

Is there a chance I can make a run for the door? But even as she thought it, he swung back to her, his eyes now clear and wide. 'Oh dear, I'll have to tie you up, Bitch. I shall call you "Bitch" from now on, it suits you, Bitch,' he repeated, his face close to hers again.

'I don't care what you call me,' said Jenny, struggling to regain her composure. How was it that the murderer was under their noses all this time and no one – she in particular – hadn't seen Andrew Einstein Luther Smith for what he actually was? One thing was for sure – she needed to play for time. Because if Peter was warning her, then they should be turning up here soon. Very soon.

Abruptly, Andrew – or Einstein, as she now thought of him – became business-like.

'Let's get you tied up, I need to work quickly. Nuisance really, I wanted to take my time with you. You see, Bitch, I don't care if they catch me now. I'm almost finished and then I'll be free!'

He took a cord from his pocket. Leaning over her, he placed his arms roughly around her neck and tied her hands at the back of the chair. 'I hope I'm not hurting you, Bitch. I'm not ready to hurt you … just yet.'

'Please, don't tie me up! I'll sit still – I will. But don't tie me up. She tried to kick out at him, but he dodged her. Fear was racing through her body – the thought of being tied up, of being helpless, was unbearable. There was nothing she could do to get away from him. Thoughts of Jonathan rushed through her mind. She needed him now, so much! She closed her eyes, breathed deeply, battling her sense of panic as he pulled the knots tight behind her back. At least Honey wasn't here, because otherwise, he would have …

'You hurt my dog! That's why you suddenly agreed to come over when I mentioned that Honey wouldn't be here. You nearly killed her!' Jenny's fury at what this brute had put Honey through swept away her fear. 'You talk of suffering and bullying – what about my beautiful girl? She's never hurt anyone in her life, yet you saw fit to inflict pain on her!'

Einstein blinked, clearly taken aback. 'She's a dog!'

'With feelings and the ability to endure pain – and totally innocent!'

His face twisted. 'Shut your mouth, Bitch! Or I'll shut it up for you. That's typical – you, getting worked up about a senseless beast while ignoring the suffering of a *defenceless child!*'

Despite his bellow, Jenny sensed that she had shaken Einstein – a feeling reinforced by his further response, when he added, with a spiteful leer, 'And for that, I'll have to tie your feet as well.' He tutted and took more cord from his trouser pocket. 'I'm going to hurt you again. Can't be helped though.' The cord cut into her legs as he tied them to the chair.

He knelt upon the floor beside her, his face not quite touching hers. 'Am I going to kill you? Hmm …' he murmured softly. 'Not sure really, not sure.' He stood, and pulled up a kitchen chair in front of her, so close that their knees almost touched as he sat down. 'Whoops, the champagne is making me a bit unsteady. Don't care really. I won't be drinking champagne any more. Don't like it anyway.'

He jumped up from the chair and moved towards the table. 'This table is a mess, I can't use a dirty table.'

He picked up dishes, knives, forks, and pans and threw them onto the draining board and into the sink. 'Can't stand a mess,' he muttered. 'I'll have to clean the table now.'

He's mad, Jenny thought, and she watched helplessly while he painstakingly cleaned and dried the table, casting his hands over the surface to feel for any debris which might have escaped.

'I think you'll do now.' He bent low to examine the table. 'Best I can do,' he muttered quietly.

He moved back towards Jenny and pulled out a transparent plastic bag from his trouser pocket. He held it up so that she could see its contents.

He looked at her. 'These are the last ones, Bitch, the very last ones, and they're the best. I wasn't sure if I needed two.' He hesitated, he lifted his hand up to his chin, stroking it thoughtfully. 'Still not sure.'

Frantically, Jenny tried to move her fingers to release the cord. The thought of dying with a peach stone lodged in her throat terrified her.

'Rather silly trying to free yourself, isn't it? You stupid girl, stupid girl, stupid girl …' He bent down, suddenly bellowing in her ear, *Stupid Girl, Stupid Girl!*

She winced. *He doesn't want to kill me – he's working himself up to do this …*

'Whoops, sorry does that hurt your ears? I do hope so ... *Bitch*. I do hope so.'

His voice was cruel and loud. 'You never tried to stop the bullying. You just let them do it. You didn't tell anyone. I'm sorry, but that makes you almost as bad as them. Actually, I think it makes you worse.' He took the peach stones from the bag and placed them next to each other on the table, whispering, 'Perfect ... Just perfect.'

'What are you going to do?' She tried to keep the fear from her voice.

'What a silly question.' He paced up and down the room. 'What do *you* think I'm going to do? You're a detective, DCI Bitch, stupid girl. Work it out.' His pacing became faster and more urgent. 'One is for me and the other one is for you, not hard to work out is it?'

He abruptly stopped yelling and added, in a voice that was chilling in its normality. 'Trouble is, I can't decide which is which.' He picked up the stones carefully, placing them onto the edge of the table. 'They are both perfect, so I suppose it really doesn't matter.'

'Funny thing is, Bitch, I don't like peaches any more. Strange that. There was a time when I couldn't go a day without eating one. My mother used to pick them out for me ... A lovely peach, every day.'

Jenny saw his eyes fill with tears.

'But I didn't have one every day. Did I ... *did I?* Tears fell down his cheeks as he moved closer to her. 'Those cretins stole them from me. And you did nothing, Bitch ... *Nothing!*

He pulled the chair close to Jenny again and sat down. 'I loved you when we were at school. You were so pretty and seemed much nicer than the other girls. I tried to talk to you so many times, but you didn't even see me. I would wait after school before I went home, just to see you. But, not once did you look my way.' He shifted forward, almost touching her, staring at her in a way that made her skin crawl.

'I followed your career, you know.' His arm wiped away the tears from his face. He touched her chin, lifting it slightly. 'Must say you did very well for yourself ... DCI, no less. Not surprised, though. You were very good at school, the highest marks all the time. We would have made a lovely couple. Just think how different things would be. But we will never know now, will we?' He wiped his hand slowly across his mouth.

Jenny wondered whether to say anything, but decided against it. Like most psychopaths she'd encountered, he was only really interested in himself.

'As for the others ... I didn't care how they got on with their life. James Williamson was a nasty piece of shit! I knew what he did.' He looked away from Jenny. 'Those poor girls, I felt sorry for them.' He sighed and shrugged his shoulders. 'Couldn't help them, though.'

'You could have gone to the police,' said Jenny, her voice shaking. She had never felt so terrified, ever. *Why aren't they here yet?* She wanted to scream. *Where are they?*

'I had made my plans over many years and the police had no part in them.' He pointed a finger at her. 'Except for you, of course.'

Jenny moved her head back to try to get away from his twisted face. 'Why do you want to hurt me now? If you never told me, how could I know about your feelings for me?' Her fingers were working slowly but steadily at the back of the chair, she could feel the cord slipping a little until one finger came free. *Must keep him talking.*

'Did you kill your mother? She choked on a peach stone as well.'

'You have done your homework, DCI Trent ...Whoops ... sorry, *Bitch*. She did die choking on a peach stone, but I didn't kill her.' He closed his eyes and took in a deep breath. 'I would have done,' he said, fixing her with that mad stare once more. 'But my father did it. You see, he hated her as much as I did. He got away with it, though. That was when I started making my plans.'

'Have they worked out as you hoped?' Her shaking fingers continued their relentless assault on the cord.

He thought for a short while. 'Mmm ... Mostly. I made a few silly mistakes, but on the whole, yes, I think they have.'

Jenny felt the cord slip from her left hand. In a few seconds, she was able to release the right one. She swung both arms up and brought them crashing down onto Einstein's head, and he fell heavily to the floor.

He turned to look up at her. 'Not a good idea, *Bitch*.' He spat the words like venom. 'I'm still here and you're still tied to the chair. Rather stupid really. Oh dear, another mistake.' He snarled, his eyes wide with hate. 'The time has come. My plan is nearly complete.' He rose quickly to stand in front of her.

Where are they? Where are they? What on earth's keeping them? Jenny wanted to scream. *Maybe this really is my punishment,* she thought, as she tried again to wriggle her feet out of the cords that locked them to the chair.

He grabbed the cord from the floor. Jenny screamed with anger as he pushed her arms behind the chair and secured them again.

'You won't untie them again.' He pulled the cord tight, making her wrists burn.

'Now, let me explain how this works.' He held the stones up in front of Jenny's face, one in each hand. 'This one is mine.' He held up his right hand. 'I'll push this one into my throat first and then before it becomes too late for me to control my pain, I'll push the last one into your throat, so far in that you won't be able to breathe, talk, or even cry out. It doesn't take too long to die, Bitch, just three or four minutes, that's all. This is all your fault. You really should have made sure someone dealt with the bullying at school.' His eyes filled with tears as he pushed the stone into his open mouth. He closed his mouth and swallowed.

Jenny wriggled on the chair. It wobbled and fell to the floor, increasing her fear and pain. Einstein fell on the floor next to her, his eyes bulging with watery, bloody veins. He spat out a loud gurgling sound, like an animal being tortured before being eaten by its prey.

She tried to move away from him, but the cords binding her to the chair were tearing at her skin. He shuffled closer to her and brought the hand holding the stone to her face. His other hand closed around her nose, forcing her mouth to open. The sound coming from his throat was so loud Jenny's head was at bursting point.

One more scream from him and he pushed the last stone into her mouth. As she tried to breathe, it moved further back down her throat. His hand holding her nose fell away and she took a last gasping breath. Her throat held the stone tight, swelling under the strain of the peach stone.

'DON'T MOVE! DON'T MOVE!'

The order thundered around every corner of the room.

Through half-open eyes, Jenny saw three heavily armed uniformed police officers with helmets and faceguards. One stood with feet and hips apart, both hands firmly gripping a handgun pointing directly at Einstein.

'Get first aid here, quick!' Two paramedics were already in the room.

'They both have peach stones in their throat.' A voice behind the firearm officers shouted. 'Move, now! See to the woman first.'

Someone cut the cords tying Jenny to the chair and she tried to move her hands to her throat. They were too heavy. The pain – the terrible sensation of not being able to draw breath.

She was dimly aware of a young man kneeling beside her, he slid his fingers up and under the bottom of her rib cage and positioned his other hand above his fingers and thrust both hands violently upwards.

Jenny strained, but the stone didn't move. And she couldn't. *This is it. I'm dying* ...

The man thrust his hands upwards once more and she felt the flesh in her throat tear as the stone moved. He moved quickly behind her and placed his arms around her body, reaching her stomach. With a quick hard movement, he thrust his fists inwards and upwards. Jenny managed a deep breath and coughed. The peach stone shot out of her mouth, onto the floor. She coughed, gasping in noisy gulps of air, tasting the blood in her mouth, suddenly aware that she was going to live, after all.

There was pandemonium in the room. Feet were moving swiftly around her. Darkness enveloped her and her eyes closed again, she felt peaceful, the pain almost gone.

CHAPTER FORTY-TWO

Jenny slowly opened her eyes. The room was white and pale green. A menagerie of machines filled the wall at the back of her bed. She turned her head and tried to speak, but only a croaky whisper came out, causing sharp pains in her throat.

'Welcome back, Jenny, don't try to speak. You're going to be fine, you just need to rest for another twenty-four hours. I'm told I can come back in the morning to pick you up.'

She saw Peter and opened her mouth to say hello, but nothing came out. He took her hand gently. 'It's over now. Thanks to you, our killer will be in custody when he recovers. Everyone back at the station is waiting for you to come back,' he squeezed her hand. 'Rest now, I'll be back first thing tomorrow.'

Jenny tried again to speak, but he was gone.

✱✱✱

One Week Later

Jenny knocked cautiously at her boss's door.

'Come in, Jenny.' Morgan-Jones opened the door before she could respond. 'Great to have you back. I just thought I should brief you before you get involved in the next investigation. Alan Hughes can bring you up to speed on a shooting that took place yesterday.'

'Thank you, Sir.'

Morgan-Jones walked to the other side of his desk and pulled a chair forward for her. 'First of all, I must set your mind at rest about Ben Seldon. He was injured in an accident with his car, not badly thank goodness, but he was concussed for several hours.'

'Why did he try to kill him before he got to me? Said Jenny.

'It seems that Ben was getting more and more concerned about the fact that the victims had been killed by someone who had a professional knowledge of surgical knives. He checked the background of all of his staff as a starting point. When he was checking Baines's employment application, he found that no check had ever been made on the qualifications he had given for the post. Ben made additional enquires and no records could be found in the name of Andrew Baines. He told me that while he was on the phone talking to someone in human resources, he heard a noise and turned to see Baines walking past the door. He believed that he had been there for some time, listening to him. It looks as though he then found Ben's car and fixed it so that Ben would have an accident. Don't quite know what he did, but we will do soon.'

He smiled slightly. 'I'm afraid his car is a write-off and he's more upset about that than his injuries. I take it that you weren't aware that Baines was in the frame for these killings?' He raised his eyebrows.

Of course, I wasn't, or I wouldn't have invited him around for a meal! Jenny wondered what it was about Morgan-Jones that always raised her hackles. Other than the fact that he was a pompous prick.

'You may already know, Sir that I had already met Andrew socially and we'd been out for dinner. To be honest, I liked him and I felt the feeling was mutual. We had a very pleasant evening and it was clear, to me, anyway, that we both wanted to do it again. So I made the invitation for him to come for a meal at my house. I told Peter to contact me if he heard anything that he knew I would want to know immediately, and thank goodness that's exactly what he did, Sir.'

Morgan-Jones held up his hand to stop her. 'I know you've made a full statement. I'm really sorry we got to you later than was ideal – a major RTA had closed the main road.' He shuddered. 'We were so nearly too late.'

'I'm fine, Sir.' *Or I will be very soon* … Jenny promised herself.

'Thank goodness you are safe and well. We've missed you.' That, at least, sounded sincere.

'Yes, and I can't wait to get back to normal, Sir.' She gave a small smile.

Morgan-Jones cleared his throat, importantly. 'Meanwhile, I'll bring you up to speed regarding Smith, or Baines. He's still in the hospital, his brain suffered badly from the lack of oxygen, so he's currently in a coma. The doctors aren't sure if he'll even recover at all. But whatever happens, if he doesn't die he will be locked up for a very long time.'

Jenny nodded. She'd known all this. She'd been to visit him and stood at the side of his bed, watching his chest rise and fall as the machines beeped and whirred. Damaged by the fruit he once loved.

Morgan-Jones rose from behind his desk and walked around towards Jenny, taking her hand. 'It's over now, Jenny, and everyone is pleased to see you back. He took her hand and held it tightly. 'You have a loyal hardworking team, Jenny, without which the outcome of this horrific case may have been so different."

'Thank you, Sir.'

He reluctantly removed his hand from hers.

Jenny reached the door to his office.

'Jenny … I …'

'Thank you again for all your support, Sir. I need to find Peter and find out what his plans are.' She opened the door and walked through. Before that need to visit Rory and his Dad, to say thank you for all the help in getting Honey to the vet, and let him know she hadn't forgotten his coat. Jenny gave a short sigh. *Just let's get on with it then.*

Acknowledgements

A big thank you to Sarah Higbee, my tutor at Northbrook College, and my colleagues for giving me the encouragement and enthusiasm to go on. And, of course, to my husband and family for the times I was writing instead of cooking!

A Few Words from Hazel Reed

I have had a wonderful fulfilling work life in Human Resources, gaining first-hand knowledge of people's desire to achieve their ambitions and witness their successes.

Through the privilege of serving as a Magistrate, I learned about people's weaknesses, but more importantly, about their strengths and determination.

I have always loved writing and seeing my first novel in print has been one of the best moments of my life.

Available worldwide from Amazon
and in all good bookstores

———————————

www.mtp.agency

www.facebook.com/mtp.agency

@mtp_agency